The Murder Game

ARTIFICIAL INTELLIGENCE. VERY REAL MURDERS.

SONNY HUDSON

p 136 — How did they know it
was Columbia?

How do they travel w/ their
weapons?

First edition: December 2022

❀ Created with Vellum

Prologue

THURSDAY, OCTOBER 20TH

San Jose, CA. Even at 9:10 pm on a Thursday night in late October, the streets were crawling with people and the restaurants and bars were packed. Santana Row had the usual mix of people tonight. Young, old, locals, visiting businessmen. The beautiful and the far from beautiful, all enjoying the gorgeous California evening. The night was perfect for the exotic cars cruising up and down the boulevard, and the cars drew at least as many covetous glances as the lovely young ladies spilling out of the bars.

It takes a lot to make yourself heard over the din created by the people, the Lamborghinis and Ferraris, and the music pumping from speakers in every bar along the street. This young lady, though, had a serious set of lungs on her, and when she let out a shriek it would have done a young Jamie Lee Curtis in "Halloween" proud. Heads turned, and a few brave souls started moving her way. Soon there was a crowd around her, drawn to her screams like flies to a piece of rotting food. She was crying and screaming to the point that she couldn't talk, but she was able to point. There, in a narrow alleyway barely wide enough for one person to pass through, lay a body. Soon more screams added to the chorus, and that was quickly followed by the lights of a hundred cell phone cameras taking pictures and videos. It took a few moments before someone in the crowd had the sense to call 911.

Several patrol cars responded within minutes and quickly established a perimeter, though it took several minutes to get all the looky-loos to put down their cameras and clear out of the way. Detective Lt. Peter Michaels was assigned to the scene, and he arrived just 10 minutes after the patrols. Doing a quick assessment of the scene, he enlisted the help of several patrolmen to help light up the dark, shadowed alleyway with their Streamlight tactical flashlights. There was no doubt that the man on the ground was dead. Slaughterhouses have less blood than what Michaels saw pooled around this guy.

"Holy shit," said Michaels, "this doesn't look like your average assault, not by a long shot. We'll need the coroner to do a closer examination, but what I'm seeing is three very precise cuts, not your typical street or rage stabbing". He shined his light along the body. "See here? Looks like someone approached him and then slashed his throat from the front, which is pretty unusual. Then the assailant slashed the femoral artery on each side of the groin. The guy would have bled out in minutes. Couldn't have been saved even if he were in the ER."

"Looks like more of a targeted execution than a random street mugging gone wrong to me," said one of the young patrolmen.

"Yeah, you're exactly right. And that makes this even scarier." Michaels felt a chill. Twenty-two years on the force and every so often there was still a murder scene that freaked him out. This was definitely one of them.

Georgetown, Washington DC

Peter Jacobsen knew that it was time to head for home. It was close to midnight, and he knew that Friday morning would start early if he had any shot of beating DC's infamous traffic and making it to work on time. Actually, he had known for several hours that he should call it a night, but his friends and coworkers kept delaying his exit by insisting on 'just one more drink', and that was several drinks ago. If he had any chance of getting any sleep tonight and of functioning at work tomorrow, he knew that he had to head out. Bidding everyone good night, and continually fending off their jokes and abuse about his inability to 'hang with the big dogs', he grabbed his coat and finally made it out the door onto M Street. The crisp autumn evening was just what he needed, and he welcomed the fresh air after several hours in a bar with a million sweaty bodies and the smell of stale beer. His car was parked just down the street in a parking garage, but he was having the inevitable internal debate about whether he should try to drive home or grab an Uber. *I'm probably OK to drive, but maybe not legally if I get stopped. An Uber would be safer. But if I take an Uber, how will I get my car later? How much will the garage charge for parking there for 2 days? How will I get to work tomorrow?*

Ultimately, alcohol won out over common sense. Peter turned and headed down M Street, the garage only about 100 yards away. As he headed down the ramp it was eerily quiet and dark, but he didn't give it a second thought; this was Georgetown, not the 'bad' part of DC, and he'd been living and partying in this area for years with no problems. Since his car was down two levels, he headed to the elevators. *OK....so this was a little creepy.* As soon as he stepped onto the elevator, he pressed the button for level B2 and then quickly pressed the 'doors closed' button, breathing a little sigh of relief when the doors closed and started down.

Peter hustled off of the elevator as soon as the doors opened, and as he looked around, he noted that there were only a handful of cars on this level. Moving quickly to his car he pressed the Unlock button on his key fob and was rewarded with the headlights flashing in recognition. As he reached for the door handle someone grabbed his shoulder and forcefully spun him around. Peter would have screamed, but before he could even utter a sound a knife plunged into his throat. As blood gurgled from his wound and from his mouth, his attacker just stood there staring at him, his eyes the only thing visible from his black clothing and black balaclava. Before Peter could fully register what was happening, how his life was already over, his attacker flicked the knife on either side of his groin, completely shredding his femoral artery. It was only a matter of time, and time was measured in minutes rather than hours or days.

When the body was discovered around 7:00am the next morning it created pandemonium. Police, EMT's, and the press all converged around the garage entrance on M Street, making an already miserable traffic situation that much worse. Washington DC Homicide Detective Nicole McKenzie was the senior detective on the scene, and she considered this to be as gruesome as any crime scene she'd ever worked. She'd seen it all: shootings, stabbings, gang violence, domestic violence, poisonings, and savage beatings with pretty much every kind of instrument of death and destruction one could think of, but this was different. This was very cold, very calculated. Her first impression was that this was definitely not a gang thing or a crime of passion between friends or lovers. She also quickly concluded that this wasn't a professional hit, at least not in the normal sense of the word. Sure, an assassin might sometime choose a knife over a gun, but they're not going to take the time for these precision cuts; they're going to plunge the knife as hard and deep as possible, maybe repeatedly, and be done with it. This murder smacked of a violent, sadistic killer – and maybe someone that enjoyed killing. Almost certainly not their first killing, and almost certainly not their last. That's what concerned her the most.

Houston, Texas

It was about 10 minutes past the 11pm closing time at Top Golf, and the 30 employees from Ragtag Software were the only remaining customers. Most groups start their events in the late afternoon or early evening, but the employees from Ragtag worked anything but conventional hours. They had arrived shortly after 9pm and enjoyed the food, the drinks, and the camaraderie, but now things were winding down. As his co-workers started drifting downstairs towards the exits, Glenn Andrews tried, with little success, to coax them to have 'one more for the road' or to hit a few more balls. Soon he was one of the few customers left on the top deck, but he was determined to finish the last of the pitcher of beer before heading home. Alternating between gulps of beer and launching ball after ball 200-plus yards, albeit most with a slice that took it far off-target, Glenn was too keyed-up to end the evening and head for home. Top Golf may be closing, but there were plenty of bars that would still be open for hours, he reasoned.

As he headed down the interior steps that lead from the top levels to the ground level exits, a hooded figure stepped-out from the doorway on the second floor and, before Glenn could react, grabbed the back of his hair, pulling his neck painfully back. With no hesitation, the attacker drove a long combat knife deep into his neck, all the way to the hilt. His eyes bore into Glenn's, never blinking, never betraying any fear or emotion. As he collapsed to the concrete floor, his blood and life flowing from his body, his attacker stood over him, motionless. Then, without a word, and with absolutely no hesitation or sign of emotion, he plunged the knife deep into both sides of Glenn's groin. His life was over in minutes.

It was less than 30 minutes before the gruesome scene was discovered by a member of the Top Golf staff as they made their final rounds after closing time. The shock, and the sheer volume of blood, made the high school senior throw-up the combination of burger sliders, chicken wings, and nachos that he'd been sneaking all evening. To say that the crime scene was contaminated would not really do justice to the volume of vomit deposited on the landing.

Detective Jeff Johnson was the lead investigator who took control of the scene. He arrived about 20 minutes behind the first responding patrol cars and only minutes before the Crime Scene units and coroner's wagon. In 26 years on the job, including 15 years as a Homicide Detective, he'd been a part of murder investigations and been to crime scenes that would give the average person nightmares for years, if not forever. While he'd seen many scenes where there were more bodies, more bullet cartridges, and more weapons, he'd never seen this much blood. And to realize that all this blood came out of one person, this one victim...... well, he was stunned, to say the least.

Johnson spoke to the CSI team. "Let's try to get multiple blood samples from around the body, just in case we might get lucky and find that the perp cut themselves during the attack. Probably a long shot, but we gotta go through the motions. And once he's back at HQ and cleaned up, let's focus on trying to ID the type of knife that was used. My first impression is that this was like a blitz attack; no hesitation, just several quick thrusts into targeted areas where death is guaranteed. The victim wouldn't have had a prayer of surviving this if he was sitting in the ER. That tells me that somebody is very skilled with the knife; they knew exactly where to cut for maximum damage."

Detective Johnson spent another 90 minutes at the scene before releasing the body to the coroner and heading back to the station. Years of experience told him that he needed to dig into the victim and his background, interview his friends, his coworkers, even the guests and staff that were at Top Golf this evening. It was those same years of experience that had him worried. In his experience, most stabbings are personal, and when they're not, a knife represents a weapon of opportunity. He already had a bad feeling about this one, though. The brutality, the precision, and the apparent speed of the attack made him think that there was a darker, more sinister explanation for this murder. He only hoped that he was wrong.

Aspen, CO

It had been more than two years since Tim Levinson had graduated from the University of Colorado, but he was still searching for his purpose in life. His parents had another term for it: 'Failure to Launch'. After graduating he had chosen to stay in Colorado rather than return to New York City, despite the fact that he had a career and a future waiting for him in the family business. His family, as one would expect, was disappointed with his life choices and constantly urging him to figure out what he was going to do with his life. They encouraged him to consider grad school. They'd even promised to pay, regardless of his field of study, if it helped him build a future instead of wandering aimlessly through his 20's. At least he had the good fortune to have been born into a very upper-crust family, truly one of the vaunted 1%, so he was not saddled with student loans and debts like so many other college kids. Plus, though his parents had threatened to cut him off financially unless he buckled down and started making something of himself, it had been nothing but idle threats. Every month his 'allowance' arrived like clockwork, and that, combined with the part-time jobs that he worked – skiing safety patrol during the season, and bartending in the offseason – allowed him to lead a pretty luxe life, especially for a 20-something.

The weather was finally starting to get cold in Aspen, and with an elevation of almost 8,000 feet, the resorts were gearing up for making snow after a warm summer and unseasonably warm early autumn. Oftentimes by this point in October the mountains had already experienced a few snowfalls, sometimes with significant accumulation, but not this year. The diehard skiers and those that worked at the ski resorts, including Tim, were bummed that the season was being delayed. While his job bartending at The Little Nell kept him busy and put some extra dollars in his pocket, he was more than ready to move on to his ski patrol gig.

With his day finally coming to an end around 9pm, Tim kicked back with a few local friends and customers to unwind after working both the lunch and dinner shifts. The beers went down easy, and quickly; after five years at the University, which, for the most part, was one long party, drinking three pints of Guinness in less than an hour was child's play. He had a nice, pleasant buzz, but the cool, crisp Aspen air would sober him right up. As he did most days, he had walked to work since his luxury apartment was only about two blocks from the bar. And you really couldn't ask for a much safer town than Aspen, especially before the high season kicked into full gear and thousands of visitors spilled in for the world-class partying and skiing. Even then, other than a few drunken idiots and the occasional theft of some rich out-of-towner's jewels or furs, crime was pretty much non-existent. Shortly after 10 he started towards home.

Two blocks. Safe, virtually crime-free surroundings. On any other night, on any other street, and at any other time that would have been enough. But not for Tim. Murders were rare, almost unheard of, in the ritzy environs of downtown Aspen. And this was a murder so grisly, so heinous, that the town wouldn't soon forget. The blood covering the sidewalk wouldn't soon disappear, either, at least not until the snows came and covered the ground until spring.

Chapter One

FBI Special Agent Mark Stevens was exhausted. Beyond exhausted, and he looked it. Wrinkled clothes, thinning brownish-gray hair a mess, and a couple of days since his face had last seen a razor. Definitely not the way the public, not to mention the recruiting posters and websites, envisions an FBI agent. He looked more like a cross between a homeless person and a used car salesman from some small midwestern city. He could at least be thankful that he didn't have his usual early morning flight and all of the crowds and hassles that go with it. Not that there had been any available seats on flights that morning anyway, but he was happy to be flying out mid-day since it allowed him at least a few hours of sleep, an easy trip to the airport, and a free upgrade to Economy Plus seating. Yes, he'd be getting home later by leaving midday, but all things being equal, this was making the best of a less-than-great situation.

Stevens had been in Irvine, CA for more than a week as part of a huge law enforcement presence sent to monitor dueling protests – which quickly boiled over into a full-blown riot – that was going on at the University of CA Irvine. In what had become an all-too-common occurrence, the crazies on the right and the crazies on the left used any pretense, real or imagined, to be at each other's throats. The situation had only been exacerbated by the 2020 election and seemed to be growing worse every day.

As a specialist on domestic terrorism, it was Stevens' job to monitor those groups and individuals that were fomenting the unrest and, in some cases, actual acts of terror, regardless of the group's ideology. After 20 years as an Agent, he had developed equal disdain for the far right and the far left. Proud Boys? He'd be happy to have the entire group jailed. Antifa? He had no love for them, either. Groups on both sides of the ideology spectrum had caused way too many problems, way too many deaths and injuries, and way too much property damage.

The impetus for the demonstrations at UC-Irvine had been, at least ostensibly, another police shooting of an unarmed black man. To make matters worse, in this case the dead person was a student, and he was killed on campus barely 100 yards from his dorm. His reported offense? Drunk and disorderly outside of a local bar, then leading the police on a short car chase and the inevitable confrontation with both local and campus police. From there the details get fuzzy and vary widely, depending on who you want to believe. Students blamed the police for being too rough and aggressive. The police swear that the young man had resisted arrest and assaulted several of the officers. Of course, the protests and the resulting riots had not waited for the official investigation – actually, *investigations*, plural – to even begin before they took to the streets. After a couple of days of mostly peaceful protests across the campus, the 'outside agitators' had descended on UC-Irvine like it was a Fourth of July block party. Hundreds of white supremacists from multiple alt-right factions, including the Proud Boys, various neo-Nazi groups, and leaders from past insurrections like the Charlottesville, VA 'Unite the Right' riots, were there in force. Not to be outdone, Antifa also showed up in force and prepared for battle. The alt-right faction openly carried guns, including AR-15's, as well as bats, flagpoles, bear spray, pepper spray, and knives, and military garb and body armor were *de rigueur*. The Antifa protestors were no better: while no guns were in evidence, there were plenty of weapons designed to crack heads and maximize damage, and as usual, they were almost all dressed in black from head to toe. It was no longer considered enough to just yell and scream at each other from opposite sides of the street. Now both sides live for the bloodshed and busted heads of their 'enemies'.

The whole situation had devolved into chaos. Cars and buildings burned. Businesses looted and set on fire. Police attacked by protesters from both sides. At times it felt more like guerrilla warfare, with millions of dollars in property damage, and dozens of injuries. Determining who was responsible for any single incident was nearly impossible unless it happened to be caught on video. Even then both sides insisted – *loudly* – that it was another instance of the 'other side' posing as one of them in order to make them look bad and bring public sentiment against them. And as one would expect, because it's become such a part of everyday life in America, the major news networks, especially the 24-hour cable news networks, were there with constant coverage. Depending on their own political leaning, they were spinning the story such that it would satisfy their ideological followers and stir their bloodlust – and their votes at future elections. It was nothing short of a miracle that no one was killed, though, if he were being honest, Stevens would not have shed a tear if leaders from both sides had been. He realized that he was becoming way too jaded; maybe after 25 years on the job in an increasingly splintered country it was time for him to hang up his spurs and move on to a new adventure. Not having a clue as to what that next great adventure might be always depressed him even further.

Now, at least, he was finally heading home. He lived just outside of DC in Alexandria, VA and commuted daily to FBI headquarters in DC. At least he did on the days that he wasn't traveling for his job, and that seemed to be an increasingly frequent occurrence with the growing polarization and 'us versus them' mentality of the American political landscape. This trip home required a 3-hour layover in Dallas, thus prolonging a week that was exhausting and felt never-ending. At least he could use the layover to grab a bite to eat, spend a few hours reading a book that had been untouched during the entire trip, and try hard to clear his mind and decompress. That was just the kind of downtime he needed.

Unfortunately, sometimes the best laid plans turn to shit. This was one of those times.

Chapter Two

FRIDAY, OCTOBER 21

M iracle of miracles: Agent Stevens' plane landed 10 minutes early and their gate was open and waiting for them to get in. Better yet, the flight was smooth and not a single disturbance or unruly passenger, not exactly a given in these crazy times. Since he was seated so close to the front, he was off the plane quickly and heading into the terminal. As much as he hated to do it, even for a trip where he had no idea how long he'd be gone, he had checked a large suitcase and brought a small carry-on with him on the plane. He'd also brought a backpack containing some of the usual must-have items for a long day of travel, like snacks, charging cords, a bottle of water, and his book. And since he was an FBI agent, after all, one other essential: extra ammunition for his service weapon. He carried his FBI-issued Glock pistol at all times, per regulations, but there were times when he wished he could forego it. Being crammed into a too small seat with too little leg room and elbow room for hours on end was definitely one of those times.

After hitting the restroom and grabbing a late lunch at Shake Shack, Stevens headed for the Skylink train to make his way from Terminal C to Terminal A for his next flight. He still had nearly an hour and a half before his connection, but he decided to head over to his gate early and relax with his book. It had been his experience that the trains were usually packed with people moving between the terminals, but since he was there in the mid-afternoon it was less crowded than he'd ever seen it, especially on a Friday. That surely wouldn't last long, since Fridays were always the second busiest day of the week, behind only Mondays. By late afternoon the place would be wall-to-wall people with planes moving in and out of the gates like a well-choreographed dance, at least if Mother Nature cooperated. Stevens said a little prayer that this wouldn't be one of those days with late day thunderstorms that played havoc with the flight schedules. Not that he had anyone or anything to rush home to, but still, he was certainly looking forward to his own house and his own bed.

As he boarded the Skylink train, he had almost the entire car to himself. He smiled to himself as he realized that this was probably the first time that there was an available seat in the many times that he'd flown through DFW and moved between terminals. He looked around at the handful of other passengers. Whether that was part of his FBI training or just part of his DNA, he prided himself on his situational awareness and observation skills as well as his ability to recall people and places and actions. Even if his career was stalled, or, more likely, coming to an early end, he was still proud that these skills came naturally for him, whereas for many others, they come only after years and years of practice and focus – if they ever come at all. He had no illusions of being considered a high performer at the FBI, or someone on the fast track. At one time he would have cared, but that was long ago. Now his life, and his career, was basically in a shame spiral and he saw no real way out. At least if he still had some of these innate qualities that all investigators need, he reasoned, then maybe he can find some way to remain useful and somewhat 'in the game' when he leaves the FBI. Or when someone asks him to leave.

Two young ladies, probably in their mid-20's, boarded at the same time as Stevens and moved to the back of the car, chatting almost non-stop. He checked them out, not because of his training but because they were both stunningly attractive. Both well dressed, very well put together. Perfect makeup, heels, and looking like young professionals returning from a week on the road. Maybe in technology, or, maybe pharmaceutical or medical device sales. They definitely looked like the stereotypical 'hot pharma girls' that he found attractive. He only wished that he could be sitting closer to them so he could overhear their conversation, maybe even live vicariously through their obviously more glamorous lives. Any other time he could have stood near them nonchalantly because of the packed cars, but not today. He was in the middle of the car, which may as well have been on the other side of the country. Of course, he had no illusions that he would ever try to talk to them or hit on them regardless of proximity; he was painfully aware, as many had pointed out over the years, that he had no game at all when it came to women, especially ones this far out of his league.

On the other end of the car was a single rider, head bobbing to the music coming through a pair of Beats headphones. Black, probably late 20's, dressed impeccably though casually. Not like a young street punk, more of a professional and educated vibe. He wasn't an especially big guy, but even in his designer jeans and designer hoodie, he looked solid. No doubt, to Stevens' way of thinking, that he was an athlete, or former athlete, maybe like a defensive back or wide receiver. He could envision him doing some serious cardio and lifting to maintain that build at an age where many men start to go a bit soft around the middle. As that thought crossed his mind, he couldn't help but to gaze down at his own expanding waistline; sure, he had at least 15-20 years on this guy, but that was no excuse. His hair was neat and professionally cut, and he sported a well-groomed beard, as well. Stevens pegged him as a professional man, not someone involved in manual labor. Not that he didn't look fit enough, because he obviously was. He just looked too well groomed, too well put together, too.....whatever.

The train ride to his next gate was only a few stops and typically takes only about five minutes. Relaxing was not in his nature, and he soon found himself scrolling through work and personal emails on his phone. He barely gave any notice when the train made its first stop, especially since no one got on or off. At the next stop, the first of two for Terminal A, he looked up from his phone to see the black guy getting off and heading to the escalator. Not giving it a second thought, he went back to his emails. That's when he heard the two female passengers trying to get his attention.

"Sir, excuse me, sir? Did that guy drop his wallet?"

Not really hearing or comprehending, he replied, "Oh, sorry, I didn't quite hear you. What was that?"

"That guy that just got off the train, I think he dropped his wallet. Isn't that a wallet on the floor up near where he was sitting?"

Stevens glanced over and saw exactly what she was talking about. "Yeah, you're right. Definitely a wallet." He looked up to see if he could spot the guy, but he must have already started down the escalator into the terminal. Normally he would have just taken the wallet and turned it in to the airport police or TSA, but since he had time to spare before boarding time, and since this stop at Terminal A would still allow him to walk to his gate, he decided to hop off the train and try to catch up to him.

Turning to the girls that had alerted him, he said, "I'll see if I can catch him. If not, I'll just turn the wallet in to the TSA or airport police and hopefully they can page him before he gets on his next flight."

Grabbing his bag and backpack he hustled off the train, barely making it through the doors before they closed. He moved quickly to the escalator and while riding down he decided to look inside the wallet to find a driver's license or other ID. At least that way he would be able to tell the police or TSA who to page if he couldn't find the guy. As he opened the wallet his cop instincts immediately started sounding the alarm. He had expected to find the usual stuff, like an ID, credit cards, maybe a business card, some money. But there was not a single credit card. Not a single business card. Not a single dollar bill. What he did find was unexpected. Not one, not two, but three different driver licenses. Three driver licenses from three different states with three different names. All the licenses had different pictures, but they were definitely all of the same man. The same man that had been sitting not 20 feet away from him on the train.

He thumbed through the licenses again. Jamie Dickson, age 28, from Clearwater, FL. Mark Hickson, age 29, Lubbock, TX. Marcus Cornell, age 28, Columbia, SC. Which one was real? Were any of them real? They were 'real' in the sense that they were official, state issued licenses, but were any of them the guy's real name and address? In his mind the answer was an unequivocal 'NO'. Twenty-plus years of law enforcement experience told him that something was definitely off here.

No way to know *why* this guy would have three different ID's, but there was also no legitimate explanation for why he should have them. No way that an undercover cop would carry around multiple ID's and risk blowing their cover should something like this happen. That's pretty much Undercover Cop 101. Create your cover, backstop the hell out of your cover, and 'live' your cover story until it's time to close the case. And it's not like this guy was some college kid that maybe needed fake ID's to buy beer; he was in his mid- to late-20's, at least, so a fake ID to make himself older made no sense.

Stevens considered his options. There was no proof that a crime had been committed, not unless it was found that the guy had used a fake ID to purchase his plane ticket and make it past the TSA security checkpoint. Certainly not any evidence of a crime that would involve the FBI, at least not yet. He thought through his options and decided that his best bet was to involve the TSA and airport police. Let them question the guy and determine if any laws had been broken. Hopefully by the time they determined that he'd be halfway back to DC and his own bed.

Reaching the bottom of the escalator, Agent Stevens moved quickly out to the main aisle and looked quickly both ways to see if he caught a glimpse of Dickson, or Hickson, or whatever the guy's name is. He had no way of knowing which gate he might be heading to, or, for that matter, which city he might be traveling to. Could it be one of the cities listed on one of the licenses? Yes, certainly, but just as likely another city altogether. Finally, he saw the guy strolling casually towards the lower numbered gates in Terminal A. Following at a safe distance, he observed the mystery man take a seat at Gate A-10; a quick check of the monitors near the gate showed that Flight 7211 would be departing for Austin in about 45 minutes. Stevens realized that he'd need to act quickly, and discretely, since the flight would be boarding in about 15 more minutes. The last thing that he wanted or needed was for the guy to board that plane. At best it would delay the flight even if the guy was escorted off by the airport police without incident. At worst – and he didn't even want to think about the worst – things could get very dicey in the confines of a plane if things didn't go well. Too little space, too many people that could get injured, and nowadays, too many people with their phones out recording every second of every such encounter on video.

Keeping the Austin gate in sight, he went to the next gate and found an available gate agent. "I'm Special Agent Mark Stevens with the FBI". He discretely showed his badge. "I need you to call the airport police and have them meet me down by the food court. Would you be able to do that, but do it discretely?"

The nervousness was immediately evident on her face. "Yes, I can do that, I suppose. But is everything OK? I mean, are we....I mean, all of these passengers waiting at the gates or walking around the terminal, are they in danger? Do we need to evacuate or raise an alarm?"

"No, no, absolutely not. I'd just like to inform the police about a situation and hand it over to them. There's no reason to be alarmed, and it's not something that needs to involve the FBI, especially an off-duty Agent. But as I said, I need to do it quietly so as not to alert the person I'm interested in and create a scene."

She looked less than convinced, but she remained outwardly calm and professional as she stepped up to the desk and reached for the phone. It took her only a couple of minutes to convey the message, and as she hung-up the phone she looked over at Stevens and gave him a quick nod as affirmation. He nodded back to her and then turned to walk to the food court which, fortunately, was only a couple of gates away. He hated to take his eyes from the suspect – *why was he already thinking of him as a suspect?* – but it couldn't be helped. He needed to talk in private with the airport police and keep them out of sight until they were ready to approach the guy and 'invite' him for a private conversation.

He arrived at the Food Court a few minutes ahead of the two DFW police officers. DFW employed around 200 police officers – more officers than many small- to mid-sized cities – so dispatching two of them to this part of Terminal A didn't take long at all. Stevens approached the uniformed officers and showed his badge, as discretely as possible, by flipping his jacket back as he neared them.

"Thanks for meeting me. I'm Special Agent Mark Stevens with the FBI out of DC headquarters."

"I'm Officer Michelle Kaplan, and this is my partner, Officer Jim Trojecki. What's the situation?"

Stevens gave them a quick explanation about the wallet and showed them the multiple ID's, and made sure to add that, while he was suspicious, he didn't have any way of knowing what the guy may have done, if anything. "At this point, it's admittedly more of a gut feeling that there's something suspicious."

"I can see why," added Trojecki. "It may be nothing, but I'd say it definitely warrants a conversation. Any indication if the guy is someone who may be aggressive or create a disturbance if we ask to have a private conversation?"

"I haven't spoken to him at all, so I have no idea. He and I just happened to share the same SkyLink car from Terminal C. At the time there was no reason to even be observing him, so I'm basically flying blind here. I can say that he looks like a guy who can handle himself, like someone with an extensive athletic background."

"So how do you want to approach him?" This from Officer Kaplan.

"While I know it's not my call or even remotely my jurisdiction, maybe I can be the one to approach him as a guy that just happened to find his wallet on the train and wanted to return it? It's possible that he might recognize me from the train, and since I'm in plain clothes maybe it's less likely to set off any warning bells or cause him to panic?"

"I'm OK with that. And to reduce the chance of spooking him, especially since we're both in uniform, I'll walk about 20 or 30 yards past his gate, and Kaplan can setup maybe 20 to 30 yards this side of the gate. Not that we expect any problems, but we'll be close but not too close."

Stevens nodded. "OK, let's do this. Hopefully we can make this quick, find that there's no reason to have more than a quick conversation, and I can still make my flight to DC."

Chapter Three

Stevens started back towards the gate for the Austin flight and felt his heart skip a beat. The guy was gone. It had been barely five minutes, but he had disappeared. Looking around and not seeing him, he felt beads of sweat breaking out on his brow. Cursing silently to himself, he slowly walked around the gate area hoping to get lucky. Clearly the guy was gone, but where? Was it possible that he was flying out of a different gate and not heading to Austin at all? In the short time that he'd been gone, was it possible that he'd already boarded another flight out of a different gate? Possible, but not probable, Stevens decided. He may have boarded another flight but no way it could have left by now. It generally takes 30-45 minutes for a flight to board and depart, and he'd been out of sight for barely five minutes.

Kaplan and Trojecki kept an eye on Stevens but had no way to communicate with him. They quickly grasped that something was wrong, though, based on his body language and growing look of concern on his face. Since they had only a vague idea what the suspect looked like, having only seen the thumbnail pictures on the fake ID's, they were relying on Stevens to spot him in the crowd. Plus, they both were trying to stick to the plan: stay close to the gate, but not too close, and don't do anything to alert the suspect that he's being watched.

Finally, he appeared, strolling leisurely back towards the gate and coming from the direction of the restrooms. Stevens breathed a sigh of relief, and then realized that this might actually play to his advantage. Instead of approaching him at the gate with a lot of people nearby, he could be approached where there were fewer people and more privacy. Sure, if the guy decided to make a run for it, he's going to be able to get away more quickly than he would if he were closer to the gate and seated, but that was a chance worth taking.

Stevens slowly approached him, and both Kaplan and Trojecki got their first good look at the guy that had aroused Stevens' suspicions. They held their ground and tried to be observant without being obvious. That might change quickly if things turned ugly, but they were hoping that wouldn't be the case. The guy didn't look like someone that would be easy to deal with if he wanted to get aggressive, and he looked in much better shape than any of the three of them; if he decided to run, they wouldn't stand a chance of catching him.

"Excuse me, sir," started Agent Stevens, "I was on the SkyLink train with you a little bit ago coming from Terminal C, and you dropped your wallet." He held the wallet up for the guy to see.

"Oh my God, I didn't even notice. That's really kind of you to track me down to return it. My name is Jamie Dickson, by the way." He reached out to shake Stevens' hand.

Shaking hands, he said, "Very nice to meet you, Jamie. I'm Mark Stevens. I'm just glad that I noticed the wallet and had time before my next flight to find you. I knew that I could turn it in to the TSA or police, but I was afraid that by the time they got moving you might have already caught another flight."

"I can't thank you enough for doing that. I'd hate to get all the way home to find out that it was missing. I'm not sure if I would have been able to figure out if I lost it on the plane, in one of the airports, in the rental car, or wherever. It probably would have been lost forever."

"Glad I was here to help. I do have one question, though." As he talked, he continued to hold onto the wallet and slowly pulled his jacket back to show his FBI badge. Dickson froze.

"Being a Special Agent with the FBI my first inclination, of course, was to see if there was ID in the wallet so that you could be found, and the wallet returned. But then what do I see, but 3 different licenses from

3 different states and 3 different names. No money, or pictures, or anything else in the wallet, just 3 licenses. You can see how, me being a cop and all, that this might make me suspicious."

Dickson was silent for a moment. Finally, "It's not what it looks like, Agent Stevens, and it's definitely nothing illegal. Maybe a little sleazy, admittedly, but nothing illegal."

"I'm listening." He expected everything that was going to come out of Dickson's mouth to be total bullshit from this point forward, but he wanted to let him talk. Lots of guilty people talk themselves right into a jail cell when they start with their lies.

"I spend a lot of time on the road in my job, and I use several dating apps to meet women while I'm traveling. I use different profile names and addresses, even different pictures and personal information. I have the licenses in case I have to 'sell' my profile to the ladies, because sometimes they're cautious about meeting guys from the internet."

"Makes sense why they would be cautious, especially in these crazy times. What with the internet, and all those dating and hookup apps. It's a wonder that these women will even consider taking a chance on meeting a stranger."

"You would think, right?" Then he smirked and added, "But I gotta tell you, I do OK. Lots of ladies out there looking for a guy on dating apps. I guess it's the 21st century version of the meat-market bars and clubs."

Stevens smiled. "Guess you're doing a lot better than me in the dating department, that's for sure. Not that you could do much worse." Time to go for the close.

"So Jamie, I want to give you your wallet back so I can catch my flight back to DC. It's been a long week; feels like a month. But there's one last thing I need to know to satisfy my curiosity and help me feel certain that everything here is on the up and up."

Dickson looked dubious, if not downright suspicious. "And what's that, Agent Stevens".

"I need to see your real ID."

"What do you mean? You have my real ID. Jamie Dickson." His tone was getting more agitated and defensive.

"I want to believe you. I really do. You seem like a nice guy and all.

It's just that I have a hard time believing your whole story. I mean, why would you keep your real ID together with two other fake ID's? I don't think you would. I think you'd keep your real one in a different place, like another wallet, where you'd probably also have your money, credit cards, and other personal items. And if you're really Jamie Dickson from Clearwater, FL, why are you flying to Austin? You could fly direct to Clearwater from DFW, so no way would you be connecting through Austin."

"Why are you hassling me? I told you why I have these fake ID's, now you're trying to make a federal case out of some minor bullshit like that?"

"No, not at all. But let me tell you what concerns me. I need to be sure that you didn't fly today using a fake name and ID, because if you did, that *is* a federal case. In a post 9/11 world, that's viewed as a likely indicator of terrorist activity. And when I see your real ID, I need to make sure that you're not someone on the no-fly list. Because if you are, and you used a fake name and ID to circumvent that, well, I'd say that you're going to be sitting in a federal prison for quite a long time."

"You got no right...."

"Actually, yeah, I got every right. At this point we're just having a conversation, so your 'rights' aren't even an issue. But before you're allowed on your flight you *are* going to have to show me your ID, and if all is clear then maybe we can forget this little dating scam you got going on. What I suspect, though, is that in addition to your real ID, you're going to have three fake passports in your backpack that match the fake licenses that you have. And once again, that is a *definite* federal offense."

"Why would you assume that I have fake passports? Or any passport, for that matter since this trip was all within the continental US?"

"It's simple, really. If you have multiple licenses with multiple names from multiple states, then that tells me there's a pretty good chance that you're involved in criminal activity. Not just scamming on the ladies, but probably real criminal activity. And you know what the smarter criminals do? They make sure that they always have an exit plan, and in the most extreme cases that means getting the hell out of the country, preferably heading to a place with no extradition. And you strike me as a pretty smart guy."

Stevens glanced at Officer Kaplan to signal him to start closing ranks. He knew that Trojecki would pick up on that movement and start doing the same from the other direction.

"So, what's it gonna be, Jamie? Or whatever your name really is. Do you want to show me your real ID here or do you want to accompany me and these two DFW police officers that are heading your way to their office? If it's the latter, I can assure you that you're going to miss your flight, and you may be leaving here in handcuffs. It's your call."

Dickson saw Kaplan and Trojecki approaching, and he knew that the walls were closing in on him, but he continued his blustery act. "I'll show you my ID to get this shit over with, but I promise you, once I get home I'm going to talk to my lawyer and sue you and every other one of these motherfuckers for your racist shit."

Stevens' attitude hardened, as well. "I'll look forward to it. Now, let's see that ID. I suppose it's in your backpack?"

"Yes, it's in my goddamn backpack. Where the fuck else you think it's going to be? You been checking me out the whole time, so you know it's not in my pocket."

Stevens watched as Dickson unslung the backpack from his shoulder and reached to unzip it. "Slowly. And don't even think about taking anything else out of the backpack other than a wallet or license. If I see anything else, even if I *think* I see something else, that will be all the excuse that we need to place you under arrest. Am I making myself clear?" His voice and his demeanor had hardened, intentionally: he wanted Dickson to be clear that there would be no more tolerating his attitude or aggression.

Dickson dug down into the backpack and as he was reaching in he made a lightning-fast move and shoved the pack into Stevens' face. All he needed was that momentary distraction. As Stevens stumbled back Dickson raised a 6" plastic, 3D printed knife and plunged it into the FBI agent's abdomen and chest with three quick thrusts. Stevens' eyes bulged in pain and terror, and blood immediately started pouring from his wounds.

Chaos quickly gripped the gate area, as people screamed and rushed away from the grisly scene as fast as they could. Dickson turned to run but only got a few steps before a deafening roar came from behind him.

Stevens, though gravely wounded, had managed to unholster his service weapon and got off a shot that went too high, but before Dickson could take another step the next bullet caught him in the right shoulder. He tried to keep running but knew that he was badly hurt, and he saw the two DFW police officers practically on top of him. Panicking, he grabbed a female passenger that stood frozen in place and used her as a shield. Putting the knife to her throat, he screamed "Everybody back away, or I'm going to kill her. Now! Get back!"

Kaplan and Trojecki stood their ground, barely 10 feet away. They could see that Dickson was seriously wounded, lots of blood soaking through his shirt, and at this point they didn't know if it was to their advantage or if it might make him more desperate and dangerous. The pain from the gunshot wound was clearly evident on his face, too.

"You need to drop the knife and let her go, right now. That's going to be the only way for you to survive this mess." Officer Trojecki circled slowly to his left as he spoke to Dickson. Kaplan stayed still, looking for an opening. Even with people scrambling in terror, there were still too many people around to open fire. But would he give them any other choice?

"You move and she's dead. I'm walking out of here, with her, and if you even think about making a move, I'll kill her". His voice was getting weaker, his body starting to shut down from blood loss and probable shock. With the knife at her throat, Dickson tried to walk slowly backwards and away from the officers. The lady was barely able to move, practically catatonic with fear. No resistance, just fear, and that meant that he practically had to drag her along. That worked against him: the more effort he had to expend to drag her, the more he bled and the weaker he got. It was still a long way to the exit, and he realized that the odds were definitely not in his favor.

It was hopeless, and he knew it. Blood was coming from his mouth with every breath, an indication of a perforation of one of his lungs. Other police were surely on their way, and he'd be totally surrounded. Even if he wanted to give himself up, and by some miracle he survived, there was no way that he would allow himself to be interrogated and bring down the others. He had to bite the bullet, figuratively speaking, and sacrifice himself.

Pushing the lady away, he raised the knife and moved towards Kaplan and Trojecki, screaming at the top of his lungs as he made one last, desperate attempt to kill them before he went down. It was not to be: eight shots to the stomach, chest, groin, and head spelled a quick and messy end for Jamie Dickson. Or whatever his name really was.

Chapter Four

FRIDAY, OCTOBER 21

I t didn't take long for things to progress from a typical day to a full-blown shit show at the FBI's Dallas field office. As the main FBI location for North Texas, they covered 137 counties spread across 125,000 square miles. The area was so vast that they had 12 satellite offices, also known as Resident Agencies. One of those satellite offices was located at DFW, but as luck would have it, the Special Agents assigned to that post were doing a two-week training assignment at Quantico.

Within minutes of the events at DFW, word had reached the FBI and quickly escalated to Special Agent in Charge (SAC) Ken Isaksen. He knew that this could put a serious damper on his weekend plans, but if an agent is killed, whether on-duty or off, everything else has to move to the back of the line. And with preliminary reports stating that the agent involved was Special Agent Mark Stevens, he took even more interest. Not that he considered Stevens a close friend, but they had attended and graduated from the Academy together many years ago. Their respective careers took them to different cities and departments, but they occasionally kept in touch and got together for dinner and drinks when their paths crossed at conferences or training.

If there was any saving grace, and admittedly, it was hard to think of an upside to any situation that involves an injured or killed agent, it at least seemed to be an open and shut case. Suspect kills Stevens, who reportedly managed to get one shot into the fleeing suspect, and then the suspect is killed by DFW police as he takes a hostage and then attacks police. Another example of suicide by cop for a dying suspect? Probably. Not open and shut – nothing ever truly is, especially with officer involved shootings – but as close to it as one can hope for.

Isaksen picked up the phone and dialed his assistant. "Angie, who do we have on the schedule for tonight and this weekend? I need to send someone over to DFW right away."

"Sir, according to the schedule we have quite a few agents working this weekend, though it looks like most of them are already working active cases. Special Agent Jansen is on-duty, and from what I can see she's not involved in any active investigations. And I know she's around here today because I just saw her maybe 15 minutes ago when I walked down to get coffee. Should I send her up to your office?"

Isaksen suppressed a groan. Of all the agents that he'd prefer *not* to have involved, Special Agent Jessica Jansen was at or near the top of that list, especially here in the Dallas field office. He considered Jansen to be a waste of space and a total burnout, but he'd been stuck with her for 10 years and counting. At least, he reasoned, she should not be able to mess up this investigation. Or at least he could hope. "Yes, please have her in my office in 10 minutes. I just need to call home first to change plans for this evening with my wife."

He hated to have to change tonight's plans, but it couldn't be helped. Luckily, his wife would understand. She was an angel. Twenty-five years of marriage and he still knew, beyond a shadow of a doubt, that he'd hit the jackpot. She was used to the life of an FBI agent's wife; sometimes that meant last-minute cases, travel, and frequent schedule changes, but she'd dealt with it without complaint. She'd taken the lead in raising their two kids, though she'd be the first to admit that Isaksen had been a great father. He made it to almost every football, volleyball, and soccer game, every school play, and key life events like graduations. Even when cases compelled him to be away, he never once failed to talk to his wife and kids every single day. His family was his life, no two ways about it. He never made a big deal about it, but he'd actually passed up two opportunities for assignments to more prestigious field offices, and even one promotion. He loved living in Dallas, as did his family, and he wouldn't for a second consider uprooting them from the home, the friends, the schools, and the life that they cherished. And certainly not to be stuck in that political hellhole that is FBI headquarters in DC. He'd rather retire and hang out his own shingle.

His wife picked up on the second ring. "Let me guess: change of plans for this evening?"

"You know me too well. But yes, you're right. Did you hear about what went down at DFW about an hour ago?"

"I just saw a quick newsflash but didn't catch any of the details."

"I don't even have a lot of details at this point. We do know that the suspect was killed, but not before taking a woman hostage and killing an off-duty FBI agent."

"Oh my God, that is terrible. Please tell me that it wasn't one of your agents."

"No, but it is someone I know. He and I actually go all the way back to the Academy. He was off-duty and just happened to be catching a connecting flight when all of this went down. Do you remember me mentioning a guy named Mark Stevens, assigned to DC HQ?"

"Vaguely. Pretty sure that I never met him at any of your Agency events, but I do recall you mentioning that name as someone that you had dinner with once or twice over the years. I'm really sorry to hear that he was killed. Are you OK?"

"Yeah, I'm fine. Obviously, I hate it when we lose any agent, but I am relieved that it wasn't someone from our Dallas office. Not that it makes the situation any better, but unless something has changed since I last spoke with Stevens, he at least isn't leaving a young family or anything. He had a nasty divorce about ten or twelve years ago and as far as I know he's never remarried or been with anyone long term since. No kids, and I'm not even sure about parents or siblings. Maybe that's a small blessing; it's an incredibly hard thing for those left living to have to deal with."

"You're right, but still, it's heartbreaking. So, what's your plan from here?"

"I'm assigning an Agent to go down to DFW to oversee our part of the investigation, work closely with the DFW police, and hopefully close this out quickly and ensure that airport operations aren't impacted for any longer than is absolutely necessary. You can imagine the political and public pressure that is going to come down with this, especially if anyone is inconvenienced or has a flight delayed for even a minute."

"Are you going down to DFW, too?"

"I'm not sure. I'm getting ready to brief the Agent that I'm assigning to the case, and it's something that I think she can likely handle without screwing it up or making us look bad. It does seem pretty open and shut, or at least as much as they ever can be." Isaksen looked up and saw Special Agent Jansen heading towards his office. "I gotta run, my Agent is here. I'll call or text you later to let you know what's going on and when I'll be home. Sorry again about our plans for tonight. I'll make it up to you, maybe tomorrow night if things don't go awry. Love you."

Before she could even knock on the door, SAC Isaksen said, "Special Agent Jansen, please come in. Sit" He noted the apprehensive look on her face, and it was not without cause. To say that they had a strained relationship would be an understatement. Based on her troubled past and work record, she knew that it's more likely that she'd been called in to be chastised rather than to receive praise or a plum assignment.

Isaksen dispensed with any warm greetings or small talk. When it came to Jansen, he felt that any attempt at that would be disingenuous, at best. Plus, this wasn't the time for it. He needed this investigation to start moving ASAP, and with velocity. "Special Agent Jansen, I'm sure by now you've heard about the situation at DFW that resulted in a woman being taken hostage, a dead suspect, and the death of Special Agent Stevens from HQ?"

"Yes sir, I have. Not a lot of details yet, but I've at least heard and seen what's being reported in the media and on social media. I assume that Special Agents Hughes and Haddad are already onsite and driving the investigation?"

"Unfortunately, they're both attending a training class in Quantico for two weeks. Let me cut right to the chase: Since they're not here to lead, as would normally be the case, I want you to head this investigation. I want you over at DFW as soon as you can get there. Find out why Special Agent Stevens was involved with this suspect, what precipitated this whole mess. Talk to the two DFW officers that were there with Stevens; in case you don't know, they're the ones that fired the shots that took the suspect down, though Agent Stevens did manage to get off a shot that severely wounded the suspect before he succumbed to his own injuries. My guess is that this is a pretty straightforward case and one that you'll be able to close, at least from the FBI's perspective, pretty quickly. Though, being as this was an agent-involved shooting, there will be eyes on this both from HQ and the public. Obviously, be *very* careful what you say and who you say it to."

"Thank you, sir. I'll head over there immediately. I assume that you'd like a sit-rep from me as soon as possible?"

"Definitely. And if for any reason you need me onsite, don't hesitate to reach out. I assume that you won't need me for the actual investigation, but if you need help with political cover, lack of cooperation from the DFW police or officials, or whatever, you let me know. I don't think that will happen; so far, the DFW police have been very cooperative and willing to work together, but you never know what can cause things to go south. This is our dead agent, and I want to know why he was interacting with the suspect, and I especially want to know how the suspect managed to have a deadly weapon in his possession. For that matter, I want to know where the suspect was coming from, where he was traveling to, and what he was doing before traveling to DFW. I've got to believe that there's a lot more to this than two guys getting into a beef over a spilled drink or reclining their seat too far."

"I'm on it, sir. I'll keep you updated as I get more details, and I'll do my best to close this out quickly." She hoped that her faux sincerity was Oscar-worthy, but she didn't kid herself. She knew that SAC Isaksen thought very little of her as a person or as an agent. As much as she wanted to resent him for it, she really couldn't. He was actually a great Agent and a very well-respected SAC, and Dallas was probably one of the most well-run Field Offices in the FBI. His reasons for not respecting her, or, if she were honest, even wanting her on his team, were legitimate. She was given this assignment probably because it seemed too straightforward to screw-up. Or, more likely she was the only agent available this late on a Friday afternoon and scheduled for the weekend. Having been beaten down for so long, both by herself and the

FBI, she lacked the self-confidence that most Agents had, often to the point of being downright cocky.

Special Agent Jessica Jansen, or 'JJ' to her friends since her childhood growing up in Scottsdale, AZ, knew that she was running out of chances to save her FBI career. Sure, she might be lucky if she kept her head down and stayed below the radar, didn't have any major screw-ups, and maybe even closed a case every now and then. But she knew that any chance of career progression was long gone, not that she had any strong desire to move to another city and another FBI Field Office. If she could move and make a clean start, not have any of her career and emotional baggage, that would be one thing. Of course, the chances of that were zero; every office and every agent would have access to her FBI history. Maybe not her medical records and other confidential parts, but that would matter little. People talk, and already too many people knew about her less-than-stellar past. And time had proven, beyond any shadow of a doubt, that FBI employees were just as capable of being gossipy little bitches as the women down at the local nail salon.

It was a well-known fact that JJ had been in rehab twice over the course of her career. While most people would probably assume that a single rehab stint would spell the end of an Agent's career at the FBI, the reality is that the Bureau is, at least *officially*, more progressive than that. They want to be 'supportive' of their agents. They pledge to keep everything 'in confidence' and to help troubled agents 'recover' and make a fresh start. Reality is usually different: while agents may not lose their job, their careers are stalled. JJ's first rehab stint had been about 10 years ago, shortly after a bitter and contested divorce. While she had, admittedly, had a problem with alcohol for many years, which she blamed on childhood traumas caused by a broken home, a mother that died from alcoholism when she was barely 16, and a distant, emotionally abusive father, she lost all control after her divorce. Fortunately for her, and probably her only saving grace when it came to her job as a Special Agent, is that she was a functioning alcoholic. On time for work, still performing at a respectable level, even closing some cases. But her fellow Agents, not to mention her bosses, the citizens she interacted with, the various lawyers and prosecutors she met with, all saw the signs. They all saw her red, bloodshot eyes, the disheveled appearance, and her declining energy levels. There were even complaints from some people that noted the strong smell of alcohol on her, even first thing in the morning. It didn't matter how many showers she took or how much she tried to mask it with scented soaps and perfumes, or mouthwash, or freshly laundered clothes, the smell just emanated from her pores. It didn't take long before her bosses gave the ultimatum: go to rehab and get clean or kiss her job goodbye. She did 30 days of residential rehab, and it wasn't at one of those posh facilities like they show in Malibu for all the rich celebrities. No massages, no horseback riding, no sushi, nothing to make it the least bit enjoyable. Instead, there were daily 1:1 and group counseling sessions, mandatory chores and tasks, and meals that were anything but Michelin-star level. After 30 days she was totally clean and looking forward to being back at work, around people, and doing a job she loved. She felt like the old JJ, before alcohol had taken complete control of her life, but people still looked at her and treated her like damaged goods. Sure, they were mostly polite to her face, but it was evident that she was no longer one of the team or an Agent that anyone wanted to be partnered with.

JJ had been sober for almost two years when she was forced into rehab a second time. This time it wasn't alcohol – she had stayed away from alcohol since leaving rehab the first time – but opioids. It was a story that seemed to be reported every day in cities big and small, rural and suburban: a person gets injured or has a serious medical problem, they're prescribed Oxy or other opioids to manage the pain, and soon they're addicted. In JJ's case, her pain was caused by a serious car accident. She always lamented that she hadn't been shot while trying to apprehend some violent felon, or at least involved in a high-speed pursuit of a suspect, because that would have garnered at least a little sympathy and understanding, maybe even a modicum of respect, from her fellow Agents. But she was not so lucky. Instead, it was just an ordinary car accident, the kind that happens hundreds of times per day across America. She was driving to the grocery store, a trip of only a few miles that she'd done a million times before. Unfortunately, this time a distracted driver ran through an intersection and t-boned her car right in front of the driver's door. She was lucky to be alive, but her injuries were significant: broken left femur, tibia, and ankle, a dislocated left shoulder and fractured collarbone; several broken and bruised ribs, and some internal bleeding. Her injuries required more than a month in the hospital, including almost two weeks in ICU. Months of physical therapy and occupational therapy followed her release. Her reliance on the pain medication continued after her time in the hospital, and she knew enough to be concerned. Concern, unfortunately, didn't outweigh the need for more pills, both physically and psychologically. Before she fell down the rabbit hole that many addicts find themselves in, namely, losing their job, their savings, their homes and families, maybe even resorting to stealing to feed their habit, she proactively reached out for help. It saved her life, for sure. It also saved her job.

If alcohol withdrawal was bad, opioid withdrawal made it look like a walk in the park. Rehab was even more soul-crushing and the facility even more austere. Still, she counted her blessings. She was alive, and she was going to beat this and turn her life around. She did beat her demons, and she did return to her life. Only the FBI didn't exactly welcome her back with open arms. They welcomed her back, one might say, grudgingly.

Chapter Five

I t took JJ 30 minutes to reach DFW, and she saved time by simply double-parking in the passenger pickup and drop-off lanes along with dozens of other first responder vehicles. The TSA and DFW Police had done a great job of keeping at least half of Terminal A open at this point, and they had setup a dedicated security line for the many police, FBI, EMT's, and other officials to pass through with minimal delay. She had to admit, that was pretty good thinking on their part. There would be dozens of law enforcement personnel from multiple agencies entering the airport and heading down to the gates, and they'd be carrying all manner of prohibited items. It was critical that security ensure that no one without the proper credentials and clearances was permitted in with any type of weapon

JJ made her way down to Gate A10 and found the whole area closed off with crime scene tape, but she was disappointed to find that both bodies had already been removed and sent to the Medical Examiner's office. There would be hundreds of pictures and videos of the scene to review, but she was pissed that she didn't get to see things firsthand. In her experience, seeing the scene as it was before things were moved and before it got trampled on by other cops or curious bystanders was critical to the investigation. Nothing to do about it at this point; there was no turning back time.

There must have been at least 15 cops from various agencies inside the cordoned off area. The TSA and DFW cops were there, of course, and at least another half-dozen plainclothes officers, presumably Dallas PD detectives. Several crime scene techs in their white Tyvek suits, gloves, and booties were still searching for evidence, and around the perimeter were a lot of grim-faced airport officials huddled in deep discussion about the potentially devastating impact on flight schedules, lost revenues, passenger inconvenience, and media coverage. The media, of course, was already onsite and more were arriving every few minutes, and as they arrived, they were escorted to a roped-off area about a hundred yards away. Of course, that didn't stop a couple of them from trying to get closer, but they were quickly rounded up and threatened with total banishment if they didn't stay in the designated area.

She made her way to the DFW officer that appeared to be in charge of securing the scene, and after identifying herself she asked to speak with Officers Kaplan and Trojecki. He called them on the radio rather than stepping away from his post, and they appeared within minutes.

Introductions were made all around, and JJ said, "Is there somewhere we can sit and talk that's a little bit more private, and a little quieter?"

"Good idea, it's so loud in here I can barely hear myself think," said Trojecki. "Let's head over to the food court and grab a table. It's closed right now, but a couple of the stands have kept on a skeleton crew to take care of all the police and fire folks. We can grab a bite to eat, if you want, or at least a cup of coffee"

"Great idea. I missed lunch, and I've got a feeling that this is going to be a long evening."

JJ grabbed a cheeseburger, fries, and a large Coke and made her way to the table where the two DFW officers were already seated and drinking coffee. "So guys, what can you tell me? I've seen only what's been reported on the news, but I'd like to hear from you. I'm sorry to ask you to go through this for probably the millionth time since it happened. At least no one is questioning the fact that this was a good shoot, I assume."

Kaplan spoke up first. "No question about it being a clean shoot, and fortunately we have dozens of witnesses and God-only-knows how many videos shot by the passengers at the gate and the surrounding area."

"Had you guys just met Special Agent Stevens?"

"Yes," said Trojecki, "He had an American Airlines gate agent call for assistance after he'd followed the suspect to the gate. According to Stevens, he had been searching for him after they'd exited the SkyLink train, and he finally found him at Gate A10. We met briefly right here, in the food court, and laid out a plan for approaching the suspect."

"Did he give you a reason why he was following this guy?"

"As I mentioned, they were on the same Skylink train heading here to Terminal A, and apparently the guy exited at the stop before Stevens planned to get off. Other passengers in the same train car told Stevens that the guy dropped his wallet, and he tried catching up to him to return it but lost him in the crowd. When he checked the wallet for ID so he could have him paged, that's when he knew something was off: the guy had 3 different ID's from 3 different states and 3 different names and pictures. And that was it, nothing else in the wallet. No money, no credit or debit cards, nothing. That made him even more suspicious, and obviously, for good reason." Kaplan looked away, still more than a little bit shook after seeing the Agent killed right before her eyes. That was even more upsetting than the fact that she had shot and killed the suspect. In her 6 years as a member of the DFW Police she had never so much as drawn her gun, and now the first time she had to take it from her holster she ends up killing a man.

"I understand that you guys secured the evidence recovered at the scene. I'd like to look through it here before shipping it to our Labs, if that's OK with you. I'll make sure to give you a detailed receipt for each item to protect chain of custody."

"Sure, as soon as you're finished eating, we'll walk you back to our office here in Terminal A. It's all locked up and secure in our safe."

"One thing I gotta know, because the curiosity is killing me," said JJ. "How in the world did this guy get a knife through security? I assumed it was a carbon knife, but 99% of the time there's still enough metal in a carbon knife to set off the metal detectors, at least if you have them setup and calibrated correctly and a halfway competent person monitoring things."

Trojecki nodded. "You're right about the whole carbon thing. Most people think that a carbon knife can be snuck on with their carryon luggage, but that's not true; they've just watched too many spy movies. The TSA guys here tell me that they catch at least 1-2 carbon blade knives every quarter. But this guy's knife was different. I'd be willing to bet my next paycheck that he created it himself with a 3D printer."

"I've never heard of a 3D printed knife. I mean, I have heard of 3D printed guns. Pretty basic firearms, generally single shot, and kinda bulky compared to regular handguns, but they will make it through metal detectors in almost all cases. Was the knife even sharp? I wouldn't think that it was something that could hold an edge."

"We haven't done any testing on the knife, but just doing a rudimentary check with evidence gloves on, I'd say that the knife edge didn't feel very sharp. The tip, however, was extremely sharp and pointed. It would easily penetrate flesh, and deeply. I'd say that it was a good knife for repeatedly stabbing someone as opposed to, say, trying to slice their throat." Kaplan made a hand motion mimicking someone dragging a knife from ear to ear.

The three of them headed to the office to look at the collected evidence. Once there they brought it to a meeting room for JJ to inspect. After she gloved-up, she started methodically going over each piece of evidence that was retrieved from the suspect's backpack. She started with the wallet and the licenses. As she'd been told, different names, different states, different pictures, but no question that it was the same guy in all the pictures. She next looked at a newer model iPhone, a cheap burner phone, passports matching the names and addresses of all 3 fake ID's, an American Express card and a VISA card in the name of Jamie Dickson, nearly $900 in cash, and a PC. She hoped that between the phones and the PC she'd hit the motherlode, but she wouldn't take bets on that. If this guy was as sharp and well organized as she suspected, it was going to take someone with skills well beyond hers to access the information on those devices.

"I assume that the crime scene team has the knife and Stevens' gun?"

"Correct," answered Kaplan. "All bagged and tagged. They also have the shell casings, some bullets pulled from nearby walls and furniture, and the contents of Stevens' pockets. And, of course, they're in charge of collecting the blood and other physical samples".

"How about the hostage? Was she injured? And do you think she has any information to contribute to the investigation?"

"She wasn't hurt, at least not physically, but she was shook-up as hell. Maybe even in shock, which is understandable." Trojecki felt certain that the woman would be traumatized for a good long while. "As far as contributing anything to the investigation, I sincerely doubt it. We're talking to her, of course, but I don't expect her to be able to add anything that would help. Just an innocent person in the wrong place at the wrong time."

Satisfied that she had given a preliminary look at each piece of the suspect's belongings, she was ready to take the next step and talk to the crime scene technicians that had collected the suspect's knife, Stevens' gun, crime scene photos, blood and hair samples, fingerprints, bullets, and shell casings and all of the other bits of evidence that make up a horrible crime like this. Most importantly, she wanted to arrange to have all of the evidence transferred to the FBI crime lab as soon as possible. She hoped that there wouldn't be any arguments or turf wars about who owned the investigation and would take control of processing the evidence. With so many agencies involved, differences of opinion and outright disagreements were almost a given. She hoped that in this situation the pecking order would be clear and easily agreed to. A dead FBI agent, inside of an airport, and a suspect with multiple fake licenses and passports? It should be a no-brainer. Then again, with all of these agencies and their tendency to have massive egos and a desire for the spotlight, brains weren't always a given.

JJ walked back towards Gate A10 with Trojecki and Kaplan, and as she went in search of the person in charge of the crime scene evidence team, she thanked them both for their assistance. She also made it a point to congratulate them on a job very well done. It was certainly not their fault that Stevens had been killed or that they'd had to kill the suspect. Because of their actions, what could have been a much deadlier scene had been averted.

Approaching the leader of the crime scene investigation unit, JJ introduced herself as the FBI agent assigned as lead for this case. "So, Lieutenant, what can you tell me about the crime scene and what you've recovered so far?"

Lieutenant George Ruffin from the Dallas PD Crime Scene Investigation team pulled-up a list of the evidence collected on his PC. "For the most part, it's what you'd expect. Weapons from both victims, lots of blood, shell casings from Agent Stevens' gun as well as the service weapons belonging to Officers Kaplan and Trojecki. All of that will need to be tested, of course, to determine which gun caused each wound and which fired the fatal shot. We've also bagged and tagged Stevens' cell phone and other contents from his pockets, plus we took custody of his roll-aboard bag and his backpack. We've sent someone down to the American baggage office to claim his checked bag, and we should have that shortly."

"Excellent. How quickly can we arrange to have that transferred to the FBI lab to start the analysis?" She assumed that if anything would start the tug-of-war, this would be it.

"We can make that happen right now. Come with me and we'll print out the evidence logs and let you sign for it, then we'll get one of our people to transport everything immediately. If we find anything else before we close-up shop this evening, I'll forward you that information via email and then have it transported tonight or tomorrow morning, at the latest."

JJ thanked the Lieutenant and breathed a sigh of relief. Turf wars take time, and time was a luxury that she didn't have. Plus, she didn't want to have to involve Isaksen in this case any more than necessary, as that would give him even more reason to think that she was incapable of handling a case on her own. She sat alone in a vacant gate area to collect her thoughts. Was there more to be done here, or was her time better spent elsewhere? How would she liaise with the other agencies? Were there tasks that she could delegate to others, in the spirit of 'teamwork'? Officially the FBI had the lead, but the TSA, DFW Police, Dallas PD, and others all had a vested interest in this case.

The top priority was getting the suspect's fingerprints into the system and uncovering his real identity, and from there she could start tracking his recent travel and spending habits. She retrieved the evidence collected by the onsite teams and headed for the exit. Much of that evidence needed to be forwarded to Quantico ASAP. As far as the suspect's PC and mobile phones, she'd get that to the Dallas office's 'secret weapon' for technical forensic analysis: the North Texas Regional Computer Forensics Laboratory (NTRCFL), which had opened in May 2021 at a new state-of-the-art facility downtown.

JJ realized that the immediate priority was touching base with Isaksen to apprise him of the situation and her planned next steps. Once she got the fingerprint analysis underway and dropped off the electronics at NTRCFL, she was going to head to the Medical Examiner's office to observe the autopsies. After that, if she wasn't too tired to function, she'd start on her preliminary report. She didn't relish this last task, but she knew that Isaksen would be looking over her shoulder. There was sure to be a lot of eyes on this investigation since it involved one of their own.

JJ called Isaksen as she drove. She was shocked to find that he was still in the office; she assumed that he'd gone home hours ago since he hadn't shown up at DFW, thankfully. She bristled under his micromanagement, but she knew that was the price she paid for her years of sub-par performance and personal challenges. She took about 10 minutes to update him on all that she'd seen and learned, and then filled him in on her planned next steps.

"That sounds like a smart plan, Agent Jansen." Isaksen, like most of the other FBI personnel, never called her 'JJ'. That was mostly just her family and friends, and there was no one in her office, maybe not in the entire FBI, that qualified as a 'friend'. "What do you need from me at this stage?"

"Nothing that I can think of yet, sir. Maybe you can reach out to the evidence team to ensure that they get everything rushed to Quantico first thing tomorrow, and maybe lean on the Quantico guys to put a rush on the evidence that we're sending them."

"Just let me know. I can have someone start on that as early as tomorrow if it's needed. I'd rather not wait until Monday, for all the reasons that we discussed earlier. Keep me updated. I'll be available all weekend, so don't hesitate to call."

JJ's interpretation of his direction: "I don't fully trust you to do the right things and get this done, so you better make damn sure to check in with me on a regular basis so I can oversee what you're doing and, if necessary, override any of your impending fuckups." Then again, maybe her interpretation was just her self-doubt and growing paranoia.

Chapter Six

T he good thing about having access to the Automated Fingerprint Identification System (AFIS) is that it drastically reduced the time and effort required to match someone's fingerprints. It was way more accurate than back in the day when a technician had to stare into a microscope to manually match the paper records with the image pulled from a piece of cellophane tape. Still, there was no way to predict how long a match would take, or if there would even be a match. It's always possible that the prints belong to someone that's never been 'in the system'. JJ had experienced this frustration before, so while she let AFIS do its thing, she set about her next task.

It didn't take long to confirm that the suspect had traveled under the alias Jamie Dickson, and he had flown into DFW from Reagan National in Washington, DC aboard American Airlines flight #1251. He'd flown to DC on Tuesday, October 18th on American #1177. *What was he doing for the two days and nights that he was in the DC area?* JJ wished that she had access to the suspect's mobile phone to see if it held anything useful, but that was out of her hands and dependent on the tech gurus. At least she had credit cards using the Dickson alias. It took a good 45 minutes, but she was finally able to confirm that he had stayed at the Four Seasons in Georgetown. Swanky. Expensive. She had expected someplace a bit seedier; she wasn't sure why. *Would a guy that says at the Four Seasons be the kind of guy that would kill an FBI agent, take a woman hostage, and try to kill a couple of police officers?*

It was no small feat to get a lead of this quality so early in the investigation. It certainly wasn't a complete picture, but it was a start. That sense of accomplishment increased ten-fold moments later when AFIS got a hit on the fingerprints from this 'Jamie Dickson'. Her pulse quickened as she read the results: real name Jamarcus Hicks, resident of Austin, TX, 29 years old. She could hardly contain her excitement. Knowing the suspect's identity should really help to get things moving. She'd start by tracing his history back to the day he was born, including his schools, his social media activities, everything. *Speaking of which, why was he in the system in the first place?* Reading through the report she saw that Hicks had been arrested in New York City for underage drinking and disorderly conduct when he was 19. He received a slap on the wrist: fifty hours of community service, no jail time.

JJ made a note to reach out to the TSA to have them check all records associated with Jamarcus Hicks and his various aliases. Hicks had a valid TSA Precheck associated with his real name and fingerprints. Could he have somehow managed to get TSA Precheck for his aliases, too, using the same fingerprints? She checked the boarding passes he'd had for today's flights: both showed TSA Precheck in the name of Jamie Dickson. As she thought this through, she realized that this must be one very smart operator with incredible skills or connections to have multiple identities and passports all leveraging the same set of fingerprints. But to what end?

It was getting late, but JJ was not about to call it a night until she handed off Jamarcus Hicks' electronics to the crackerjack forensic specialists at the NTRCFL. On the way she would call Isaksen to update him on her findings, and then call ahead to the ME's office. It was only about a 20-minute drive from her office to the NTRCFL, and she planned to take advantage of every minute to keep things moving.

Isaksen picked up on the first ring. "Special Agent Jansen, I hope you have some good news. The public and media rumblings are already starting, and I'm sure that a spate of lawsuits will be next."

"Yessir, I've been able to make some progress in the past few hours.

Most importantly, I have a positive ID on the suspect. His name is Jamarcus Hicks, from Austin. No rap sheet to speak of, just a D&D about 10 years ago in New York. I found that he traveled back from DC today using one of his aliases, Jamie Dickson. He'd been in DC for a couple of days, and while I don't yet know all of his movements, I was able to confirm that he stayed at the Four Seasons Hotel."

"That's certainly progress, especially on a Friday evening. Good job, Agent Jansen."

Wow. Was that actually praise coming from SAC Isaksen? "Thank you, sir. I'm on my way now to NTRCFL to drop off the electronics we recovered and then heading to the ME's office. One last thing, sir: I know that we're early in the investigation, but my gut is telling me that this is more than some random encounter in the airport. We've got a guy with multiple aliases and passports, and apparently four different TSA Precheck approvals all tied to the same set of fingerprints. That's not easy to do. This reeks of organized crime, or maybe state-sponsored terrorism."

"Let's not let your 'gut' make this into something it's not. At this point all we know is that we have two men dead, including an FBI Special Agent, and a public relations nightmare at one of the busiest airports in the US. What I want you to do is get the electronics to NTRCFL and ensure that the rest of the evidence gets expedited to Quantico. Then by close of business Monday, have your completed reports ready for my review and forwarding to the US Attorney. Is that understood?"

Are you fucking kidding me?! JJ had to count to ten in an attempt to calm herself. It didn't help. She was barely able to control the outburst that was forcing its way out. She looked down at her hands and saw that her knuckles were white from trying to squeeze the steering wheel into dust. Arguing would get her nowhere, except maybe out the door. "Yes sir. Understood." She quickly disconnected and then let loose a string of profanities at the top of her lungs. Frustrated, humiliated, and on the verge of tears, she had to fight the temptation to pull off the road at the next bar and drown herself in tequila. But she resisted; not because of her years of sobriety, or because she might lose her job. She simply refused to let Isaksen continue to beat her down and make her feel 'less than'. *Fuck him.*

Before heading into the NTRCFL, JJ called the ME's office and they agreed to start the autopsies on both victims when she arrived. She thanked them profusely and promised to arrive within the hour. Fortunately, the drop off to the electronics forensics team only took a few minutes, and they promised to have a preliminary report waiting for her by 9am in the morning.

The ME's office was only about 10 minutes from NTRCFL, and as she approached she was psyching herself up for the sights, sounds, and smells she was about to face. This wasn't her first rodeo; she'd attended dozens of autopsies, for all manner of deaths, and she took pride in the fact that she'd never once fainted or vomited. Not many could say the same. Still, there were a few things that always messed with her mind, like the formaldehyde smell that permeated your clothes and lingered on everything you carried into the building, or the sound of the Stryker saw cutting into the corpse's head or chest cavity. She may be able to 'handle it', but if she had her druthers, she'd never attend another one.

Donning protective clothing, a face shield, and gloves, she entered the theater. She knew from experience that blood and other liquids tended to splatter, and bone 'dust' gets in the air as the power tools are used. Plus, she always wanted it on the record that she wore proper protection to avoid accusations of contaminating or mishandling evidence. That was one of the lessons drilled into their heads in the Academy: never give the defense an opening to question your handling of evidence, including chain of custody.

The two autopsies were conducted at the same time in adjacent rooms. JJ moved between the rooms as each autopsy progressed, and she watched from a respectful distance unless the pathologist asked her to come closer. The examiners paid special attention to Stevens' stab wounds, photographing them, measuring the depth of penetration, and determining blood loss. The report would show that any one of the wounds could have been fatal on its own, but with three wounds, one that pierced his heart and one on each side of his groin that nicked the femoral arteries, death was a certainty.

"So, Dr. Kleinman, anything else to add regarding Agent Stevens' wounds?"

"No big surprises, Agent Jansen. Any one of the wounds would have been fatal. I am of the opinion, though, that the person who stabbed Agent Stevens was highly skilled. Take, for example, the stab wound to his heart. The knife was thrust at an upward angle and went perfectly between two ribs and into the heart muscle itself. Either the suspect's aim was extremely lucky, or he was highly skilled and well-versed in anatomy. My money is definitely on the latter."

"Why is that?"

"If you combine the accuracy of the stabbing to the chest with the perfect placement of the stab wounds to the groin area – hitting the femoral triangle area and piercing the femoral artery on both sides – that takes skill. And I say that for one other reason: usually when someone's femoral artery or arteries are cut, they're slashed with a knife or a scalpel. It's not the stabbing that cuts the artery, it's the slashing motion of the blade. In this case, though, it appears that this knife had no real sharp edge, just a very sharp point."

"I saw the knife for myself, Doctor, and I'd have to say that you're spot-on. It wasn't your typical knife; it was a 3D printed knife made of a strong but lightweight plastic."

"I could tell for certain that it was not your average kitchen or hunting knife. There were no teeth marks consistent with a serrated hunting knife, and I didn't find a single bit of metal filings or remnants, even when looking under a microscope."

Satisfied that she'd learned all that she could from the examination of Stevens' body, JJ went back into the room to observe the rest of Hicks' posting. "Any news yet, Doctor Johnson?"

"Yes, please come in Agent Jansen. I've extracted the bullets from the deceased and can say definitively that the shot from Agent Stevens' 9mm hit the suspect in the right shoulder. A serious injury, to be sure, but not the fatal shot. As for the other wounds, there were a total of eight bullets retrieved, and all were .40 caliber rounds, which is consistent with the weapons used by the DFW officers. One of those .40 caliber bullets nicked the aorta, which I've determined to be the cause of death. We'll have to wait for the Lab to determine which officer fired that shot."

"Any reason to suspect that the deceased was under the influence of illegal drugs, or even too much alcohol?"

"We'll have to wait for toxicology tests to confirm, but my preliminary opinion is that is not the case. We found nothing in his clothes or belongings, no trace of any drugs as we examined his clothes under the scope, no trace of drugs around his nostrils, no needle marks anywhere on his body, not even any alcohol when we examined his stomach contents. Perhaps the blood work will turn up something to surprise me, but indications are that he was not under the influence at the time of this incident."

"Did you find any marks or scars on his body that makes you think that he'd been involved in a lot of violence before? Like healed bullet or knife wounds? Or maybe gang tats of some sort, you know, like the kind that some gangs flaunt to show that they've been in prison, killed someone, or been jumped into a gang?"

"No, nothing like that, but his X-rays do show that he'd had a broken right ankle and surgery on his left shoulder. The ankle injury was fully healed, and my best estimate is that it was at least 15 years ago. The shoulder injury is more recent, I'd estimate within the last 10 years. In both cases I'd ascribe them to sports injuries, though I can't be certain. But I can say that there are no scars associated with those injuries to make me think that they were the result of any kind of violent behavior."

"Alright, Doctor, thank you for doing both posts tonight. I'll look for your report on Monday, as you mentioned."

JJ headed for the exit, lost in her thoughts. All things considered, she'd accomplished a hell of a lot this evening. She'd learned the suspect's real identity, as well as where he'd been before arriving in Dallas and turning a typical Friday in DFW airport into a shooting gallery. She had learned about his multiple aliases and apparent penchant for sophisticated technology and organization, including the creation of absolutely perfect passports. And she knew, deep, deep down, that she was involved in something much deeper than it at first appeared. Her mind spun with a million possibilities, but she was determined to keep an open mind and let the evidence guide her. SAC Isaksen, on the other hand, didn't seem interested in looking too deeply. He had the 'who' for Agent Stevens' death and seemed much less interested in the 'why'.

Without question, JJ was viewing this case through a much different lens. And she knew, undoubtedly, that she was once again putting her reputation and career at risk, but she was determined to follow wherever the evidence led. *Fuck Isaksen.*

Chapter Seven

SATURDAY, OCTOBER 22

The three surviving members and founders of The Murder Game, who referred to themselves, collectively, as The Slayers, were inconsolable at the loss of their good friend and partner, Jamarcus Hicks. They had learned about yesterday's incident at DFW, but not in a million years did they expect it to be Jamarcus. It was only this morning that the names of the dead FBI agent and his assailant were released, but in less than an hour they were on their hastily called meeting via secure video conference.

Graham Robbins was the first to speak. "How the hell could this have happened? Jamarcus was meticulous in his planning for the Game. Do you think this had anything to do with the hit in DC?" Robbins was in his late 20's, as were all of the Slayers, and he was easily the most unassuming member of the group. The quintessential bookish nerd, he was the youngest of three children, and his closest sibling was almost 12 years older. He never had many friends growing up in NJ, and the guys in the Slayers felt more like family than his actual family ever had.

"I don't see how it could involve DC, at least based on the what's been reported so far. To hear the news reports, it sounds like the DC police haven't the first clue as to what happened to the guy in Georgetown. What was that guy's name again?" Mark Saxe was distraught; he loved Jamarcus like a brother. They hadn't seen each other in almost three years, partly due to COVID and partly due to their constant security concerns. One of their most sacred rules was to minimize time together in person, and all get togethers had to be outside the US. COVID had put a real damper on travel in general, and on international travel, in particular.

"News reports said that his name was Peter Jacobsen. By all accounts, Jamarcus did a great job of making it look like just another random street crime, so I can't believe that what happened in Dallas has anything to do with DC." This from Calvin Mitchell. Now the only surviving black member of the Slayers, he was taking Jamarcus' death especially hard. They had roomed together at Columbia for several years, and they had remained close since, though, again due to the rules of the Slayers, they didn't get to see each other nearly as often as they wished.

Mark added, "I don't understand what could have possibly happened to bring these two together and end up with Jamarcus and this FBI agent dead. News reports are saying that the FBI guy flew in from Orange County, CA, so they definitely weren't on the same flight. And Jamarcus would never do anything to bring attention to himself."

"I definitely agree," said Graham. "He always preached the importance of keeping a low profile and trying to be as invisible as possible. If someone was starting any kind of confrontation, he would have just walked away."

"I wonder when they're going to release more details. The news is saying that half the cops and Feds in the country are working this." Calvin wiped a few tears from his eyes. "A million witnesses and videos of the confrontation and killing but not a single soul seems to know *why* it happened. Or, at least, no one is talking."

"My best guess is that those two DFW cops that shot Jamarcus know something. Maybe everything. Whether or not they'll be allowed to talk about it is another matter." Graham was getting angrier the longer they talked about it.

"I don't know any way for us to get to the bottom of this beyond tracking the news reports and anything that may be posted on social media. Although......maybe I do have one idea," said Mark. "I could build a simple web crawler to grab everything that gets posted about this and then we can sift through it looking for anything that sounds like a reasonable explanation."

"I like that," said Calvin. "Maybe we can carry it one step further and access the texts and voice mails of the two DFW cops. Even if they can't talk publicly, they might be communicating with each other, their families, maybe some lawyers."

Mark replied, "Yeah, that's doable. Might take a little longer, but nothing that we can't handle. Let's divide and conquer. I'll build and launch the web crawler, and you guys split up the two cops and access their mobile records, and while you're at it, maybe start looking at their online presence."

Graham added, "Plus there might come a time when we want to avenge Jamarcus. We can't do anything about the FBI agent that confronted him; he's already dead. But maybe those two cops deserve some payback."

"Let's not even go there," replied Calvin. "At least not yet. No one is more pissed than me at losing my 'brother', my best friend. But if we go after those cops now it's only going to make them dig deeper into Jamarcus, maybe even lead them to our doorstep. If we decide to terminate these two, it needs to be after this shit dies down."

"Agreed", responded both men. Satisfied that they had a path forward, the surviving Slayers ended their video call and dove into their respective tasks.

* * *

The Slayers had been friends since their sophomore year at Columbia University when they were all in the same Computer Science class. Despite their different backgrounds and personalities, they became friends after being assigned to the same group project. They soon discovered that they all had an aptitude for computer gaming and coding. While the class project sucked up a lot of their time, they spent as much time playing *World of Warcraft*, *Call of Duty*, and other multiplayer video games.

The assigned project was simple and straightforward: build a computer game that works on multiple platforms and hosts multiple players. They invested hundreds of man hours, but in the end, they were awarded first prize among more than 50 entrants. The game became the talk of the campus after being featured in the school newspaper, and it was safe to say that the guys were enjoying their newfound popularity.

The game was deceptively simple and meant to be fun, all while taking a good-natured jab at popular culture and the biggest names and pseudo-celebrities in the entertainment industry. They called the game "Kill Starter", a play on the crowd funding application Kick Starter. Kill Starter was conceived as totally tongue-in-cheek, but as its popularity grew so did the volume – and comic genius – of the postings sent in by the growing legions of fans. Social media was feeding the pop culture machine and highlighting our own worst behaviors, and the comments became increasingly snarky and rude. The meanest comments were consistently the ones that got the most 'likes'. They knew they'd hit the big time when reposts from their site were shared on Facebook, Twitter, and late-night talk shows.

Each week there was a new game and new winners, and the cash prizes continued to grow. Players nominated the pop culture figure(s) that they would love to see die. Then, for each celebrity that they nominated, they had to pay $1 and provide their justification; and the funnier the better. A computer program stack ranked the 'winning' celebrity from the thousands of votes cast, and then it was up to the four of them to pick the funniest submission for the #1 most-hated celebrity of the week. So long as players stayed away from political figures, lest the Federal authorities come down on them, all celebrities were fair game.

Within months the game had grown so popular that the weekly grand prize was $5000. They worked with their faculty advisors and members of the law school faculty to establish an LLC to keep things legal and aboveboard. After two years of running the game, they decided that the time was right to sell the business to one of the many Silicon Valley companies that were pursuing them. Their business and legal advisors helped them structure a great deal worth well into eight figures, and even after all expenses and a generous 'gift' to their faculty advisors, they walked away with several million dollars each.

Selling Kill Starter wasn't just a financial windfall, it represented freedom. Freedom from student loan debt, and freedom to think about life after college. And mostly, the freedom to think about their next project. Launching and running Kill Starter had shown them that they were smart, creative, and incredibly talented at developing online multi-player games. They spent hours outlining their plans for a new game, a game that would take things to the next level. Make that a *lot* of levels.

Chapter Eight

SATURDAY, OCTOBER 22

We don't often hear the word 'begat' in everyday speaking. In its simplest terms, begat means that someone had children/offspring. The Bible has 139 verses spread across 17 different books that mentions begat, as if the (supposed) history referenced in the Bible was an ancient predecessor of *23 & Me*. If one were so inclined, we could say that Kill Starter begat The Murder Game. And just like the Old Testament, with its many stories of killings, plagues, and world devastation, the Slayers were vengeful, cruel, and without remorse. That is to say, the idea and execution of The Murder Game was much more akin to the God of the Old Testament than the God of the New Testament.

At its core, The Murder Game was one of chance hosted on the Dark Web that allowed players to bet on the performance of the Slayers. The parameters for each game were specified by 'Oz', the software program they developed that leveraged Artificial Intelligence (AI) and Machine Learning (ML) to constantly learn and refine the game. Mark Saxe, the Slayers' specialist in AI, ML, and complex networking security, was the primary creator and project manager for Oz. Under his guidance, the application evolved into an almost omnipotent, sentient being made up of ones and zeros.

The game itself was straightforward, and Oz stipulated the parameters for the executions that the Slayers would have to perform, and the Slayer that most closely adhered to those parameters would be awarded the most points. Online players would bet on the total number of points that the winning Slayer would be awarded, and the player coming closest to the number wins; there were prizes – *very* generous prizes – for 1st, 2nd, and 3rd place. Of course, there are a lot of underlying details that impact how points are amassed.

There was a new game every two months, and for each game a Slayer could earn up to 1,000 points. Each game starts with Oz picking four cities across the US, one in each time zone, and a Slayer is assigned to each. Oz further stipulates the type of weapon to be used, the exact date and time for the execution, and the age, sex, and ethnicity of the victim. The Slayers can never know for certain the exact age and ethnicity of their targets, and they might not be able to complete the hit at the exact moment stipulated. That's where the point variability comes into play; for example, if Oz dictates that the target should be a 23-year-old white male, fewer points would be awarded if the victim is actually 25 years old, or if he's African American instead of white. Similarly, if Oz dictated that the killings should be at 7:15pm ET, the number of points awarded for the killing would decrease for every minute before or after that time that the Slayer completed the kill. Every murder was recorded and time-stamped with a modified Go-Pro body camera and uploaded to a secure server to be 'scored' by Oz. In addition to evaluating the uploaded videos, Oz would scour the web and all news sources for seven days following the murders to gather and validate all of the relevant information to aid in the scoring. The points were then totaled for each Slayer and the winning online players were announced.

The weapons used by the Slayers were not overly exotic or special-ized. Semi-automatic handguns were off-the-shelf Glocks, and sniper rifles were generally Remington M24's. When a knife was called for, as it had been just a few days ago, the weapon of choice was the venerable KA-BAR. Sturdy, strong, and solid, it easily tackled the toughest jobs and kills. Learning how to use a garrote was a little bit trickier. It's not like you find them in your average sporting goods store, and there are certainly no training classes or places to practice the skill. Luckily for them, they had their own area of expertise: the Dark Web. If you know how to search the Dark Web you can find pretty much every kind of killing, maiming, and torture device that man's sick mind has ever created. For that matter, if you know where to look, and are willing to pay, you can find somebody to take on virtually any task, no matter how depraved. When it comes to illegal activities, the two greatest enablers in modern history are the Dark Web and cryptocurrencies, and The Murder Game leveraged them both heavily.

In fact, it was the Dark Web that made The Murder Game possible and profitable. They were able to conduct their game, with complete anonymity, by leveraging the TOR browser. With the ability to enable anonymous communication through an overlay network of more than 6,000 relays, TOR was the Holy Grail of privacy. It was ironic that TOR had been developed by the US intelligence community to protect their secrets, but then they turned around and made it available to the world as free open-source code. In effect, the best tool ever created for secure communications was now in the hands of the world's worst actors, enabling them to carry on their illegal activities with little concern that anyone, even the US government, can track them.

Once The Murder Game launched, it quickly developed a world-wide following of people who considered murder to be just another form of entertainment. Whereas their college gaming project, Kill Starter, had been innocent and entertaining, Murder Game was anything but. People died. Violently. Online players wagered on the deaths of innocent victims; the minimum bet was $1,000 in Bitcoin, Etherium, and other selected cryptocurrencies, and from there the sky was the limit. Typically, more than $1.5 million was wagered on each game. Most people would consider that a sad commentary on where we are as a society. The Slayers considered it affirmation of their genius.

To keep their players engaged and the money flowing, the Slayers took a page from the Vegas online betting apps. Several times per day there were opportunities to wager on *something* and win thousands of dollars. *How many murders would be recorded in the US in the next 24 hours? How many shootings in Chicago this coming weekend? How many 'active shooter' instances this week in US schools?* While these daily bets kept their online players entertained, the heaviest site traffic and betting days were in the week leading up to the next executions. The volume generally went up tenfold because that's when things started getting real. That when the bets focused on Oz's proclamations: *Which cities would Oz choose for the next round? What would be the exact date and time? What weapon would be used? What would be the victim demographics?* The possibilities for betting were almost endless, and that was good for the game's sustainability and the Slayers' bank accounts. While they paid out thousands of dollars every week, not to mention the large Grand Prize paid after each game, the Slayers were still raking in hundreds of thousands of dollars each per year. No fees to lawyers or accountants. No taxes. No employees. It was the perfect money-making machine.

Chapter Nine

MONDAY, OCTOBER 24

After having a lot of early success in the first few hours after the DFW debacle, JJ was frustrated that the weekend had not been as fruitful. She didn't make it to bed on Friday evening until, well, early Saturday morning, but she was still ready to hit the ground running when she made it into the office around 9am that morning. Her disappointment grew as the hours dragged on and no new information came in from the forensics teams. By lunchtime she was absolutely crawling the walls and getting more and more pissed off by the minute. She knew that some things could not be rushed, and ofttimes science was one of them. Still, she couldn't help but wonder if forces within the FBI were aligned against her and simply putting her things on the back burner. Her rational mind said that would be unlikely, especially when her case involved a dead FBI agent. Her lack of self-confidence, coupled with a healthy dose of paranoia, made it hard to stay focused.

While the weekend was a bust, on Monday morning the dam broke and she was flooded with new information, thankfully. Around 10am she received a detailed history of all travel booked by Jamarcus Hicks, including travel booked under his known aliases. He certainly got around. DC. Boston. LA. Spokane. Milwaukee. Detroit. Nashville. Tampa. And that was just the last twelve months. *Were these personal trips, or did he travel as part of his job?* She noted that virtually all his travel was on American Airlines, but that was no great shock since DFW was their HQ and primary hub. With Jamarcus living in Austin, he would have to connect somewhere to reach many of the distant cities that he traveled to, and DFW made the most sense.

There were so many travel dates and cities that it wouldn't fit easily onto the whiteboard that JJ used to map out her cases, so she plugged the data into a simple spreadsheet. Her mind raced. *I should look for crimes, especially murders, that occurred within a 100-mile radius of these cities during the dates that Hicks was there.* JJ made a note to dig for more credit card charges on those target dates to find out where he stayed, where he ate, where he shopped, everything. The numbers could be huge with parameters that covered that many dates and locations, but that's what investigative work came down to. *Maybe Isaksen will take pity on me and assign me some help to run all of this down.* She smiled to herself at the absurdity of that thought. *That's OK, maybe I'll get all the glory when I bust this case wide open.*

The rest of the day she spent heads-down focused on the intersections between Hicks's travel and major crimes. It was slow going, but she was starting to see some definite connections, too many to be just a coincidence or even confirmation bias. No, she was certain that she was onto something real. Just before 5pm she got a call from the forensics technicians at the NTRCFL letting her know that they were still working to gain access to Hicks' PC. "What's the problem?" she asked. "I thought there was nothing that you guys can't crack."

"Thanks for the sarcasm. It's just what I needed to cap off a day of banging my head against the wall," responded Ted Dwyer, one of seemingly hundreds of 20-somethings working their magic at the NTRCFL. "This guy had a seriously strong password on the PC, and we still haven't been able to get around it. It appears that he used an application that uses a combination of letters, numbers, special characters, and even symbols to make it nearly impossible to crack."

"Any chance that you can try parallel processing to get more computing power and brute force your way in?"

"Wow, I'm impressed Agent Jansen. That's some pretty good techno-speak for a field agent. Do you have any real idea what you're talking about or did you just Google a few buzzwords to try to impress me?"

"A little bit of both," she said lightly, not taking offense at the question. "I mean, I've read articles over the years talking about criminal groups taking control of thousands of computers to run their Denial-of-Service attacks against unsuspecting victims."

"That's one example," said Dwyer. "There are legitimate uses for networking a lot of computers together, which is basically the poor man's version of a massive super-computer. The processing power from those networked PC's can make a huge difference when it comes to crunching numbers, searching databases, or looking for patterns in data."

"Well, thank you for the education on this amazingly exciting subject," she added with a sarcastic tone, "but can it be used to get me the information on this PC?"

"It might. We have two possibilities, and we should work both possibilities in parallel. Here's what I propose: I'll reach out to my network of engineers and enlist their help to create our own massively parallel processing computer network. With enough PC's networked together we might be able to change the brute force timeline from literally thousands of years – seriously, no shit – to something more manageable. Maybe even hours or days."

"And the other route?"

"You and your team should focus on the social engineering aspect. See if there's anything on his phone that might lead us to a password: his texts, his emails, his social media, all of it. Check out his home, his friends, and anything else you can think of that might give us a place to start."

While JJ completely agreed with Dwyer's logic, she also recognized that this would increase the volume of work and research exponentially. She would need someone to check out Hicks's home in Austin, for starters. Damn, now she was going to have no choice but to involve Isaksen. She could feel the acid churning in her stomach just thinking about it. This would not be an easy conversation. They never were.

Chapter Ten

TUESDAY, OCTOBER 25

"**S**o let me get this straight," said Isaksen. "You've positively identified Jamarcus Hicks as Special Agent Stevens' killer. You've worked with the ME team to determine cause of death for both victims, and the ME determined that Stevens did not fire the shot that killed Hicks; the lab will have to determine whether that shot came from Trojecki or Kaplan, but regardless, they've been cleared of any wrongdoing. And, the physical evidence is being processed at Quantico, but it's not expected to change the current narrative, namely, that Hicks killed Stevens before being shot by the DFW officers. So tell me, Special Agent Jansen, why isn't this 'case closed'?"

Well, this certainly went to shit in a hurry. "Sir, while I agree that we know who killed Agent Stevens, and how, we still don't have a clue as to the *why*. I realize that since Hicks was killed there's not going to be a trial, but I think we owe it to Stevens' family, and the Bureau, to find out what led to two men being killed."

"Maybe they accidentally bumped into each other and words were exchanged. Maybe Hicks cut in front of Stevens in line at Starbucks, or Stevens was wearing a Washington Redskins jersey and Hicks was a Cowboys fan. It could have been any one of a million things."

"Yes sir, it could have been anything, but we haven't found a single witness that saw Stevens and Hicks so much as speak to each other prior to their confrontation. Officers Trojecki and Kaplan witnessed the whole thing, and Stevens had made them aware that he'd recovered the dropped wallet with multiple ID's. Prior to that, we know that they rode on the same SkyLink train between terminals, but according to witnesses the two men never spoke a word or had any interaction. The only thing out of the ordinary is Hicks losing his wallet and Stevens trying to return it to him."

"And you're suggesting, what? That Hicks was an international spy, or assassin, or domestic terrorist? That perhaps he targeted Stevens?"

God, he is frustrating. "No sir, not at all. As I stated, I've found multiple instances where Hicks has been in the same city, at the same time, as numerous unsolved murders. It's possible that with a bit more digging we'll find more instances that connect him to a whole range of murders spanning several years. I've only had time to go back two years so far, and I've already found eight instances that are suspicious."

"What is it about these murders that suggests Hicks' involvement? Besides the fact that he just happened to be in the same city or town when a random crime occurred. And, from what you've said, some of these cities are experiencing *hundreds* of murders every year."

"Admittedly, sir, the murders that align with Hicks' travels seem to be truly random. Different races, various age ranges, both men and women. Some victims were wealthy, others barely one step from being homeless. And the weapons used in these murders ran the gamut, so there was definitely no signature method."

"So, the fact that you don't find any pattern to point to Hicks as the perpetrator is proof that it was, in fact, Hicks that is responsible for them?"

JJ wanted to scream. It was all that she could do not launch herself across the desk and claw his eyes out. He was being an asshole, even more than usual, and she didn't know what pissed her off more: the way he was treating her, or the fact that his logic was spot-on. "Sir, I get that it looks that way. But I think there's more to this than we're seeing at this point. We have absolutely no idea what led to this confrontation. I'd really like to continue digging into this to see if I can find more information, maybe even some point of intersection between Stevens and Hicks that we don't know about yet."

Isaksen was silent for a moment, considering his next words carefully. "Agent Jansen, let me be frank. I think this whole line of investigation around Hicks is going to be a dead-end, but I do admit that there are two possible avenues that have been troubling me. I want you to investigate them both and see if it helps solve the '*why*', as you put it."

"Alright, sir. I'd love to hear your angles on this. And I'll do my best to investigate them thoroughly." JJ was being sincere; she needed another perspective since so far, she'd been the proverbial Lone Ranger on this investigation. Forensics had certainly contributed, but only with the facts and not the interpretation of the facts. Only she had seen all the puzzle pieces that had been collected and started trying to assemble those pieces into one complete picture.

"OK. Avenue #1: Special Agent Stevens was flying home after being in Orange County, CA for the past week during the protests and riots. Stevens' job was focused on Domestic Terrorism, so he was monitoring both the white supremacists and the antifa mobs. We should investigate the possibility that his killing is tied to those events. Maybe it was someone he arrested, or maybe someone he argued with during that week. Maybe it was as simple as retribution against a federal cop for making arrests and doing their job."

"That's an interesting idea, sir. But do you recall that I've already established that Hicks was in Washington, DC during the time that those riots were going on in CA?"

"Yes, I'm aware. I'm considering the possibility that Hicks targeted Stevens at the request of someone involved in the Orange County event, like maybe a radical group that he's affiliated with. I think it would be a stretch to assume that Hicks, being a black guy, was affiliated with the Nazis or other white supremacists, but it's not inconceivable that he's part of a radicalized splinter group loyal to BLM, antifa, or maybe some group of anarchists."

"I agree that's a definite path for investigation. I'll reach out to the other Agents that were there that week and see if they can help shed some light for us."

"Avenue #2: Perhaps this has ties to an old case that Stevens worked, and even if Hicks weren't the focus of the investigation, maybe it was someone connected to Hicks. Or maybe Hicks was paid to target

Stevens for something from his past. This certainly wouldn't be the first time that a cop was targeted for doing their job."

JJ thought this unlikely, but she couldn't dispute Isaksen's logic. Love him or loath him, he was still a damn good Agent, and he had great instincts as an investigator. "Agreed, sir. If you could reach out to your counterparts in DC to clear the way for me to get access to Stevens' case files that would expedite things."

While the avenues of investigation he ordered were reasonable, they would definitely add to the workload, and she wasn't about to push aside her instincts to follow his. She needed help, and there was no time like the present to ask. She had held her tongue the entire meeting and not argued or pushed back on any of his ideas. That was partly to stroke his ego and, admittedly, because the ideas were valid. She had been as charming as she was capable of, far from an ass kisser, but definitely respectful. "Sir, I agree that these are necessary paths for investigation, but I think it will require additional resources to help cover all these angles. Perhaps an Agent in DC working his old cases, and an Agent in LA working the riots angle."

"Not a chance, Agent Jansen. I don't have the manpower locally, and I'm not about to go begging for help just so you can focus on your theory about Hicks being some serial murderer or spy. Let me make myself very clear: You are to focus your investigation on the two avenues that we just discussed, and I want this wrapped-up by the end of the week. I don't want another minute invested in trying to make Hicks into the next Ted Bundy or Aldrich Ames. Turn over your information about the possible murders to the respective local PD's and let them take it from there, if they think it's warranted. But you're out of it. Are we clear?"

JJ had to fight back tears of rage and frustration. She'd always prided herself on having a great poker face, a huge asset when conducting inter-rogations, but she knew that her face betrayed her now. There was no hiding the hatred and rage that she was feeling. No doubt he saw it, too, and surely took pleasure in reminding her who was in charge.

JJ stood and barely muttered a 'Yes, sir' and then abruptly walked out of his office. She ducked into the restroom as the tears started flow-ing, not wanting to give anyone the satisfaction of seeing her cry. Thankfully, there was no one else in there and JJ shut herself in a stall and buried her head in her hands, sobbing. She was hurt, humiliated, and angry. Isaksen had treated her like shit for years, and she was the first to admit that some of the ridicule and disrespect were warranted. How many times can you go into rehab and maintain your reputation and your leader's respect? If you're a female FBI employee, the answer seemed to be zero. Maybe once if you're a man, especially if you can attribute it to something 'manly' like being injured on the job. But for her, a female agent? Double standards are alive and well in the FBI.

Well, fuck Isaksen. She vowed that she wouldn't be beaten down again. She *was* going to break this case, with or without help. She would do Isaksen's bidding, but there was no way in hell that she was putting her own instincts aside. Whatever it took to crack this case, she would do it: long hours, 'bending' the laws, working until she dropped. This was quite possibly her last case; if she failed, it was a certainty. Even if she succeeded, she'd be labeled as insubordinate and definitely not a 'team player'. *Fuck them.*

Chapter Eleven

S ome cops absolutely hate reporters. Others tolerate them, at best, and usually only if the reporter could be used to leak a story at the right time to help drive an investigation. If the reporter crossed them, or put something in an article that showed the cop in a less-than-favorable light? They'd effectively be 'dead' in the cop's eyes, regardless of the accuracy of the report. JJ had no strong feelings either way. She'd been insulated from most media inquiries since she was rarely the lead agent on anything that was hot, juicy, and newsworthy. This case was different, so she wasn't really shocked when a reporter contacted her. It was more shocking that it took a week to happen. Not that she was complaining.

JJ had never heard of this reporter, Kristyn Reynolds. Like most people, she no longer subscribed to the local paper and rarely read it online, preferring to get her news from online sources and the usual smattering of slightly-left-of-center cable news networks. Still, she was far from a news junky. Politics bored her to death. World economics? The stock market? Snore. She did spend too much time following American pop culture, but she led such a boring, lonely, monastic life, that's what passed for entertainment. The first call from Kristyn Reynolds came in on her office line mid-morning on Wednesday. *Thank God for small favors that she didn't call yesterday*, thought JJ.

The conversation had gone the way they typically do with a reporter, with Kristyn explaining that she'd been assigned the DFW shooting story since it first broke, then listing some of the other big stories she'd worked on in the past. She went on to assure JJ that she always protected her sources. Again, typical. Now she was digging into the 'why' behind the DFW events, especially since, in her words, "the police and FBI haven't even released a possible motive." *Bingo!* That piqued JJ's interest. Taking a chance, she did something almost unheard of: she invited Kristyn to lunch to talk about the case.

They met at a small but popular Mexican restaurant just a few miles from the FBI Field Office at 1pm, and luckily the lunch crowd was starting to thin. JJ was already seated at the table when she saw Kristyn walk in. Her first impression was that she was the kind of woman that other women usually hate on sight and hope that she's dumb as a bag of hammers or a stone-cold bitch, while deep down envying her and hoping to become her BFF. It was immediately evident that Kristyn was neither. JJ had, of course, checked Kristyn out in advance with a little cyber sleuthing, including a quick check of LinkedIn. There JJ found that Kristyn had done her undergraduate work at Texas A&M and then received her graduate degree in Journalism from Northwestern. She'd been with the Dallas newspaper for almost 10 years and in that time had won a slew of awards, both local and statewide. Bottom line, she was impressive on many levels. JJ was still halfway hoping for her to be bitchy and cocky and conceited to go along with the beautiful, smart, and accomplished. *Maybe I've watched too many Real Housewives of Beverly Hills.*

It took mere minutes for JJ to realize that any hopes of Kristyn being any of those things was out the window. She was lovely, and JJ immediately warmed to her despite her usual propensity to be more of the standoffish type, particularly with other women. The two of them clicked on many levels, and JJ now understood why some women immediately gravitated to someone like Kristyn and made it their mission to become BFF's. She couldn't deny that, in this case, she was one of them. After some small talk and placing their lunch orders, they got down to the topic of the DFW shootings.

"So JJ, I recognize that you can't share every detail of the investigation with me, and I respect that. Would you be comfortable ff I told you some of my ideas and areas of interest and then maybe you let me know if you think I'm heading the right way, or if we're on a similar path?"

"Sure. I'd like to hear your perspective, and I'll be as forthcoming as possible at this stage." *What the hell? Why was she being so nice and friendly and accommodating to this reporter that she'd known for less than an hour?* It wasn't like JJ to be a fangirl, but that's how she was acting. *Embarrassing.*

"Great. For starters, I'm at a total loss to explain what led to this confrontation and shooting. I've talked to a number of witnesses, including the DFW officers, and the only thing being talked about is the fact that Hicks was in possession of multiple ID's and passports. To me, though, that sounds like something that might lead to an arrest on some minor charges, but not likely to spark the events we saw last week."

"I would have to agree with you on that point."

"Thanks. Having the lead investigator validate my assumptions is always appreciated. Now, I can think of any number of different scenarios where a person might have multiple driver licenses, passports, credit cards, etc., but none of them strike me as 'normal'. The least criminal thing that I can think of, not counting the fake documents themselves, is that we have a guy cheating on his wife, maybe with another wife and family in another city."

"I'd considered that too," responded JJ. "But I think you'd agree that murder seems like an extreme reaction if all we're talking about is bigamy. Not saying that it couldn't happen, especially if a nasty divorce was going to cost him a lot of money, but I think it's one of the less likely scenarios."

"Agreed," said Kristyn, as she swirled her glass of wine and thought about her next statement. "So, I'm sure that if this Hicks guy was a government agent it would have leaked by now. I mean, that might be some rationale for the multiple ID's, but I can't imagine that he'd murder an FBI agent to protect his cover. I think the idea that Hicks is an operative for the US government is totally off-base."

"I love how your mind works. You think just like a cop," JJ said with a smile. She immediately blushed and felt self-conscious, realizing that she was acting like a giddy teenager with her first crush. If JJ didn't know that she was a newspaper reporter she would have sworn that she was a TV news anchor, the stereotypical 'Barbie'.

"I've always thought that there's a fine line between a reporter and a cop," smiled Kristyn. Again, with that thousand-megawatt smile, and a little giggle. Nothing about her came across as fake or pretentious, just someone genuinely friendly and confident.

"So, you've shared a few ideas and scenarios that you think have holes big enough to drive a truck through, so tell me your thoughts about what might be going on." JJ was anxious to hear her thoughts and see if it validated many of her own.

"There's definitely a criminal element to all those ID's and aliases, to say nothing of murdering Agent Stevens. At the risk of sounding like someone who's seen too many *Jason Bourne* movies, he strikes me as a professional assassin. Not for our government, but possibly a foreign government. My money, though, is on a freelancer who conducts his business via the Dark Web. There are a lot of bad people out there that will do anything for money. Or, more accurately, for cryptocurrency, diamonds, gold, or other forms of payment that are virtually untraceable."

"Interesting," said JJ, not revealing, at least not yet, that this was an angle that she and the forensics teams were exploring. "Any chance, in your estimation, that he could be doing something else on the Dark Web besides murder for hire? Like maybe child porn, human trafficking, illegal weapons sales, or large volumes of illegal drugs?"

"I've actually considered all of those, and more. And I can certainly see where being confronted by an FBI agent for any one of those crimes could lead to someone desperately trying to escape. I've not seen anything that would positively point to, or eliminate, any one of those possibilities. I think this whole Dark Web angle warrants a lot more investigation."

"Did I already mention that I love how your mind works?" giggled JJ. It was not like her to be so 'girly' but she couldn't seem to stop herself. "OK, cards on the table. I am totally onboard with the fact that Hicks was into some bad shit, and somehow that led to a confrontation with Stevens. My guess is that Stevens had absolutely no connection to Hicks before that day; Stevens found that wallet, thought something was suspicious when he found the multiple ID's, and he was killed when he confronted Hicks about it. Now the tough part is figuring out why Hicks had them in the first place and why it's important enough to him that he would kill an FBI agent, take a woman hostage, and try to kill two DFW cops to keep it from getting out."

"Is that where you're going to focus your investigation moving forward?"

"Yes and no. Sorry, I don't mean that to be evasive. What I mean is that I've been ordered to spend some time reviewing Stevens' old cases and his last assignment at the Orange County riots. There are other irons in the fire, including our forensic technology specialists and the Lab at Quantico, still working on the evidence that we collected at the scene. And at some point, I need to get down to Austin to do a thorough search of Hicks' home."

"Wow, that's a lot to cover. Let me ask you this: my editors are anxious for some new and exciting updates on this story to keep our readers engaged. What can I write about at this point that won't risk compromising your investigation?"

JJ thought about that for a moment before speaking. "I appreciate that you have a job to do, and I know that I can't stop you from printing everything that we talked about, especially since I never uttered those magic words, 'off the record' at any point. Ideally, I'd love it if you wrote that we have no definitive connection between Stevens and Hicks, and that we're searching back through old cases as well as his involvement last week at UC Irvine. I'd ask you to hold on the speculation regarding Hicks' possible – more likely *probable* – criminal background and our searching for information on the Dark Web. I'd like to be a little further down the road with that investigation in case there are others involved in this with Hicks."

"Any reason to think that there are others?"

"I'd say it like this: there's no reason to assume there *aren't* others, and all the illegal activities that I mentioned aren't usually one-man operations. If our assumptions are correct, we're going to find that this is a large-scale conspiracy and ongoing criminal enterprise. And I want to be able to shut them down permanently, not give them a chance to pull the plug for a few days and then start up again."

"That makes sense. And you have my word, I'll hold on that part of the investigation. When you think the time is right, then I'll report it. And not until."

"Wow, you'd really do that? Don't you know that conventional wisdom says that reporters and cops have no integrity or scruples?" JJ smiled again, a little less self-conscious this time.

"I'd like to think that you and I are the exceptions to that rule," answered Kristyn. She raised her glass to clink 'cheers' with JJ.

"Agreed. And in return, I'll do everything I can to ensure that you get the exclusive when this is over. And you have *my* word on that."

"I appreciate that. Here's my card so you can reach me if you want to discuss things further."

"And here's my mobile number. Call anytime. But before you go, I do have one more idea I'd like to run past you. It's probably something that will push my boss right over the edge, which is probably why I find it so appealing. Got a few more minutes?"

"You kidding? Now I'm totally intrigued!"

Chapter Twelve
WEDNESDAY, OCTOBER 26

"This is a bit unorthodox, maybe even unethical from your perspective, so you can absolutely say 'no' and walk away. No hard feelings if you do." JJ was hopeful that Kristyn would at least consider the idea before blowing her off.

"Like I said, I'm intrigued. Let's hear it."

"What would you think about working together on this investigation? We'd divide and conquer to cover more ground, but it would be a joint effort in every sense of the word. I'll feed you information along the way, like results from our Labs, to help you stay on track and moving forward. And, of course, you'll then have the inside track for writing another award-winning piece, and this time it will be the very definition of 'investigative journalism'."

"I think calling this 'unethical' from a journalist's point of view, and my editor's, is a huge understatement. *Huge*. But what about for you? Couldn't this get you fired, or maybe even prosecuted?"

"I'm not too worried about myself. Truth be told, my boss would like nothing more than to find an excuse to fire me. He's been looking for one for years. I've been able to keep a low profile and stay employed, but because my boss and coworkers don't respect my abilities as an Agent, I've never had that one big, high-profile case that can make or break a career. Until now. My boss still isn't convinced that it's big; if

72

he'd had any inkling that it was, he never would have given me the assignment. I'm willing to take my chances, to really push the envelope on this. If I end up getting fired, then so be it. There is life outside of the FBI. Or so I've been told."

"Someday you're going to have to tell me the whole, sordid history of why your boss and coworkers don't think you're worthy of respect and having the big cases thrown your way. From what I've observed, you seem like the ideal Agent."

"Thanks. And I promise: '*someday*' I will tell you about my less-than-stellar past, maybe sooner than later. You deserve to know what kind of damaged goods you're hitching your wagon to."

Kristyn smiled at that. "I doubt that you're 'damaged goods' in any sense of the word. Sounds to me like the people you work with are damaged." She looked around to make sure no one was paying them undue attention. "How should we stay in touch with each other moving forward? Not to be paranoid, but should we consider getting burner phones for staying in touch? Seems to me it would be wise to have zero evidence on our regular phones if someone starts investigating us."

"Good thinking. We can never be too careful. We should each buy one, in cash, today or tomorrow. I'll stop on the way back to the office and purchase one and then share the number with you. I'd suggest that we download an app called Signal that provides encrypted text, voice, and video for our communications about the case. For everything else continue using your regular iPhone. Nothing is ever 100% foolproof, but this would definitely make it harder for anyone to track us, should they ever become suspicious."

"I'll stop at Best Buy on the way back to my office. So, let's dig into the details of this partnership. How are you thinking that we'll split-up the work?" Kristyn was anxious to hear more. She liked the idea of partnering with JJ and appreciated the trust that was being shown and the access that she was being given. Of course, trust was a two-way street, and she was putting as much on the line as JJ, maybe more. Still, the possibility of winning a Peabody or other prestigious journalism award was definitely worth some risk.

"Remember when I said that my boss wants me to investigate the possibility that Stevens was killed because of a connection to the UC Irvine riots? And he also instructed me to dig into Stevens' old cases to see if I can find any connection to Hicks?"

"Yes, I remember us discussing that....."

"I think you should run with those."

Kristyn gave her a quizzical look. "OK.....you'll have to explain that one to me? I'm not necessarily disagreeing, but admittedly, that's a bit of a curveball."

"It's like this. I'm being given access to all of Stevens' old cases, so I can pass those on to you. And as far as the UC Irvine angle, I think you can dig into that pretty much on your own by talking to the FBI and local cops that were onsite. Plus, there's a ton of video evidence already available on YouTube. We're hoping to find anything that points to Stevens being involved in any kind of confrontation, or someone that seems to be focusing on him. We know that it can't be Hicks because he was in DC at the time, but it's possible that someone could have had a grudge against Stevens and hired Hicks to deal with it."

"You said earlier that you don't think either of these lines of investigation are going to pay off. Is that why you're dumping them on me while you follow the other leads? You think I can't add as much value as an investigator since I'm only a journalist?" She sounded a bit hurt, coupled with disappointment. As a highly competent reporter, and someone with a lot of years of experience, she was not used to being sidelined from the most promising leads or stories.

"No! Definitely not, I swear! The only reason that I want, *correction*, the reason I *have* to follow the Dark Web angle is because I'm working with an incredible team of electronic tech specialists at the North Texas Regional Computer Forensics Laboratory." She saw the confused look on Kristyn's face. "You may have heard references to them by their initials, NTRCFL. They are the best of the best, but they can't work with anyone outside of law enforcement. They prefer to be hidden in the shadows to anyone that's not a Fed or State cop. The NTRCFL techs are partnering with other electronic specialists around the world to combine forces as they work on accessing Hicks' PC and do some digging on the Dark Web. There's no way that I could bring you in on that part of the operation, or anyone outside of the Bureau for that matter."

"I'm surprised that they haven't already accessed Hicks' PC."

"It surprised me, too. It's really rare for them to be stymied on anything technology related, but the techs told me that Hicks' computer had a level of security that would be the equal of pretty much anything any government agency in the world has, including ours, the Chinese, and even the Israelis. In fact, if the NTRCFL were to continue working this alone, they estimate that it could take 10,000 man-years to brute force their way in. That's why they've reached out to other researchers to link thousands of computers together to create a computing system that would rival the world's top super-computers. In fact, that's how they referred to it: *the poor man's super-computer.*"

"What do you think you'll find on his PC, assuming that you ever get in?"

"I don't know at this point. But my gut says there must be something important on there, otherwise why this security-from-hell? It's the same logic that Special Agent Stevens followed at DFW: he didn't know if Hicks was guilty of anything, but the fact that he had multiple ID's with different names, addresses, and pictures definitely raised his antenna. I gotta believe that there is some incredibly important information on that PC that we need to break this case."

"That seems logical," agreed Kristyn. "Is it the same team of specialists that will be digging into the Dark Web side of things?"

"Definitely. We have some techs that spend half their lives on the Dark Web investigating every type of crime you can imagine. Navigating the Dark Web and gaining their trust enough to be granted access to many of the sickest sites takes a special talent. I have zero skills in that area; actually, I don't know anyone within the Bureau that has those skills and talents outside of these guys."

"I know what you mean. Those skills are highly specialized, and the people I've met that have them are scary smart. I did an article about the kind of people and crimes that are found on the Dark Web a few years back, and as bad as it was then, I have to believe that it's probably gotten much worse."

"Yeah, things never seem to get any simpler, and for us mere mortals, we just seem to fall further and further behind the technology curve every year."

"OK, I'm willing to partner together on this, and I see the logic in how you want to proceed. Admittedly, it wouldn't be my first choice, but your rationale is solid, so I think it's in our best interests to proceed this way. I don't want there to be any miscommunications or misunderstandings, so I tend to over-communicate; I hope that doesn't bother you. I think we should plan on getting together at least 2-3 times per week, in person, to compare notes and brainstorm. Would that work for you?" Seeing JJ smile and nod in the affirmative, Kristyn added, "How about we plan to meet this Friday evening after work?"

JJ couldn't deny the little tingle she felt, and she was glad that Kristyn broached the topic so that she didn't have to. Putting aside the fact that she wanted to spend more time with her, if they were going to be partners then it was imperative that they stay in close contact to review progress, plan next steps, and share ideas. Bringing Kristyn into the case was a risk, on many levels, but it was the right thing to do. Isaksen had made it perfectly clear that he wasn't going to assign any other agents to help her, much less put together any kind of interagency task force, and without help she had no chance of getting to the bottom of this. At least that was her rationale. If she were handed her walking papers? Fine. If the time came that she needed to talk with a lawyer, well, she at least knew several good ones that to call on. Whether or not any of them would want to represent her against the FBI and the Federal government was another question altogether.

Chapter Thirteen

THURSDAY, OCTOBER 27

The surviving members of the Slayers all agreed that it was too risky to try to find a replacement for Jamarcus Hicks. Secrecy was their top concern; the four original members had been together for nearly 10 years and trusted each other with their lives. There had to be complete trust that each member would take the group's secrets to the grave, especially since they had, collectively, committed 80 murders. Staying off of Death Row was more important than recruiting a fourth Slayer to stay with the game's original intent of four simultaneous murders.

"Anybody think that it's time to pull the plug?" asked Mark. "Personally, I don't want to. This game has become more than my livelihood, it's become my reason for getting out of bed in the morning."

"We're lucky to be comfortable financially since we did well on the sale of Kill Starter, and Murder Game has been a veritable cash cow. But I'm with Mark. I don't want to walk away, and I honestly don't see any reason to walk away. We're all devastated by what happened to Jamarcus, but nothing we do is going to bring him back. Not to be cliché, but I think Jamarcus would want us to carry on." Graham looked at the others for affirmation.

Calvin nodded his agreement. "I definitely want to keep it going, and I'd actually like to start the planning for the next game ASAP. We can't tell our players about losing Jamarcus, obviously, but we have to consider how losing one of the four principals is going to affect the game, both from our perspective and theirs."

They spent the next few hours considering the impact on the game's rules, how it would affect the players and their wagers, even how they would determine a grand prize winner moving forward. They considered every facet of the game and decided to relaunch it as 'Murder Game 2.0: Bigger. Better. Richer'.

"I'll get started on rewriting the rules and logic for Oz," said Saxe. "Can you guys handle the communication to the players explaining the changes, and maybe have it ready to announce and go live in a couple of weeks? I could probably rush my end a bit more, but I'd like to take some time to test the logic and code to ensure that it's perfect before our 'go live' date."

Calvin added, "Do you guys have concerns that doing our next game on November 1st seriously shortens our normal interval between killings? Is anyone worried that if we rush this, we might fuck something up and risk exposure? I'm not suggesting that's what happened to Jamarcus, but something happened to get him on the FBI's radar, and let's not kid ourselves: the FBI is not a bunch of bumbling idiots. It's not out of the realm to think that they'll tie the rest of us to Jamarcus at some point."

"I don't necessarily disagree, Calvin." Mark chose his words carefully. "But I think that's actually all the more reason why we should schedule the next game as soon as we can. Hell, if we weren't re-writing the code and introducing new rules, I'd be up for doing it this week. After what happened to Jamarcus, I need something to take my mind off this constant grief and anger." He paused to gauge their reaction. "Let's get together tomorrow and finalize our plans and make sure we've considered all the downstream effects. Like always, security and anonymity are paramount, so we don't want to do anything that puts us in jeopardy. That goes for our players, too." Mark saw that the others agreed.

Graham added, "Protecting our players' identities is critically important, as you said. If the authorities get onto them, it's not a leap to think that they'll soon be on to us."

"While we're considering changes, I've got one more idea that's been kicking around in my head for a bit, and with all that's transpired and our plans to launch a new 2.0 version of Murder Game, this may be the perfect time." Seeing that he had their attention, Calvin continued. "What if we post a list of our greatest hits – no pun intended – and sell an access token that allows our players to view the video clips that we recorded? The three of us will decide on the Top 10 and then post them on a secure server."

"That sounds like something that our players would love, and it could help ensure that the players hang around until the next execution date. It might even be an enticement for them to keep an open mind about the new rules we'll be introducing as part of 2.0." Graham liked any idea that helped drive a marketing focus.

Mark added, "It also sounds like a great little revenue generation idea, and one that requires very little effort or cost on our side. The only possible downside is that it adds to our considerable workload over the next couple of weeks, but I think we can pull it off. Especially if we divide and conquer."

"I'm happy to take the lead on our Top 10. I'll pull together a list of 15-20 potential hits and share them with you guys tomorrow and then we can decide which ones we want to have to make available for one-time viewing. I'll pick a cross-section that represents all four us, different methods and victims, everything. Cool?"

Calvin's idea inspired the others and lightened the somber mood. They actually looked forward to reviewing some of their most popular and challenging kills from the past. For most people this would be a very macabre exercise, but for the surviving members of the Slayers, it was part tribute to Jamarcus Hicks and part Academy Awards.

Chapter Fourteen

THURSDAY, OCTOBER 27

How to pick the best killings when each of them were, from almost any perspective, true masterpieces? With 80 murders to date, was it even possible to pick the Top 10? And what criteria would one use to pick the best? Should there be some kind of arbitrary 'degree of difficulty' rating like they use to judge Olympic gymnastics and diving events? By its very nature, aren't the murders using knives or garrotes more difficult because it's a one-on-one, in-your-face (or maybe in-your-back) killing? At the very least, aren't they more difficult than a long-range shot with a sniper rifle? Or does the simple act – not really so simple – of building a bomb, placing it unde-tected, and detonating it at the *exact* time also constitute a high degree of difficulty? The bottom line is this: no matter how simple an execu-tion appears, there is always a tremendous amount of planning that goes into the act. Yes, Oz picks the exact time, the locations, the methodol-ogy, and the general victim persona, but from there it's all on the Slay-ers. There is so much to plan for and take into consideration, like scouting the locations, choosing a victim that closely matches Oz's crite-ria, learning the target's habits and schedules, understanding police response times, planning for the perfect getaway, and, of course, ensuring that they leave no clues. The fact that none of their murders had ever been solved, or even risen to the level of law enforcement identifying a 'person of interest', is proof that the strategic and tactical planning that goes into these games would do a McKenzie and Company consultant proud.

Calvin researched each and every murder committed since the inception of The Murder Game. He knew every detail of his own killings, of course, and could still recall every sight, every sound, and every smell associated with the event. The same for the dates, the weather, any last-minute hiccups or hesitations, like unexpected passersby, or a police cruiser turning down the street or alley where he was about to commit the act. He was proud of the fact that he had never once failed to complete his mission. As a group they had experienced a few close calls, and on several occasions, events had occurred to push the killing a few minutes, maybe even a half-hour, off of the planned schedule, but the real world often trumps the best laid plans and timelines.

Calvin decided not to limit the potential Top 10 to only the game winners from the past few years. Looking through the victim profiles, Calvin could see that they ran the gamut of the 'allowed' profiles. That is, the Slayers didn't consider themselves monsters despite how many murders they committed. They believed themselves to be more 'evolved', which is why they created limitations and boundaries when coding The Murder Game logic that ensured that certain personas would be off-limits in the selection process. Oz prohibited targeting anyone under the age of 18 or over 65, pregnant women, anyone obviously handicapped, and anyone in the military or law enforcement. Beyond those few limitations, they were an equal opportunity killing machine.

Calvin started by identifying what he considered his finest kills. In some cases, he had won the respective games with those hits, but not always. He fondly recalled the night that he had killed a corporate bigwig, later identified as Rick Johnson, along Prospect Street in La Jolla, CA. After observing Johnson for several days, he had watched as he met up with a few others at Georges at the Cove restaurant for drinks and dinner. It was several hours later, and obviously several drinks later, when Johnson walked out. Calvin was ready but curious as to why Johnson had parked a couple of blocks away instead of using the restaurant's valet parking. Then the reason became apparent as the driver of the car parked next to Johnson's stepped out. She was young, gorgeous, and most definitely *not* his wife. He observed them for a good five minutes as they groped each other like teenagers before finally climbing back into their cars and heading east. Calvin assumed that Johnson was going to follow her to her place, or maybe he had an in-town *pied-a-terre* where he took his girl *du jour*, but regardless, the game's schedule dictated that he needed to take Johnson out now. Not later tonight, not tomorrow as he headed to the office. *Now.*

By the time that Johnson reached his car, Calvin had donned the 'killing kit' that he'd put together for tonight. This was a tricky kill; it was right in the middle of town, it was only 8pm local time, so plenty of people were still up and about, and there was not a lot of natural cover. Still, Calvin was jazzed and eager to roll. He pulled a large black garbage bag over his head and, with arm holes cut into it, donned it like a poncho. He had black gloves attached to black Tyvek sleeves that went most of the way to his shoulders. And, of course, a black balaclava that covered almost his entire face. As Johnson opened the door to his Mercedes, Calvin struck quickly and viciously with his KA-BAR knife, first viciously wrenching his head back by the hair, and then plunging the knife in right below his ear and up towards his brain. Immediately shoving Johnson into the car, he closed the driver's door and slipped quickly into the passenger side and extinguished the interior lights. A quick check of Johnson's pulse confirmed what was already obvious to the naked eye. He took a minute to admire his handiwork. Compared to killings where the victim's throat is slit, there was relatively little blood and no arterial splatter. Even though he had 'dressed for the occasion' in case there was a lot of unintended blood, Calvin had barely any on his disposable coverings. Despite the last-minute arrival of the victim's young friend and parking in an open and public area, the killing had gone perfectly. After disposing of his clothes and the knife, Calvin casually made his way out of town. The local police never identified a motive, never identified a person of interest, never found any blood or DNA evidence, and never found the murder weapon. In other words, the perfect crime.

* * *

Jamarcus had more than his share of winning games, but probably his most impressive kill was one that took place about 18 months ago in Mendocino, CA. Compared to the cities and towns usually chosen by Oz, Mendocino was small. *Really small.* Like, so small that most small towns look like NYC by comparison. It only made the list of potential towns for the game because it was a tourist destination along the northern California coast, and people often stopped there if they were visiting the San Francisco area or wine country. For this particular game, Jamarcus had to target a younger male victim and make the kill at 11am – broad daylight – and the designated weapon was a garrote. This game presented more than the usual number of serious challenges. Because this was a small tourist town, people often only stayed one or two days, so it was hard to establish the victim's patterns. Plus, very few people were there alone; if they were tourists, they usually visited as a couple or family. He could choose to focus on locals, but the pool of potential targets was still very small compared to games set in larger cities.

Jamarcus finally found his mark. He could have found someone easier than the eventual victim, but he liked the challenge. The greater the challenge, the greater the chance of winning the game. He settled on Ward Grady, a former defensive back for the USC Trojans that had been a starter for three of his four years in college. Ward was 6'3" tall and a solid 235 pounds; unlike many former athletes, he had not lost his impressive physique after his football career ended. It didn't matter to Jamarcus, in fact, he liked the extra element of danger that it added, especially with an up close and personal execution. Of course, the trick was finding a time when Grady would be alone since he was traveling with his fiancé; the Slayers considered it a point of pride that there were never multiple victims or collateral damage. They focused only on the target and having anyone else killed due to their miscalculation or misfortune would mean disqualification from that game. Collateral damage and the resultant disqualification were not good for their repu- tation or for the players that saw their bets go up in smoke.

Finally, Jamarcus saw his opportunity. Grady and his fiancé had just finished a late breakfast along Main Street, and he observed the fiancé heading towards the numerous shops while Grady headed across the street to walk along the water in Mendocino Bay Headlands State Park.

It was a beautiful and scenic place with 7,400 acres and several miles of trails, but on this day, it was cold, wet, and foggy. In other words, a perfect day for hunting another human along the trails and cliffs. Jamarcus followed Grady but sometimes on parallel or intersecting paths so as not to raise suspicion. When the time was right, both from the game's perspective and from the situational perspective, Jamarcus made his move. As he slipped the garrote over Grady's head, he immediately pulled back hard and saw a line of blood form where the wire was cutting into his flesh. Grady was strong, but it didn't matter. Once the garrote is in place and pressure applied, it's almost impossible to escape even if the attacker is smaller and weaker than the victim. To minimize any chance of that happening, Jamarcus kicked the back of Grady's knee and pulled him to the ground. While Jamarcus had no real desire to roll in the wet grass, pulling Grady to the ground had the dual benefits of shielding them from view and letting Jamarcus increase his leverage. It took less than 60 seconds for Grady to die, and because of Jamarcus' own strength and the leverage that he had, Grady's windpipe was completely severed. It was, to put it mildly, a very gruesome murder. Taking advantage of the location, Jamarcus rolled Grady off the cliff and down to the crashing waves and rocks below, figuring it never hurts to give himself extra time to head out of town. In this case, a lot of time: though Grady's fiancé reported him missing within hours, it was four days before his body was found. Another perfect murder. And another game winner.

Graham had also had many impressive kills, but to Calvin's mind, his most impressive hit wasn't even a game winner. He thought that Mark and Graham would agree. Viewed through the same lens as many of the other top kills, Graham's seems simple by comparison. Look beneath the surface, though, and it was anything but easy. The game was being played in the winter almost two years ago, and Graham was assigned to Burlington, VT. This game called for victims to be eliminated via sniper rifle; the only stipulation on distance was that the shot must come from at least 250 yards away. All of the Slayers had developed proficiency with their weapon of choice, the Remington M24 Sniper Weapon System (SWS). Graham, more than others, was fanatical about his weapons training and routinely shot 1,000 or more rounds per week between his handguns and the Remington M24.

He had a constant run of bad luck in this game. Burlington, and the whole Northeast, was hit with a lot of snow so his arrival was delayed due to canceled flights. He even ended up having to rent a car to drive from Boston just to get there in time for the game. That left him little time to scout locations or even identify his intended target. Oz's chosen profile was for a 48-year-old Hispanic woman, and that proved to be a problem due to the low percentage of Hispanics in Burlington. Graham scouted the downtown area for a place to setup, somewhere with elevated but minimally obscured views. Burlington isn't a large city, but there were still several buildings that were high enough to view much of the downtown area. He finally found what he was looking for, a hotel that overlooked one of the downtown parks and one of the busier intersections. He checked into the Hilton using one of his aliases.

On the day of the game, his bad luck continued. More heavy snow, and this time visibility was further reduced by high winds blowing the snow sideways and creating drifts on the streets. Now he had to contend with both reduced visibility, winds that would play hell with his accuracy, and the probability that his exit would be slowed, if not halted, by the terrible conditions. Still, he refused to concede. He loved the game, and he loved that many of the players had wagered on him because of his reputation as a crack shot. As the designated time approached, he came to the realization that he probably couldn't win because there was very little foot traffic and, to make matters worse, visibility was so limited that he couldn't be 100% certain that the target that he would focus on through his rifle scope was a man or a woman. Finally, about 25 minutes after Oz's specified time, he spotted what he had to assume was his perfect target: a portly, middle-aged woman - *presumably* - wearing a heavy winter coat with a pink hat and a huge pink scarf. Bingo!

He had calculated that a target walking from his left to right, which is where most of the foot traffic was coming from, would be visible for five seconds at most, depending on how fast they walked. That gave him five seconds to acquire the target, ensure that his range and sight adjustments were as optimal as possible, and take the shot. With the winds blowing and swirling between the buildings, with gusts of 25-30 miles per hour, there would be no shame in missing. Still, Graham was determined. The range was only about 400 yards, and under normal conditions that distance would be like a chip shot. But not today. As the target, later identified as Carol Dresser, moved into view, he was ready. The M24 was set on a tripod just inside the hotel window which was able to be opened just enough for him to have the needed range of movement. Graham had designed and built his own suppressor, and in these conditions it was more than up to the job; no one reported hearing the shot, whether in the hotel or down on the street. It took a few minutes before another pedestrian took notice, but only because they literally stumbled across the dead body. Graham had made a perfect shot, under absolutely shit conditions, and put a bullet right into the side of her head. There are better snipers out there, some of whom have reportedly hit targets from a mile or more, but they would put Graham's shot that day up against any shot ever taken. Since Graham was late making the hit, and the victim was non-Hispanic and substantially older than the game's chosen persona, he didn't win. Still, everyone agreed that this was one of the most impressive killings in the history of The Murder Game.

**

Mark Saxe was not the biggest Slayer, or the toughest or the strongest. But he was, by everyone's admission, the smartest and most technically gifted. Not that the others weren't smart, probably brilliant, as well. It's just that Mark seemed to operate at another level, which is why he took the lead on most projects requiring coding or long-term, strategic planning. Mark could handle himself, without a doubt, and had played the game extremely well against all targets. He'd won his fair share of games, too, owing as much to his toughness in the field as to his brilliant and painstaking planning. Where he really excelled, though, was in creating explosives. He *loved* the games where explosives were called for, and while the others used rudimentary explosive devices culled from the internet, Mark went a more specialized and elaborate route. He tweaked the design of his devices to obscure any possible signature or pattern that law enforcement might notice, and he specialized in shaped charges that could be hidden in plain sight until detonated. Sure, the end result was the same, but he loved the 'art' aspect of his creations. He compared his craftsmanship to swatting a housefly with a newspaper rather than a shotgun.

His most creative explosive, and to Calvin's mind, Mark's most impressive hit ever, happened just six months ago down in Sanibel, FL. The game stipulated an explosive device as the weapon of choice against a 41-year-old Caucasian female. While Calvin, Graham, and Jamarcus had crafted relatively simple devices with black powder, ball bearings, and a mobile phone trigger, Mark went the extra mile. His creation was as much a work of art as it was a weapon of destruction. He'd already identified his target, Jade Cooper, a 40-something widow living the good life in her 12,000 square foot home smack-dab on the Gulf of Mexico. He spent time learning all he could about her in the few short days he had for onsite planning. Luckily for him, besides being a local socialite, she was prolific on social media so it was easy to learn about her favorite places to eat, favorite places to drink, dance, and party, and her favorite types of art and home furnishings. It was the art angle that intrigued him. Crafting a lovely sculpture from modeling clay and C4, he inserted a small camera into the base before sealing it, and then readied it for delivery. Rather than using FedEx or UPS, he placed it in a box from one of her favorite art and furnishing stores and left it in her mailbox. It was simply a matter of time. Being too vain to question why one of her favorite stores was sending something to her that she hadn't ordered, she took the bowl into her house.

Mark was able to see her every move, at least during the time that she was in the same room. But he'd planned that part perfectly, as well. At the appointed time, which was 7:25pm on the East coast, Mark called the number of a small mobile phone that he'd concealed in the base. He could have simply used a timer set to go off at 7:25pm, but his goal was not widespread destruction but rather total carnage within a very limited area. She heard the phone ringing but couldn't figure out where it was coming from. It took her several minutes, and at least 15 rings, before she re-entered the room with the sculpture. When Mark saw her

approach, he triggered the explosion. The blast was large and very
narrowly focused; death was instantaneous, but property damage was
minimal due to his impeccable design and craftsmanship. Most of Jade's
face was obliterated by the blast, and her remains had to be identified by
DNA. That was one of Mark's many wins, and most players agreed that
it was one of his very best.

Cold blooded assassins. Meticulous planners. Shrewd businessmen.
Killers with a conscience. These, and many other labels, could be
attributed to the Slayers. A few labels that definitely did not apply
include sloppy, impulsive, or reckless. That's why they had a perfect 80-
0 record. It's also why they were starting to grow concerned that their
perfect record, like any team's, could eventually come to an end.

Chapter Fifteen

FRIDAY, OCTOBER 28

J J arrived at the Dallas Field Office early on Friday morning, and not just because there were a million-and-one details to follow-up on. She intended to leave by 4pm so that she'd have time to run home and freshen-up before meeting with Kristyn that evening. She smiled to herself, realizing that she was probably looking forward to it just a bit too much. It had been a long time since she'd felt this anxious, this giddy. And other than a short 'bi-curious' period during her sophomore and junior years in college, she had never been this attracted to another woman. Why now, smack-dab in the middle of the most important case of her career? Yes, the timing sucked, but she couldn't deny the feelings.

Around mid-morning JJ received a call from the Lab in Quantico. The technician, a young specialist in the DNA lab named Keith Haddad, was reaching out with information ahead of his official report. "Please tell me that you found DNA from multiple sources when you ran the knife."

"Sorry to disappoint you, Special Agent Jansen, but no such luck. The only DNA on the knife belonged to Special Agent Stevens, in the form of blood, and a bit of 'touch DNA' from the suspect, Jamarcus Hicks."

"Damn, I had a feeling that that would be the case. I was hoping to find DNA from another victim, someone that we could connect back to Hicks, to help us understand why this interaction turned violent."

"Sorry that I can't be of more help in that area, but the evidence is what it is. But I'm curious: why are you still investigating Hicks when there's no question that he killed Stevens, not to mention that Hicks is already dead?"

"That seems to be the question on everybody's mind, especially my boss." JJ sighed. She knew that the consensus was that she should be done with this case, and when people asked why she wasn't, she felt that she was being judged and second guessed. "Well, It's a couple of things. First, we still don't know why this happened, what caused things to turn violent. Stevens and Hicks weren't on the same flights or coming from the same city, and there's no record that they've ever met or crossed paths. And second, based on the information that we've uncovered, I think there's still a lot about Hicks that we don't know. In fact, I'm looking to tie him to other crimes that may have set this whole thing in motion."

"Wish I could help you, Special Agent Jansen. My understanding is that Hicks flew from Reagan National to DFW the day of the murder. I'm guessing that you're already looking at his movements here?"

"I am, and in fact, I'm getting ready to reach out to the DC Homicide investigators as soon as we're done. I was hoping to already have a solid lead on another victim based on DNA from the knife, but if it's not there it's not there. Still, you and I are aligned: DC may be the key."

After JJ hung-up from her call with Haddad, she reached out to Detective Lieutenant Drew McKinnon, head of the DC Homicide division. Shockingly, McKinnon picked up the phone on the second ring; JJ was so caught off-guard, fully expecting to either get screened by multiple assistants or transferred directly to voice mail, that she was momentarily stunned into silence.

"Hello? This is Detective Lieutenant McKinnon. How may I help you?"

Recovering quickly, she dove in. "Lieutenant, this is Special Agent Jessica Jansen with the FBI in Dallas. I'm working a case that you may have heard about that occurred about a week ago at DFW, the one where an FBI agent and a suspect were killed."

"Yes, I'm certainly familiar with that case, Agent Jansen. Terrible thing, to lose an agent and have a shootout right in the middle of one of the busiest airports in America. I trust that your investigation is going well?"

"Well, yes and no. We know that the suspect, Jamarcus Hicks, stabbed Special Agent Stevens and then was shot by two DFW officers. No real mystery there. But we're still trying to understand what led to their confrontation. The fact that Stevens found Hicks' wallet with several fake ID's inside was enough to start a conversation, but we think it's a stretch that this was enough to get two men killed."

"I have to admit, that's been bothering me, too."

"I'm glad that you agree, Lieutenant, because that's why I'm coming to you now. For obvious reasons we've kept some things out of the press, but one thing that we've learned is that Hicks was in DC before taking the flight to Dallas. I've tracked his movements as best I can, and I've verified that he stayed at the Four Seasons in Georgetown while in town. What I don't know is why he was there; nothing we've found seems to tie him to DC."

"So, you're thinking that maybe he was up to no good while he was here in our fair city, right?"

"Exactly, sir. I was hoping to connect him to something that occurred there on October 19th or 20th. I'm starting with DC because it's where he stayed, but if I need to look at Northern VA and Maryland, I'll try them next. But if I'm taking bets, my money is on DC."

"Assuming that it was a murder, any leads on the possible victim or cause of death?"

"No sir. He stabbed Stevens with a homemade 3D printed knife, but lab testing showed that it hasn't been used as a weapon in any other killings. So that's a dead end. No pun intended." JJ collected her thoughts. "If he did kill someone while in DC, I can't say for certain what kind of weapon was used. Any possibility that you had any unsolved murders during those two days last week that might fit the bill?"

"It's rare for us to go two days without at least one murder," sighed McKinnon. "As I recall, my team picked up five new homicides last week, but let me see what we have."

JJ paced the floor waiting on McKinnon to share the information. The wait felt interminable, even though it was less than two minutes.

"OK, Agent Jansen. We did have five homicides last week and three of them fell on the days that you gave me. One of those cases was domestic violence, so that's definitely not your guy. Another one was gang related, and in that case, we were able to make an arrest on the spot." McKinnon took a minute, re-reading the last report that the system had provided. "This last one is interesting. We found a dead body on Friday morning in a Georgetown parking garage. Victim's name was Peter Jacobsen. He'd been stabbed sometime the night before, sometime after 11pm. Body was found hours later, around 7am. We didn't find any prints or any murder weapon, but our ME determined that the assailant used a military type of knife, sharp with a serrated edge. And it says here that the ME was quite impressed with the precision cuts that the assailant inflicted; the victim had one stab wound to the throat and cuts made to both femoral arteries in his groin area. Even without the wound to his throat, he would have bled out in minutes from the femoral artery wounds."

Yes! That has got to be connected to Hicks! JJ was practically bouncing with excitement and could barely contain herself. "I think there's a definite connection, Lieutenant. I'll share with you, in confidence, that Agent Stevens' wounds also included cuts to the left and right femoral arteries. Not 100% conclusive proof, but I think we're onto something here." JJ decided to take advantage of the moment. "Sir, would it be possible for me to talk with the lead Homicide investigator on the case to follow-up on this? With a little luck it will answer my questions about Hicks and help you guys close your case."

"Actually, I'd appreciate very much if you two connected. My investigator is Detective Nicole McKenzie. Give me your email address and I'll forward our report along with her contact information."

JJ thanked him profusely. This was the break she'd been hoping for, and it immediately lifted her spirits. Her first inclination was to call Isaksen and share the news - *or maybe rub it in his face* - but she resisted that urge. She didn't want to do or say anything until she was 100% certain that the information was airtight. She really wanted to call

Kristyn and share the great news, but she resisted that urge, as well. It would have to keep until this evening.

When the homicide report arrived from Lt. McKinnon, she found it to be pretty much as she'd expected: no motive, no suspect, no murder weapon. *So, if Hicks did this, what was his connection to the victim?* Obviously, this murder was premeditated; he'd traveled to DC, taken a hotel, flown home the next morning on a flight that was booked in advance. Was the victim, this Peter Jacobsen, targeted in advance or was he just a victim of opportunity?

McKinnon had provided the contact for his detective, as promised. JJ called her. "Good afternoon, Detective McKenzie. This is Special Agent Jessica Jansen with the FBI. I spoke to Lt. McKinnon earlier and he suggested that we connect."

"Yes, Special Agent Jansen. Lt. McKinnon filled me in on your case and your theory that Jamarcus Hicks was Peter Jacobsen's killer. I think you're onto something. How can I help you at this point?"

"I'd like to understand some of the details of the investigation. Like, were there any witnesses, any theories about why Jacobsen, in particular, was the victim, if you uncovered anything out of the ordinary about Jacobsen. I'd love to hear it all. "

Detective McKenzie spent the next fifteen minutes going through the investigation step by step. JJ was impressed with the thoroughness and professionalism of the DC Homicide team's investigation. They had talked to all the right people, looked for evidence in all the right places, and come to the right conclusions. By all accounts, Jacobsen was a decent guy with no known enemies, no radical views or known associates, and no criminal record. He'd had drinks that night with friends but was the first one to leave, and everyone they talked to agreed that he was far from sloppy drunk. No one that was interviewed knew of anyone with a grudge against him, much less a reason to kill him. Despite spending hundreds of hours interviewing witnesses, they still had no clear motive. The detectives were certain, though, that this was not some random street crime. They saw it as a violent crime committed by a skilled and experienced killer. That actually concerned them more than the usual street crime since they had no idea why a deranged killer would target Jacobsen.

"One last question, Detective: did you look for other similar murders in DC and the surrounding areas to see if any of them matched Jacobsen's?"

"We did. Like we talked about, it's an almost certainty that whoever did this, it wasn't their first rodeo. We looked at murders going back five years, across DC, Maryland, and Virginia, but we didn't find any case, open or closed, that came close to matching this. We did find some stabbings, but very few were unsolved cases, and those that were unsolved didn't have the kind of precision, or the violence, of Hicks' work. We also looked at similar victimology, but we found nothing that aligned closely with Jacobsen's killing."

JJ was a bit disappointed, but not surprised. The investigation would be easier if DC were always Hicks' hunting grounds, assuming that he'd committed other murders. *And she had no doubt that he had.* But why would a guy travel from Austin to DC to do his killings? Maybe part of his MO was only committing murders when he traveled for business, or in cities where he vacationed. Committing multiple murders in a single city, particularly when it required travel each time, certainly increased your chances of being recognized or caught. And she had a feeling that Jamarcus Hicks was much too smart for that.

"I'll send you everything I have," JJ was telling Detective McKenzie, "so hopefully it will be enough to help you close your case, officially, on Jacobsen. Admittedly, it's all circumstantial, but I'm guessing that with a little legwork you'll uncover some video evidence from around the area that captured Hicks on the evening of the murder. Maybe, with a little luck, even some witnesses that saw him near the bar or parking garage."

"Thanks, Agent Jansen. I'll keep you posted as things progress. And I owe you one; it never hurts, career-wise, to close a murder around here. God knows that we get enough chances, but sadly, our close rate is barely above 50%. That means there are a lot of families that never really get closure, much less justice. At least for Peter Jacobsen, I think we're going to be able to give his friends and family that little bit of comfort. I'll take that win any time I can get it."

JJ agreed with her on that point, but she couldn't shake the feeling that there were a lot more families out there that deserved the same closure as Peter Jacobsen's family. She was making it her mission to uncover every murder committed by Jamarcus Hicks, no matter how many and how spread out across the country. She wanted those families to find peace.

What she didn't count on – *and who would?* – was the sheer number of murders that Hicks had committed. Had she known, she would have demanded, career be damned, that Isaksen create a task force involving the FBI and other state and Federal agencies. Would Isaksen even blink an eye when she tells him about Hicks' ties to the Peter Jacobsen's killing? She'd find out soon enough, but she wasn't optimistic. She had the weekend to continue working on the case and consider her options for approaching Isaksen on Monday morning. She'd learned long ago, as she was being subjected to ridicule and abuse from her bosses and peers at the Bureau: *never do today what you can put off until tomorrow*. And she did not intend to let thoughts about Isaksen or his reaction to her findings and theories ruin her weekend. Especially her Friday evening meeting with a certain someone.

Chapter Sixteen

FRIDAY, OCTOBER 28

Hen the alarm on her iPhone went off at 7:30am Friday morning, Kristyn was anything but ready to get out of bed. To say that she'd had a lousy night's sleep was an understatement. She couldn't blame the hotel, the street noise, or even noisy neighbors in the next room. No, this was all on her. She should have known better than to eat so much BBQ and drink so many beers the night before, not to mention all of the side dishes that were just impossible to resist. And the desserts! The cops were more than impressed with how much food Kristyn put away, and they teased her about it unmercifully. If last night had been an eating contest instead of a friendly dinner among friends? Well, she would have been the hands-down winner, for sure. God knows she paid the price for it later that night, though. The heartburn was enough to practically catch the sheets on fire. And now she knew, beyond a shadow of a doubt, that the much talked about 'meat sweats' were a real thing! And here she thought it was just guy-talk mixed in with a bit of urban legend. But now? She couldn't have sweat any more if she'd run a marathon in the middle of the summer.

Luckily, she didn't have to rush back home. She was convinced that she'd found a lead at Jamarcus Hicks' home, and she was anxious to share it with JJ when they met for dinner that evening. *God, I can't even think about food! And I don't need to see any more alcohol for weeks, maybe months!* She did the only rational thing under the circumstances: she reset her alarm for 9am and rolled back over to get some more sleep.

Before heading to Austin on Thursday, Kristyn had been heads-down for a couple of days digging into Steven's past cases, and as she suspected, nothing stood out as a likely cause of his murder. Sure, he had made many arrests over the years for all manner of crimes, including organized crime, domestic terrorism, drug trafficking, human trafficking, hell, even endangered animal tracking. Some of those arrested, and the people around them, could have held a grudge, but nothing really felt right. Plus, as she dug into Stevens' involvement at the UC Irvine riots, she didn't find any evidence that someone targeted him or had ties to his past cases. The deeper she dug, the more frustrated she became. Was the fact that she couldn't find any evidence that someone had targeted him, either personally or via a hired surrogate, proof that it hadn't happened? The old adage, *'you cannot prove a negative'* sprung to mind; it's impossible to find positive evidence for something not existing.

She wasn't ready to give up, but after looking at written files, computer screens, and hours of video until her eyes were glazed over, Kristyn felt that it was time to shift her focus to Hicks' day-to-day life in Austin. If new information came to light that warranted her refocusing on Stevens' past cases, she'd dive back in, but she didn't expect that to happen. She was determined to keep an open mind, but right now her open-but-tired mind needed a break. She left early Thursday morning to make the three-hour drive from Dallas. Leaving early meant a couple of extra cups of coffee – which then necessitated making a couple of extra stops along the way – but at least she reached Austin at a reasonable time and was able to get something accomplished.

Her first stop was Jamarcus Hicks' house. Normally, if anyone other than law enforcement had shown up at Hicks' house they would have been turned away, maybe even arrested if they were bold enough to trespass. Fortunately for Kristyn, JJ had greased the skids by reaching out to the Austin PD. The detectives who had investigated Hicks' life in Austin met her there and led her inside, and they explained that their team had gone through Hicks' home with a fine-tooth comb and were disappointed that they hadn't found anything especially useful. Kristyn was thankful for the opportunity to talk to the detectives that had led the local investigation. When JJ had talked to the Austin PD team, she had emphasized that Kristyn was talking to them off the record. An unusual request, to be sure, but it seemed to relieve any reluctance on the part of the Austin cops.

The lead detective for Austin PD was Robert Swain, a 21-year veteran of the department and a seasoned homicide detective. He was friendly and outgoing, which was more than Kristyn expected from someone that had been in the trenches for more than two decades; she had expected old, crusty, and world-weary. And probably someone who hated reporters in general, and female reporters especially. *Hell, maybe a misogynistic asshole who hates all women, especially if they're not stay-at-home moms that are barefoot and pregnant.* As it turns out, Swain was none of the above and he and Kristyn got along well.

As she neared Hicks' house, Kristyn was struck by how nice the homes were in the neighborhood. Homes were in the 3,000-5,000 square foot range, a mix of older Craftsman and Victorian houses along with some newer construction from the early 2,000's. Curiosity got the better of her, so she did a quick Zillow search and found that homes there were valued between $500K and $1.2M. *And this guy was only like 28 years old? WTF?* As they walked through Hicks' house together, Kristyn asked questions about the investigation. "So Detective, did you find anything that helps us understand why Hicks would end up in a violent confrontation with Special Agent Stevens? Or maybe anything that showed why he was in Washington, DC before all of this went down?"

"Unfortunately, we didn't. We went through the house for several days, top to bottom, with a full forensics team. We even looked extensively for any hidey-holes in the walls, under the cabinets and floors, both in the house and in the garage. Nothing. At first, we were concerned that we didn't find any electronics; in his home office we found multiple monitors, the usual broadband modems and routers, etc. but no PC. Later we found out that he had traveled with his PC and the FBI was in possession of it as well as his cell phone; again, nothing unusual in that. Lots of people travel with their computers, particularly if they're traveling on business. Do you know if the FBI has been able to pull any data from that computer?" For Detective Swain, it was highly unusual to be asking a reporter to tell him what's happening in an investigation and not the other way around, but he decided to roll with it.

"The latest report I have is that the forensics team still hasn't been able to access his PC. Apparently, it has some world-class security on it just to boot it up; I can't imagine what the encryption will look like on the files and folders if and when they do get in."

They continued walking through the house. Kristyn was impressed with the tasteful décor and the evident neatness and cleanliness of the place. Not what one would normally expect of most 20-something males. "Detective, how long was Hicks living in this house?"

"We pulled the real estate and tax records, and he bought this place about five years ago. He had a mortgage on the place, but it wasn't a huge mortgage in relation to the purchase price and present value. Had to have put down a sizable down payment."

"Hicks would have been all of about 23 years old when he bought this place? How the hell does that happen? Just out of college, I would imagine, a time when most kids are saddled with a ton of student debt, and this guy buys a house that costs probably a half-million dollars?"

"Actually, he paid about $710,000, and the latest assessment puts it north of $1.1M. I guess that you and I are in the wrong lines of work because there's no way I could afford this neighborhood. I'd be lucky to afford the taxes on this place."

"Yeah, and he definitely spent a lot of money on the furnishings. Every room is tastefully decorated with really high-quality furniture and materials. It was more of the same when I checked out his closet. Everything in there, from his dress shirts to his dress shoes, hell, even his athletic wear, are all high-end and designer labels."

"I noticed that, too."

"Have you found out exactly what Hicks did for a living? He apparently claimed to be a 'consultant' in the technology and gaming industry. There are a lot of young people in Austin making good money working for big technology companies, but have you seen many that could afford this type of home and lifestyle at twenty-eight years old?"

"Not really, no. Our investigation came up with the same thing, technology consulting. Supposedly his expertise was in developing software for multiplayer video games, at least according to his tax filings. We reached out to some of the companies that he'd worked with and confirmed that he was an absolute rockstar, so I imagine that he commanded a pretty high fee for his services."

They continued walking through every room of the house, Kristyn hoping to get a better sense of Jamarcus Hicks. After looking through every room, including the garage, she made her way back to Hicks' office. "If you don't mind, I'm going to look through his desk and bookcases just to see if anything pings for me. I won't remove anything, of course."

"The whole house has been processed, so that shouldn't be a problem."

Kristyn took her time looking around. As she looked through the built-in bookcases, she noted books on coding and gaming, as well as a handful of classics that appeared to be, at least to her untrained eye, authentic first editions. *He had a wide range of interests, and almost as many non-fiction books as fiction.* Her focus shifted to the framed pictures that occupied several shelves. She had noted the very nice, and very expensive looking, Nikon D850 DSLR camera on his credenza and recalled hearing some of the photographers at her paper gushing and lusting after that particular model. She assumed that Hicks had taken the pictures that were displayed, including pictures of beautiful spots like Big Sur, the Grand Canyon, Zion and Arches National Parks in Utah, and Key West. Then she focused-in on several pictures of Hicks and, presumably, some friends. *Scratch that 'presumably' – these same people appear in almost every picture. These people must be an important part of Hicks' life.* Knowing that she couldn't remove anything from the house – JJ could secure a warrant, if necessary – she did the next best thing and used her cell phone to take pictures of the photos that showed Hicks and these unidentified friends.

"Detective, any idea who the people are in these photographs? I noticed that it's the same people in each of them, and it appears that the pictures were taken over the span of several years, based on their appearance."

"No, we have no idea. We didn't find anything on the pictures themselves, front or back, that provided any clues. If they're friends, we've found nothing to help identify them."

"My best guess is that these pictures were taken while a group of close friends were vacationing together. In fact, as I look more closely, several of them appear to have been taken outside of the US. One of them certainly looks like Ireland or Scotland." She pointed at one of the pictures. "And this one, it sure looks like pictures I've seen of islands in the South Pacific like Tahiti or Fiji."

Swain was duly impressed. "You know, you'd make a helluva investigator. I don't know if it helps us identify these guys, or if identifying them will bring us any closer to understanding Jamarcus Hicks, but it certainly can't hurt. You going to share that with your friends at the FBI?"

"I am, for sure. If we can track down enough people that knew Hicks, we might finally get to the 'why' behind this case. And we're hoping that it leads us to other bad acts that he was involved in prior to this. I don't think anybody believes that he was just an average guy who snapped and lashed out at Agent Stevens."

They spent about another hour walking through the house and property, but nothing set her senses tingling the way those pictures in Hicks' office had. By this point it was getting late in the day, and Krystyn hadn't even checked into her hotel. She'd gotten up early to get on the road, so she was starting to drag a bit, but she felt energized not only because of what she'd found – *if what I found really has any bearing on the case* – but because of the opportunity she'd been given to participate in the investigation, not just report on it. It had been years since she'd felt this excited, probably all the way back to her first days as a 'real' reporter.

"So, Kristyn, do you have any plans for this evening?" Wanting to make sure that he wasn't giving her the wrong impression, Swain quickly added, "Me and a few of the guys are going out for some BBQ tonight. If you're not busy, why don't you join us? Beats the hell out of eating alone."

"You're telling me that a bunch of cops would actually welcome a reporter to sit down and have a meal with them? Usually, they'd rather put reporters on the spit and slowly roast us." Kristyn smiled at Swain and had to admit it sounded like fun.

"You kidding? These guys will love you, and they'll appreciate someone classing up the evening a bit. Plus, today you were more of an investigator than a reporter, and as I said, you are a helluva investigator. Great eye for detail, real talent for reviewing the evidence and developing well-reasoned conclusions. Trust me, if you ever wanted to step away from your reporter gig and join the boys in blue, I think you'd be a superstar."

Kristyn blushed. Spending the evening with some guys from Austin PD had to be better than sitting alone in her room at the Hilton Garden Inn. "Well, I'm not sure about all of that, but thank you. I just hope that we're taking the investigation in the right direction."

"From what I've observed, I'd say that it's definitely heading in the right direction. I believe it's exactly like you said: there's a lot more to Jamarcus Hicks than meets the eye."

"Thanks. The fact that you agree means a lot. So, being as you're an Austin guy, I assume you know a little bit about BBQ? You won't steer me wrong this evening, especially since I only have this one night in the best BBQ town on the planet?"

"Oh, you don't have to worry about that, young lady! They don't call me '*Bobby BBQ*' for no reason!"

"Bobby BBQ? You're kidding, right?"

"No, absolutely not. I actually have a little side hustle where I put together BBQ tours for the tourists that flock here. People tell me what they're interested in and then I put their tour together to all the best places, whether it's huge mega-restaurants or little hole-in-the-wall places. And they're accompanied by me or one of the guys on the force. Can't get a better and safer tour than that!"

Kristyn couldn't help but smile. "Count me in. I love great BBQ, and it's been a while since I've been to Austin. We've got some good BBQ in Dallas, but let's face it: it ain't Austin. I probably won't be able to keep up with you guys when it comes to putting away the food, but I'll give it my best shot."

Chapter Seventeen

T o say that it had been a long, stressful week was an understatement. Still, JJ was upbeat since she had uncovered some great leads in the case. She was even more upbeat and excited because she was looking forward to dinner tonight with Kristyn. Yes, she was eager to discuss the case, share everything that she'd uncovered, hear from Kristyn on her progress, and plan next steps, but she didn't kid herself: she couldn't wait to see Kristyn again.

She rushed home from work around 4pm and threw herself into looking as attractive and put-together as possible. There was no denying that she had to pull out all the stops if she wanted to look like someone even remotely in the same league as Kristyn. Right now, on her way to the shower, she barely felt like she was even the same *species*. Not that she was bad for someone in her mid-30's, but Kristyn was in a whole different league. JJ couldn't deny that she had let herself go. After being alone and beaten down for so long, she made only the minimum effort most days, and it showed. Sure, she was at least 15 pounds heavier than she'd been in college, but who the hell isn't? And yes, she wore too many unflattering pant suits and 'sensible shoes', but most female agents did. It wasn't a job that leant itself to high fashion and even higher heels. Her daily makeup regimen was minimal, basically just a touch of foundation and some mascara, never much more. If she were honest with herself, she was maybe a '6' on a good day. There just weren't a lot of good days, mostly because she didn't care enough to try.

JJ took extra care getting ready, spending at least an hour longer than she did most days. She was far from an expert on using the blow dryer and curling iron, since she rarely used either, but she did her best to add a bit of style to her otherwise drab hair. It took several attempts to get her makeup just right; at first, she went overboard to the point of looking like a streetwalker from the bad side of town. Finally, she felt that she had it right; classy, appropriate for evening, and colors that were complimentary without being garish or whorish. It didn't take long to decide which dress to wear. When you only own two dresses, and one looks like something an Amish school teacher might wear, it was a slam dunk that she had to go with the trusty Little Black Dress. She paired that with her nicest, frilliest, black bra and panty set. Make that her *only* frilly bra and panty set, still unworn after almost two years. *Like there'd ever been an occasion to wear it.* The dress was coupled with her nicest shoes, a pair of 3" black pumps that she'd bought at Nordstrom, and her best jewelry. As she checked herself out in the mirror, she was pleasantly surprised with the results. *Maybe not a '10', but a solid '7.5'. That's a lot better than a '6'.*

Kristyn had recovered, more or less, from her marathon eating and drinking session in Austin, and after making the long drive home she had taken advantage of the opportunity to climb back in bed to grab another couple of hours of sleep. She slept like she was in a coma, and when her alarm went off, she awoke having no clue where she was or what time it was. Groggy as hell, but at least not hungover. *Small favors.* Heading to the bathroom to start getting ready, she was shocked when she passed by the mirror. Hair a mess, eyes bloodshot as hell, makeup smeared, and just generally looking like death warmed over. *Nothing that a good, hot shower and a little makeup can't fix. Hopefully.* An hour later, she was back to her usual stunning self. Most importantly, she felt like she might actually live to see another day. The restorative powers of sleep and a hot shower had once again saved the day. *And the older I get, the more I have to count on those magical restorative powers, because I sure as hell can't bounce back like I used to.*

Their dinner reservations were at The Henry, and JJ arrived first and allowed the hostess to show her to the table. She was as nervous as a teenager on a first date, and despite trying to reassure herself that this was simply a business meeting between two women who had just met, it did little to calm her butterflies. And then, when Kristyn walked in, she literally got weak in the knees, and she noticed that every man in the restaurant was practically drooling. Of course, it was all that she could do not to stare, too. *Stunning. Play it cool, JJ.*

"Hi, JJ," said Kristyn, as she smiled brightly and threw her arms around JJ in a friendly hug. "I'm glad that we could get together, I've got a lot to share with you."

JJ practically melted in her embrace, and it was all that she could do to break away. If it was up to her, she'd stay wrapped in those arms all night. *Not doing a very good job of playing it cool, JJ.* "Same here. Lots of exciting details to catch you up on."

"OK with you if I order us a bottle of wine to go with dinner?" Kristyn saw what she perceived as a bit of hesitation on JJ's part but then saw her smile and nod in agreement.

As they scanned the menu, Kristyn smiled and said, "After last night's dinner, which more closely resembled a Roman bacchanalia centered around Texas BBQ, I didn't think I'd ever eat again. Or drink, for that matter." She looked across the table at JJ, impressed at how nice she looked this evening. "Do you know what you're going to order?"

"I think I'm going with the Short Rib Potstickers as an appetizer, and the Roasted Half-Chicken for my entrée. And I'm happy to share both if you want. I'm not sure that I can eat that much." That was a lie. She had skipped lunch to make sure that she was hungry for dinner tonight, plus she rarely left a morsel of food on her plate at any meal.

"Mmmm, sounds great. I think I'm going to do the Shrimp appetizer and the Seared Ahi Tuna for my entrée. I don't think I can look at another piece of red meat today! But don't you dare let me order dessert later. I don't need the calories, and I definitely don't want to feel as miserable tonight as I did last night." At JJ's urging, Kristyn told her all about her dinner the night before in Austin, and they both laughed almost nonstop.

They both cleaned their plates, and, despite their protestations, ended up splitting the Warm Croissant Bread Pudding for dessert. "Oh my God, that whole meal was incredible, and the dessert was one of the best I've ever had. Ever." JJ was glowing. "Though I'm embarrassed that I ate that much in front of you. I feel like a real heifer. I probably look like one, too."

"Bullshit. You look fantastic tonight. And no reason to be embarrassed; it's not like my dinner last night where I ate more than every single cop in the place. So ladylike!" She and JJ both had to laugh at that.

After the plates were cleared, they decided to move to one of the sofas in the bar area to be more comfortable and have more privacy. "One more glass of wine while we talk business?" asked Kristyn. JJ's smile was taken as an affirmative.

For the next hour they exchanged the details about what they'd learned. JJ was super excited to hear about the pictures that Kristyn had found at Hicks' house, and she examined them closely on her phone. They both agreed that this was a thread that they needed to follow. Kristyn was excited to hear about JJ connecting Hicks to the murder of Peter Jacobsen in Georgetown, and they both wondered how many other murders Hicks might be connected to.

"I know that we need to talk about next steps, but since this place is getting ready to close, why don't we take this over to my place for a nightcap or a cup of coffee? I only live about 10 minutes from here," suggested Kristyn.

JJ didn't want to sound overeager, but she could barely contain herself. "I guess that could work. I took an Uber here just in case I had a bit too much to drink. Which is exactly what has happened," she giggled. What she didn't say was that this was the first drink she'd had in at least two years and the few glasses of wine definitely had gone straight to her head.

"I took an Uber, too, and for the same reason." Kristyn smiled at her and said, "Let's head over then. You can always have an Uber pick you up at my place later to take you home. Worst case, I have a guest room that you're welcome to use if it gets too late or you get too tired."

JJ was starting to get aroused, and the wine wasn't helping matters. *And I may never want to go home again.* It took barely 10 minutes for their driver to arrive.

Once they arrived back at Kristyn's home, a beautiful brick rancher situated in a decidedly upscale neighborhood, they both opted for a cappuccino rather than another glass of wine. Getting comfortable on the huge sectional sofa in the family room, which was perfectly situated in front of a giant fireplace with a massive flat screen TV mounted above, they got down to discussing next steps. They agreed that JJ would focus on Hicks' history to see if she could tie him to any other homicides. Kristyn suggested that her next step should be writing-up a report detailing her investigation into Stevens' past cases and the incident at UC Irvine, as well as her search of Hicks' home in Austin.

Feeling that they had covered all the important points regarding the investigation, Kristyn switched gears. "So, since we've been friends and working together for such an incredibly long period of time – like at least 3-4 days, right? – what are the chances that today is the 'someday' that you mentioned for sharing your story with me? I want to know why you think you're not the most loved and respected FBI agent in Dallas, if not the entire Bureau?" Kristyn gave JJ that thousand-megawatt smile to help put JJ at ease.

JJ didn't speak right away, deciding what to share and how best to say it. Her palms were sweaty, and she was fidgeting practically nonstop, clearly uncomfortable. She wanted to be open and honest with Kristyn, not only to build trust and a strong bond between them, but because of her growing attraction towards her. She hoped that Kristyn would reciprocate and share her backstory, both the good and the bad, in the spirit of trust. "OK. Let me give you the Cliffs Note version, otherwise we could be here for hours." She looked at Kristyn and smiled meekly.

"I'm sorry, I feel like I put you on the spot and made you uncomfortable. If you'd rather not share, it's not a problem."

"No, I'd like to tell you. You deserve to know; you're putting as much at risk here as I am. So here goes: I grew up in Scottsdale, AZ and was raised in a pretty dysfunctional family. My father was a raging alcoholic and was extremely abusive to me and my mother. Lucky for me the abuse never got physical, but it did with my mom. She died when I was 16, from breast cancer, and that just made my dad worse. I mostly stayed with friends until I graduated, and then I went to Arizona State University on an academic scholarship."

"So, you were super smart, I take it?"

"Not really, I had to work hard for it. I'm not one of those lucky people that can skate through without cracking a book. I was kind of a nerd, to be honest, and not exactly the kind of girl that attracts a lot of guys. But still, I had a great time at ASU once I came out of my shell. I started partying way too much, out drinking with friends almost every night, barely passing my classes and basically majoring in partying and sleeping with random guys. Ended up marrying some guy that I had met at a frat party and slept with a few times, but it was a huge mistake and we both realized it. We finally split after about 2 years, though we had no real relationship after the first few weeks. Not my proudest moment."

"But even through all of that, you did graduate?"

"I did, and even went on to graduate school to major in Criminal Justice. I graduated near the top of my class, and that's when I got recruited by the FBI. Happiest moment of my life. But then I fucked it all up by letting my drinking get out of control. I started drinking to the point of having blackouts, and God knows how many times I woke up in my bed and had no idea how I'd gotten there. Bottom line, it affected my work and my bosses 'encouraged' me to check into rehab. Luckily the Bureau likes to have this public image that they're 'enlightened', especially for their female agents, so they supported it. I was there for 30 days and came out clean and ready to get back to my job. I guess I was naïve in thinking that they'd forgive me and welcome me back."

"Please don't take this as being judgmental, at all, but I'm curious: you're a recovering alcoholic ..."

"So, why I was drinking this evening?"

'Yes. Sorry if I'm being too personal or nosy. I guess it's just the journalist in me, if that's any excuse."

"The fact of the matter is that recovering alcoholics should not drink, or that's certainly the conventional wisdom and the AA party line. I don't disagree with their position, at least in general, but I will admit that on very rare occasions I drink a glass of wine or have a beer, and for me, it's never presented a problem. The wine we shared tonight was actually the first alcohol I've had in about two years, if you can believe that. AA might not agree, but I feel that I can control my drinking; I don't feel the *need* to drink, and I never get even close to the point of losing control or exhibiting risky behavior, like drunk driving. Maybe I'm just lucky. Maybe one day my luck will run out. But I still try to take life one day at a time."

"I'm sorry that you had to experience all of that, but I'm very impressed with your resolve, your inner strength. To battle your addiction and then survive all the bullshit that you described with your boss and coworkers, well, I'd say that's pretty impressive."

"Well, there's actually more to it. Sure, I was kinda cast aside after my stint in rehab, and even though the Bureau would never admit it, my career was effectively stalled as soon as I stepped back in the office. Unfortunately, a couple of years later I was involved in a bad car accident – off the job – and ended up alone and in the hospital. Lots of painful injuries, lots of time spent in the hospital and then in physical and occupational therapy. Being out for so long also didn't make me Ms. Popular around the office."

"How long were you out?"

"About two months for the hospital and therapy, but that was not the end of it. Then, like half the people in America, it seems, I continued to need help dealing with the pain."

"Oh, no....."

"Oh, yes. Here I am, a 30-something professional, a Special Agent with the FBI, and I end up getting hooked on opioids, just like millions of others. Rich, poor, white, black, brown, urban, or suburban or country. It doesn't matter; we're all the same when it comes to our addiction to pain killers. Drugs don't discriminate."

Kristyn was fighting back tears as she listened to JJ's story and imagined the hell that she'd been through. "How did you get off the opioids? I imagine that was even harder than the alcohol."

"It was definitely harder. Much harder. I can't tell you how many times I prayed for death. Anything to stop the pain, which in this case was the continuing pain from my injuries and the sickness from the oxycontin withdrawals. But I did it. I won. It took several months, but I did it. And once again, the Bureau welcomed me back with open arms. At least officially."

Kristyn wiped away her tears; she could no longer hold it all in.

"And since then, they've treated you like shit and looked for a good excuse to push you out, right? "

"Yeah, that pretty much sums it up. My boss, and his bosses above him, wish that I'd just fade away. And my coworkers, well, let's just say that I'm not really one of the boys around there. I just keep to myself, do my job as quietly and effectively as I can, and try not to make any waves or bring any attention to myself. At least that's how it's been for a long time. I have a feeling that this case is going to change all of that, one way or the other." JJ took a second to compose herself. She wasn't yet sure what she felt after sharing her story like that. Was it relief? Was it cathartic? Was it something that would send Kristyn running for the hills? She forced a smile and tried her best to put on a brave face. "So, is turnabout fair play? Are you willing to share your dirty secrets and sordid past with me?"

"I almost feel guilty sharing because my life has been so average and uneventful, maybe even boring. I'm not complaining; I know that, by comparison, I'm blessed, and I don't take that for granted. Does that make me dull and uninteresting?"

"No, and you should never apologize for having been raised in a good home and a good family. Are you still close with your family?"

"I am. My parents still live in Fort Worth, and I have one brother that lives in Denver and a sister that lives in Houston. We're all really close, and I'm grateful for that. They've always been there for me when I needed them. Like, when I got divorced."

"Oh, I didn't realize that you'd been married before. Not that I'm surprised, at all. I mean, my God, look at you!"

"Well, thanks. Yes, I was married for about five years, but then we divorced after I caught him cheating on me."

"Oh my God! Why in the world would a man cheat when he's got a beautiful wife and a seemingly great life waiting for him at home? Men, they just suck sometimes!"

"Can't argue that point. As it turns out, though, he didn't leave me for another woman. He announced to me, after five years of marriage and three years before that of dating and living together, that he realized that he was gay."

"No!"

"Yes, and he'd met a guy and was ready, in his words, "*to stop living a lie*" and follow his heart."

"Wow. That must have hurt! Did you have any hint that he was gay before he came out to you?"

"You mean, like, was he into all the 'gay cliché' things? No, not at all. See, Steve is a 6'4", 240-pound former football player, a total jock. And he's a high-end custom home builder so most of his time is spent on construction sites. He's the very definition of a 'man's man'. And he was a great husband and lover, too, if I'm being honest."

"Just...wow! I guess you threw him out on his ass and told him you never wanted to see him again."

"You would think. But, no. He and I – and his husband, the same guy that he cheated with – are great friends. In fact, when they got married, I acted as 'best man'. Being cheated on was a shock, admittedly, but I'm happy for him. He's beyond happy and living his truth. And I'm doing OK, too. I have a great job, great friends, a home I love. Maybe I'll find someone new someday, but I'm not rushing into it, and I don't feel desperation. I love my life!"

They talked for about another half hour, just gossiping and reminiscing like old friends. Soon they realized that it was well past midnight. Kristyn touched JJ's hand and said, "I really had a great time tonight, and I really appreciate how you shared your story with me. It's getting really late; that offer still stands about using the guest room. It's ready and waiting for you, so I hope you'll stay. By the time an Uber gets here and then gets you home it will probably be at least 1:30. Stay here, get a good night's rest, and I'll make you some coffee in the morning before you head home. Deal?"

JJ was hoping that the offer to stay would be brought up again, though her heart and her head were both wishing that the offer would be to share Kristyn's bed. *Baby steps, JJ. Baby steps.* She wasn't sure which was going to rule the night, her arousal or her exhaustion from too many hours of work, too much food, and too much wine. Luckily, it was the latter. Otherwise, she might have pretended to sleepwalk and 'accidentally' ended up in Kristyn's bed. The thought did cross her tired but exceptionally horny mind.

Chapter Eighteen

SATURDAY, OCTOBER 29

L uckily, JJ had no intention of going into the office today. There were a ton of things that she needed to get done today, but at the top of her agenda was a few more hours of sleep. It was close to 12:30am when she finally made it into bed at Kristyn's, and she was too keyed up, and mostly, too damn horny, to fall asleep. After a half hour of tossing and turning and letting her mind run crazy with lustful thoughts, she finally gave into temptation and let her hands explore her aching body, slowly driving herself insane. It took only minutes to bring herself to orgasm, and God, what an explosion of pleasure it was. She buried her head in the pillow to make sure that she didn't scream so loud that she woke Kristyn, if not the neighbors. After such an intense, mind-blowing orgasm she should have fallen right out, but it was not to be. JJ barely stopped long enough to catch a breath, and then she was right back into it. After another earth-shattering climax, exhaustion finally took over and she fell into a deep sleep. Deep sleep with a very satisfied look on her face.

As soon as she'd gotten home from Kristyn's, she crawled right back into bed. She finally got moving around 10:30, but not before getting herself off one more time, and as before, a certain someone was the fantasy running through her head. This time, being as she had the 'home court advantage', she had a little assist from her favorite 'toy' and the release was every bit as explosive as the ones she'd had last night. Not that she was complaining. Stepping into the shower, she went well beyond her usual daily routine. Today she took it far beyond washing her hair and shaving her legs, even though, admittedly, shaving her legs was a once or twice per week event, at best. *One good thing about wearing those ugly pantsuits.* On the off chance that things progressed romantically with Kristyn, she wanted to make herself attractive and desirable. When she exited the shower, she was as smooth as a newborn baby. Or as smooth as every millennial and Gen Z girl in America.

As she stepped into her closet to get dressed, a new realization hit her: she really needed to up her game in the wardrobe department. Her closet was full of old, drab, and shapeless clothes. Her shoes were no better, nor was her lingerie. Actually, she couldn't even refer to it as 'lingerie', it was just cheap bargain-bin underwear from the outlet stores. Not the kind of underwear that you'd want to wear if you're in a relationship. For that matter, not the kind of underwear you'd want to be wearing if you were rushed to the hospital. JJ made a mental note to plan on some serious shopping before the end of the weekend. Seeing herself as she passed the full-length mirror, she also made a mental note to setup an appointment to get her hair cut and colored.

Around 1pm she was ready to head out to run a few errands, and just as she reached for the door handle her mobile phone rang. At first, she considered ignoring it, but then her old-fashioned work ethic kicked in, especially when she saw that the call was coming from Quantico. "This is Special Agent Jansen."

"Hi, Agent Jansen. This is Chad Cook from Quantico. I'm glad that I was able to reach you. Sorry to call you on a Saturday, but I thought you'd want to know right away that we were finally able to get past the encryption on Jamarcus Hicks' laptop and we've retrieved a lot of data that you're going to want to see."

JJ's heart literally skipped a beat. "Fantastic! You were right to call me on a Saturday, no question. I can't wait to review what you've recovered. What kind of data did you get?"

"I haven't reviewed any of the data to see if it's meaningful or case-critical; I'll leave that to you to determine. But I can tell you that we recovered emails, some financial transactions, and some communications between Hicks and others from the Dark Web. All totaled, we've recovered about 20-25 gigabytes of data so far that I need to compile and forward to you."

"Do you think this is everything, or do you still have more files and sites to access?"

"There's definitely more. It might take the rest of the weekend to get through it all, but I'll have it waiting for you no later than Monday morning."

JJ talked to Cook for another 10 minutes and agreed to have him transfer the data to her electronically. As soon as she hung up with him, her next call was to Kristyn.

"Hey JJ. I heard the new phone ringing, but it took me a second to realize what it was. What's up?"

It was one of those rare times where JJ could not contain her excitement and she was talking a mile a minute, explaining what the Labs had come up with. "I won't have the files until Monday morning, but my plan was to spend tomorrow tracking all of Hicks' travels as far back as I can go to see if we can correlate it to any unsolved murders. I know that it's not the most exciting way to spend a Sunday, but would you want to come over to my place and we'll dig through the data together?"

"I don't have any big plans for tomorrow, but even if I did, I'd put them aside to work on this. What time should I come over?"

"Want to say around noon? And maybe I'll order us some lunch when you get here?"

"Perfect! Need me to bring anything other than my PC?"

JJ wanted to tell her to bring whatever she needed to be able to spend the night – or several – but she resisted the urge. "No, I think I have everything that we need. And I'm sure that I have a few bottles of wine hanging around here someplace."

"This is exciting! I can't wait to dig into it with you. See you tomorrow then."

As soon as she hung up, JJ rushed to the kitchen. She'd told a little white lie – actually, a real whopper – when she'd said that she had 'everything we need' in the way of food to snack on, decent bottles of wine, or even decent coffee or sodas. All the errands and shopping that she'd had planned for today would just have to be pushed back a couple of hours;

priority number one was to hit the grocery store. The thought of having someone over, especially Kristyn, and have her find that the only things in her refrigerator were some condiments, a carton of out-of-date milk, and a box of baking soda, was not the impression that she wanted to make. She rushed out the door and headed straight to the Kroger's just a few blocks away. *Thankfully.*

By mid-afternoon she was finally headed to the Galleria for some serious shopping, something that was completely foreign to her. She'd never been much of a girly-girl, and fashion had never been anywhere near the top of her priorities. The only upside to her decidedly down-market tastes in fashion is that she saved much more money that she spent. Today was going to change that. By the time the stores closed, she'd burned through several thousand dollars. Shoes. Makeup. Dresses. Designer jeans. Dress slacks and matching tops. Lingerie. Even a nice designer purse that she found on sale, though its $550 'sale price' was still more than she'd spent on every purse she'd owned in the last 10 years. *Money may not be able to buy happiness, but it can definitely buy you the things that make you happy.*

Chapter Nineteen

SUNDAY, OCTOBER 30

T he doorbell rang right at noon. and when JJ opened the door she was once again struck by how Kristyn looked so effortlessly beautiful. Even on a casual Sunday afternoon dressed in jeans and a top, she still looked flawless. Hair, makeup, jewelry, everything; just perfectly put together. "Wow, do you ever have a day when you don't look great?"

"Oh, yeah, trust me. I have *lots* of days like that." Kristyn closed the door and turned to give JJ a hug in greeting. "Today feels like one of those days."

JJ held onto the hug for at least one or two extra beats. She couldn't help herself. "Well, *you* trust *me*. You certainly don't look like it's 'one of those days', and in my limited time knowing you, I haven't seen one yet."

They grabbed some snacks and headed into the dining room so they could spread out their work. As she shuffled some papers from the files she'd brought home, she shared her ideas. "I've sorted through Hicks' credit card bills from the last year, but I think I should search even further back, say five years, and focus on his travel destinations, dates, and related expenditures. And then when we find where he's been, you dig into police and news reports about any murders that may have coincided with the dates and locations of his trips. Sound like a good plan?"

"A very good plan. If you'll pass me what you have for the last 12 months, I'll start there. I assume that you already have it broken down by dates, cities where he traveled, where he stayed, etc.?" Seeing JJ nod in the affirmative, she continued, "Great. That will help me structure my search for murders in the surrounding areas, starting with murders in a 25-mile radius of his destination. If I don't get anything, I'll expand the search out maybe another 50 miles."

Kristyn looked through the information that JJ had compiled and found that he'd made a total of 11 trips. Of those, only one was outside of the US – to Belize – so she ignored that one for now. She looked for multiple trips to the same cities, any discernible pattern for certain days of the week or month, or even similarities in the types of industries or attractions. She didn't expect to find something as innocent as Hicks regularly traveling mid-week to cities with major theme parks so he could ride rollercoasters without long lines, but she was determined not to start with too many preconceived notions. A cardinal sin for reporters is falling victim to confirmation bias, and she was always on guard not to fall into that trap.

They worked quietly for about an hour, barely speaking as they concentrated on their respective tasks. "I've got a list of 10 cities to check into scattered across the US, and I've noticed that most of his trips are spaced about every other month, usually the second week of the month. There are a few that don't fit that pattern, but I'll dig into them, too."

"I'd say start by looking at those cities that most closely fit the pattern that you've observed. Save the outliers for last."

"Exactly what I was thinking. One other thing that I've noticed, and this could just be coincidence: of all the trips that he's made, at least those that fit the pattern that I mentioned, none of them are here in the Central time zone. He made multiple trips to cities in the other time zones, but none in Central. Weird. Maybe it's nothing...." She trailed off.

"Or maybe it's something. You have great instincts, so keep that as one more data point to consider as you dig. And as I look at earlier years, I'll try to focus on itineraries that fit the same pattern. Just curious, what cities are you seeing that you believe fit the pattern?"

"In addition to Washington, DC, which we already know about, I've found Santa Fe; Ogden, Utah; Spokane; Hartford; Temecula, CA; and Savannah. In a couple of cases, like Temecula and Ogden, he flew into airports that were a bit further away but then drove to those cities. Like for his trip to Temecula, he flew into Orange County/Santa Anna, and that's almost 50 miles away. It was still easy to follow the trail, though, since we have credit card receipts for his rental car, his hotel, and some restaurants."

After a few more hours of heads-down work, interrupted only by a pizza delivery, opening a bottle of wine, and several bio breaks, they pushed back from the table to talk about all that they'd found. "I don't know about you, but I am totally blown away! We've got more than 30 possible cities over the past five years; do you think it's possible that we've stumbled on one of the worst, most prolific serial killers of the past few decades?" JJ knew that she should be more tired but was running on pure adrenalin at this point.

"I'm thinking the same thing! Let me show you what I've come up with based on my research of the past 12 months." Kristyn pulled up her notes. "In all the cities that we talked about earlier that fit the pattern, I've found at least one unsolved murder during the time that Hicks was there! That can't be coincidence!"

"Oh my God! And were all of them the same MO as the Peter Jacobsen stabbing in Georgetown? And similar victims?"

"No, there's a whole mishmash of killings and victims, but let me throw out a theory: what if Hicks used different MO's in his killings so that he stayed below the radar? If he committed these murders – and I'm definitely leaning that way – no one has ever even put together that these homicides are related."

"Tell me about the other victims and how they were murdered."

"In this case, I think the lack of a pattern is, in and of itself, a pattern. There are men, women, young, and old. Multiple races. And as far as how they were killed, they ran the gamut. One person was killed by blunt force trauma, which police believe was a baseball bat to the back of the head. Another was shot at close range, while another was also shot but by a suspected sniper rifle. There was one woman that was stabbed, though with a different wound pattern than Jacobsen, or from

Agent Stevens, for that matter. And finally, one was killed by garrote; that's not something that you see every day. I don't know about you, but I would think that the chances of having all those different types of victims and weapons during the very weeks that Hicks was in those cities is like one in a billion."

"I have to agree. I'm not a big believer in coincidence, and this really pushes past any reasonable boundaries for coincidence." JJ looked at her files for a second and then offered up an idea. "I don't know about you, but the only way that I can make sense of this volume of data is to put it in a spreadsheet. Basically, I 'think' in Excel. I guess it's a character flaw, one of many," she smiled.

"Oh, I get it, totally. I'm a reporter, so my mind tends to 'think' in Word, but in this case, I think you're right: Excel is the way to make sense of this data, especially if we have to present it to others."

JJ started on the spreadsheet, setting up rows to correlate with dates when Hicks traveled and columns that correlated to cities where he traveled, the name of the unsolved murder victim, the date and time when they were killed, and how they were killed. While she worked on that task, Kristyn continued digging into possible murders for the other years that JJ had identified. It was close to 11pm when they finally had all the data crunched, all of the variables and data entered into the spreadsheet and were able to sit back and really take in the magnitude of what they'd uncovered.

"Are you fucking kidding me? We've got more than 20 likely murders that we can tie to Hicks, at least by circumstantial evidence. But pretty damn convincing circumstantial evidence! I've seen convictions based on a whole lot less." JJ was so keyed-up that she couldn't stop pacing as she talked, even after 11 hours hunched over her PC, and barely taking time to stand up and stretch. Or, as she was starting to realize, eat any dinner or stay hydrated.

"Even assholes like your boss won't be able to deny the connections that we've identified. Like we said earlier – I can't remember if it was earlier today or days ago, I'm so tired – we may have uncovered one of the most prolific serial killers in decades."

JJ poured them each another glass of wine – from their second bottle, the first one being long-since gone – as they sat on the couch to relax after a grueling day. "We really accomplished a lot today. I don't want to jinx us, but I'd say that we cracked the case. Cheers to that!" She clinked her wine glass with Kristyn's. "Look, I know it's getting late, especially for a 'school night', so let me return the favor: why don't you stay here tonight and just head home in the morning?"

"I am tired, and I've probably had a bit too much wine to drive. And I've still got a half glass to finish," she smiled. "You sure you don't mind?"

As if, thought JJ. "Absolutely not. But full disclosure, my guest room is a wreck, and the third bedroom is what I use for my office. Would you be ok sharing my king-size bed for the night? And I'm happy to lend you some pajamas or whatever you like to sleep in."

"Sure, I'm fine with that. It would be like a grown-up slumber party," she giggled. 'You're sure that I won't be keeping you from getting a good night's sleep?"

JJ could barely suppress a smile and laughter. "Me? No way! After a day like this I'll probably be out as soon as my head hits the pillow." Another whopper, even as she tried to convince herself that is was just the tiniest little white lie.

They stayed up another hour talking and winding down from their long day. JJ was growing tired but was really nervous about getting into bed. Would she be able to maintain her composure and keep her hands – and body – to herself? Thank God that she had a king-sized bed rather than a double or queen; as much as she'd give anything to fall asleep snuggled up to Kristyn, she knew that it was a bridge she shouldn't try to cross. At least not yet.

When they finally headed to bed all of JJ's resolve was sorely tested, because Kristyn came out of the bathroom and climbed into bed in just a tee-shirt and panties. *God, give me strength* she thought to herself, though she wasn't convinced that she really meant it.

"Thanks for inviting me over today to help with all of this. It was a great day," Kristyn said quietly to JJ as she turned to her and embraced her in a long, warm hug. "I think we make a great team," she said as she gave her a quick kiss on the cheek, then smiled and turned over to go to sleep.

How the hell am I going to sleep now? Despite how tired she was, JJ's arousal was stronger as she lay there staring at the ceiling and fantasizing about the beautiful woman lying next to her in bed. The chorus from one of her favorite songs kept playing in her head, a classic from the Divinyls: *When I think about you, I touch myself.* God, it was going to be a long night.

Chapter Twenty

MONDAY, OCTOBER 31

Most Monday mornings, JJ was none too anxious to get to work and even less anxious to see SAC Isaksen. Luckily their paths rarely crossed, but today was different. She knew that he'd be tied-up in meetings throughout the day, so she did the politically correct thing and reached out to Angie Claxson, his Executive Admin, to request time on his schedule. That was risky; Angie was not a huge fan of JJ, and as the official 'gatekeeper' for Isaksen's precious time, she took pleasure in being a roadblock. Fortunately, that wasn't the case. JJ had been prepared to go full-blown bitch and either go over her, around her, or through her, but luckily that wasn't necessary. JJ was granted 30 minutes to meet with Isaksen at 10:30am.

For the next two hours, JJ reviewed the spreadsheet over and over, anticipating every possible question and objection. She expected both, with the objections tainted by the personal animosity that Isaksen had for her and numerous 'gotcha' questions where he hoped to catch her in a mistake or moment of uncertainty. No matter. She intended to be on top of her game and maintain her cool. This was too big, too important, to allow her feelings or ego to keep her from successfully presenting compelling evidence that might close 20-odd murders. *Make that 20-odd murders that no other cop or FBI agent anywhere in America had any clue were connected.* If this were any other agent, Isaksen would probably lead a ticker-tape parade in their honor, but that didn't faze her in the least. *Fuck them*. All she wanted was to have Isaksen and his bosses acknowledge that she was onto something and let her close these cases. Beyond that, she knew that a single 'attaboy' could never erase the years of ridicule, abuse, and second-class treatment that she'd endured.

At 10:30, on the dot, JJ presented herself at Angie's desk. "Thank you for your help in getting me in to see him, Angie. I know that his schedule is always packed, especially on Mondays." JJ tried to smile sincerely but wasn't sure that she pulled it off very well. Still, as the old saying goes, *you catch more flies with honey than with vinegar*. She at least had to make the effort.

"Certainly, Agent Jansen," Angie responded without so much as a smile, even a fake one. "He's ready for you, so you can go right in."

JJ stepped up to Isaksen's door and knocked politely. No response: one of his more irritating traits was making his underlings wait unnecessarily until he granted them entry. Purely a power play and a way to stroke his own ego. *Prick*. After about five seconds he invited her in.

"What do you have for me, Agent Jansen?"

Wow. No 'good morning' or no 'how are you' or 'how was your weekend?'. Isaksen was never the king of small talk, especially with her, but this was to the point of being rude. She hadn't even started to talk about the case and already he'd gotten under her skin. Instead, she went the opposite way and spoke as sugary-sweet as she could muster – or stomach. "Good morning, sir. I hope you had a great weekend." As he raised up from his work, giving her an awkward look, she continued. "I've been working all weekend on the Jamarcus Hicks case....."

Before she could even complete this thought, he interrupted, "Why are you continuing to waste time on this case, despite our earlier discussions? I asked you to focus on Steven's past cases and his last case at UC-Irvine. And since we know that he killed Special Agent Stevens, and we know that Hicks was subsequently killed by the two DFW officers, we should be wrapping this up. End of story."

They weren't 30 seconds into the meeting and already she was having a hard time maintaining her composure. She knew that's exactly what Isaksen hoped for. *Asshole*. "Sir, when we last spoke you agreed that we'd like to understand a bit more about the 'why' of this case.

That is, why was there a confrontation between Hicks and Stevens, and why did Hicks have multiple ID's and aliases, etc." She took a breath in hopes of calming herself, to little avail. "That's exactly what I've been doing. And now, with the help of evidence collected from Hicks' PC by the guys in Quantico, I've been able to delve into his travel and spending for the past five years."

"And to what end if I may ask? And more importantly, can it bring this investigation to a close so that we can focus on more important cases?"

"Actually, sir, no. In fact, just the opposite." JJ let that hang in the air for a moment, relishing the look on Isaksen's face as he went from merely annoyed to ready to blow his stack.

"Now listen here, Agent Jansen. I'm tired of you wasting your time on this so-called investigation and then, by extension, wasting my time by trying to convince me that you've done anything worthwhile to bring this to a conclusion....."

Cutting him off, showing that she could be just as forceful and rude as he, "No, it's time for *you* to listen, goddammit." She saw Isaksen's eyes get as wide as saucers as he was rising from his desk. "If you would put your disdain for me aside for one damn minute, you'd see that I am bringing you evidence, *compelling evidence*, that Hicks may have killed 20 or more people over the last four to five years."

"Bullshit! Just because you found evidence that Hicks is likely to have killed that guy in Georgetown before his run-in with Stevens, that does not make him the next Ted Bundy or Son of Sam. And it sure as hell doesn't make you God's gift to the FBI or the 'chosen one' to uncover a serial killer."

"No, it doesn't, but it does make me the one person that has been willing to take her head out of her ass and actually do the work to find out what the hell made him tick!" All pretense of trying to remain calm and under control was out the window. She knew that she was beyond the point of insubordination, but she was also beyond the point of caring.

Trying to calm the situation and reassert himself as the one ultimately in control, he said, "OK, Agent Jansen. I'm going to give you 15 minutes to show me this so-called 'compelling evidence' that you claim to have uncovered. But make no mistake, I'm giving you just enough rope to hang yourself here. If I'm not convinced, then two things are going to happen. One, I'm going to write you up for this little outburst and you're going to have a sit-down with the Office of Professional Responsibility (OPR), and if they take it all the way to the Inspector General and end up washing you out of the Bureau altogether, I won't lose a minute of sleep. And I doubt anyone else will, either. And number two, you're going to be done with this case as of today. No argument, no grace period, no nothing. You're off the case, and if I catch you spending even one more minute on it, I'm going to recommend your termination up the food chain. So, bottom line, you better think of this as the most important 15 minutes of your career, otherwise it's very likely to be your last."

JJ couldn't even begin to keep the contempt out of her voice. "Fine. You got it. Fifteen minutes should be more than enough time to convince even the dumbest, most pig-headed person alive that what I've uncovered is real. And please, feel free to add that little comment to your complaint to OPR. I almost welcome that investigation, and if I do sit down with them, I'll be sure to share all of the documented examples I have of you and dozens of other agents harassing me and treating me like a total piece of shit for years. I'm sure that will do *your* career a whole lot of good, as well."

For a few minutes both were quiet in an apparent stalemate. Both looked furious enough that they might start throwing punches at any second. Finally, Isaksen spoke. "You have 15 minutes to show me what you have. Put it up on the big screen and walk me through it."

JJ connected her laptop to the large 65" monitor mounted on Isaksen's wall but held off putting up her spreadsheet. She wanted his attention, without distractions, and she wanted to set the stage before sharing it. "Let me start at the beginning. When I started investigating Hicks, I checked into his travel and spending in the days immediately preceding the events at DFW and found that he'd been in DC, in Georgetown, specifically. I talked to the DC Homicide detectives and learned that they'd found a stabbing victim on the same morning that Hicks flew to Dallas; the victim had been stabbed and killed the night before. I got them to dig through area traffic and business cameras and we were able to establish that Hicks had been in the same part of Georgetown at the time of the killing, and the victim's wound patterns were very consistent with the wound patterns on Agent Stevens."

"But not the same knife, correct?"

"Yes, that's correct. The knife used to kill Stevens was a 3D printed plastic knife, while the one in DC used to kill Peter Jacobsen was a military style knife, most likely a KA-BAR. It was never recovered."

"OK, go on."

"After establishing that Hicks had almost certainly killed Jacobsen, I decided to look at his past travels. My logic was simple: why would he fly to DC to kill Jacobsen? There is no evidence that they knew each other or in any way ever crossed paths, had mutual business or personal acquaintances, nothing. It seems that he flew to DC specifically to find a victim to kill, as cold and unbelievable as that sounds. There is no indication that Jacobsen was the intended target when he left Austin to fly to DC, so it seems more likely that he picked this guy, seemingly at random, once he was in DC."

"So, at this point the DC police consider the killing of Jacobsen closed, correct?"

"Yes, sir. They have notified the victim's family and closed this out." JJ took a sip of water to calm herself further, as she was now getting into the part of the discussion where she expected the biggest pushback. "While I am convinced of Hicks' involvement in Jacobsen's murder, the whole scenario of him traveling to DC *specifically* to kill someone kept bugging me. I mean, if he wanted to kill someone, why not in Austin? I hypothesized that it was possible, maybe even probable, that his trips around the country were simply a pretext for murder, so I dug into every single trip he's taken over the past five years. I checked the flights, the destination cities, the hotels, and restaurants, basically every financial record that I could get my hands on."

"And what did you find, pray tell?"

At that, JJ put the spreadsheet up on the big screen. "What I found was this. More than 20 trips over the past five years, and in almost every instance I've been able to identify at least one unsolved murder that happened during the period that he was in town."

"But there are unsolved murders that occur virtually every day, all across the country. Wouldn't you agree Agent Jansen?"

"Yes, sir, but if you look at this from a statistical perspective, the chances that an unsolved murder happened in every one of these cities during the short period of time that Hicks was there, well, it's off the charts. The odds are a lot less than your chances of winning Powerball or MegaMillions."

"I see. So, tell me about these other columns showing the victims, the murder weapons, etc. It seems that both are all over the place, and historically, most serial killers – and that's what you're suggesting that we're dealing with here – follow a consistent MO when it comes to victimology and methods of killing."

"Agreed, sir." JJ saw Isaksen's surprise when she stated her agreement on that point. "But I'm working on the assumption that Hicks is smarter than that, maybe even a true psychopath. I think he mixed it up to keep the cops around the country from ever tying all these murders together. And it's worked; I can't find a single instance where detectives in one city contacted detectives in another city to inquire about similarities between their cases. Bottom line, Hicks has stayed off the radar completely, has never even been named a suspect or person of interest in these crimes, or any others, for that matter."

"I noticed that your spreadsheet shows the various weapons that he allegedly used, but I don't see any kind of pattern to when or where he used them, do you?"

"No, sir. His choice of weapons seems to be entirely random. I even dug into the logic, if you will, of why a particular weapon was chosen for each kill. That is, why was this killing in Bangor, Maine done with a knife but the next one, in Vancouver, Washington, done with a sniper rifle? As I investigated, the location in Vancouver was a terrible place to use a sniper rifle. A pistol would have made a lot more sense. Similarly, how often is a garrote the weapon of choice? From what I've found, in the cases where a garrote was used, almost any other weapon would have made for an easier kill, much less risk, and an easier escape. I think there's something else driving the choice of weapons, but I don't yet know what that is."

"And am I to understand that, in all of these cases, no murder weapon has ever been recovered?"

"Yes, sir. That means that the police have never been able to match bullets that they recovered to other bullets in our systems, never been able to pull DNA off of the knives or garrotes that were used, though in every case I've found that the knife was consistent with a KA-BAR. I think Hicks was the ultimate planner and pro; he knew when and where he was going to hit, he knew his escape route, and he knew how he was going to dispose of his weapons, cost be damned."

"I'm no profiler, but if Hicks did kill all of these people, he's not one of those serial killers that reportedly longs to be caught and stopped."

"I would definitely agree with that, sir. I think that this was a guy that loved to kill, loved to prove his superiority over his victims and the authorities. It didn't seem to matter whether the victim was young or old, big or small, or even male versus female. And he really didn't seem to have any proclivity about race or ethnicity, either. He was an equal opportunity killer."

Isaksen was silent for a few minutes, and JJ chose not to say anything more. She'd made her case, and while she would not put it past Isaksen to shoot her down just because of his dislike for her, she was satisfied that she'd laid the facts out in a simple, logical, and easy to follow way. Nothing more she could do. They'd gone beyond their planned 15 minutes, but she didn't consider that to be a bad thing since he had stayed attentive and engaged.

Finally, "I don't often say this, or even admit it to myself, but...... Agent Jansen, I can see that my assumptions on this case may have been totally off-base. I was ready to close this one out, but admittedly, your instincts seem to be spot-on. I want you to focus on this full time, wherever it leads." He saw that JJ was nodding in agreement. "I think the first order of business is for you to reach out to the Homicide teams in every one of these cities and share what you've uncovered with them; let's hope that this helps them close out all these cases. Hopefully we can provide answers and closure to these 20-odd families that have lost their loved ones."

"Thank you, sir. I will start contacting the cities right away, and I'll try to compile a report that summarizes our findings for each victim and provide that information to the respective detectives. And I assume that you'll want those reports, along with my spreadsheet and other files, so that you can share this with DC?"

"Yes, definitely. I know that DC will want to be all over this since it involves so many different jurisdictions. And Agent Jansen? I will make sure that you are given the proper credit for this. That's a promise."

"Thank you, sir. I'll get started on this right away."

She packed up her PC and papers and headed back to her desk. She could hardly suppress a smile. It was the first praise that she'd had from Isaksen, or pretty much from anyone, in several years. It was a great feeling. *Of course, I guess it would have been too much to ask that he actually apologize! Let it go, JJ. Let it go. Take this small victory.*

Chapter Twenty-One

MONDAY, OCTOBER 31

For the next several hours, JJ was heads-down working on a summary report of her findings and tracking down the Homicide detectives from each jurisdiction. It was slow going due to the age of many of the cases and the fact that, in several instances, the original detectives were now in different roles or no longer with the department. That's to be expected; people burn-out and want a change, or maybe they get promoted. Maybe they get pushed out for any of a million reasons, real or contrived.

She looked up as she heard one of her least favorite agents in the Dallas Field Office approach her desk, and she could barely contain a grimace. Special Agent Chad Mills was one of many who took pleasure in ignoring her, ridiculing her, and basically being a misogynistic asshole. She braced herself.

"Congratulations, JJ. I heard about the incredible work that you've done linking Jamarcus Hicks to a whole slew of unsolved murders. That's great work! Isaksen knows that I'm not working anything hot at the moment, so he asked me to lend you a hand with all the contacts you have to make. I know that's a time-consuming task. Can I take some of that off your plate?"

It was all that she could do to hold her tongue and think before she spoke. Not once in all the years that she'd worked here had he called her

JJ, if he even bothered to speak to her at all. Not once had he been friendly, or initiated a conversation, or offered to help her on any case or task. Her first instinct was to tell him to decline his offer, but she decided to take the high road and be gracious. Besides, she could use the help with all this administrative work. "That would be a huge help, and I'd really appreciate it. Thank you." She pulled out roughly half the files – intentionally sticking him with the cases likely to require the most digging and effort. She was willing to act gracious, but she would be damned if she'd act like they were suddenly BFF's. "This is about half of the cases, and I'll email you a copy of my spreadsheet and the summary that I've created in just a few minutes. Those two documents should be helpful as you get started. Thanks for offering to assist." she added with the best fake smile that she could muster.

"I'll keep you informed as I track the information down. Would you like to reach out to the local Homicide detectives personally, or would you like me to take that step, too?"

"Actually, I'd like to be the one to have those conversations. I suspect that they'll all have some questions and I'm probably in the best position to answer them. My bet is that the local DAs would be reluctant to file charges based on this circumstantial evidence if Hicks were still alive, but since he's not they may be willing to close the case."

Mills headed back to his desk with the files that JJ had given him, and she just shook her head in wonder and amazement that someone had acknowledged her and treated her like, well, a human being. Maybe not exactly like a member of the team, but baby steps. *Maybe they're just hoping to ride my coattails and get some recognition of their own. Or maybe I'm just being a bitch.* Before diving back into the work, she texted Kristyn to let her know about Isaksen's 180-degree turn around and his support for her continued investigation. She didn't expect to hear from Kristyn until later, maybe even this evening, since she was working. Much to her surprise, the response was almost immediate.

OMG! That is SO great! Good for you. It's about time that he took his head out of his ass and recognized how awesome you are.

That's funny – I may or may not have said something about people needing to take their head out of their ass and follow the evidence. Making friends wherever I go – NOT!!

They texted back and forth for a few more minutes and then JJ reached for her files to get back to the task at hand. No sooner had she gotten back into the groove than her phone rang. "This is Special Agent Jansen."

"Hi Agent Jansen, this is Gerry Ruggiano from Quantico."

"Thanks for calling. You've got something for me?"

"I do. I mean, we do. It was a team effort, took us all week-end.....Anyway, I have good news and bad news. Which would you like first?"

God, like I have time for these games. "Well, since I've had a pretty good day, all things considered, I can probably handle a little bit of bad news. Hit me with that first."

"We've run those pictures through every facial recognition database that we can access, and the individuals in those photos with Hicks didn't come up at all. Not any of them."

"Wow, that's kinda surprising. I just assumed that they would be in the system and have some criminal record, being as they obviously spent a lot of time with Hicks. I'm guessing that you tried military and government employee databases as well, right?"

"We did. We got zilch everywhere we looked."

"Well, that's disappointing but I'm not giving up on them. I'll just have to find another way to track down their identities. OK, so that was the bad news. Not what I was hoping for, but not the worst that could happen in the larger scheme of things. So, let's hear the good news."

"OK, we finally finished our forensic analysis on the PC. Sorry that it took longer than we had expected, but we were hitting roadblocks and firewalls and different encryption algorithms at every turn. But the good news is that we got a *ton* of data."

"Fantastic. I know that you guys were focused more on accessing the data than analyzing it, but did you come up with anything earth shattering that jumped right out at you?"

"We did, actually. You may want to sit down for this. We found something that I'm pretty sure is going to change the whole size and scope of your investigation."

JJ was a bit skeptical. "You may not be aware, but we've already taken a deep dive into Hicks' past travels and are pretty confident that we've identified around 20 murders, from all over the US, that we can tie him to. I'm not sure how much more you can give us on Hicks at this point."

"That's just it, Agent Jansen. What we recovered isn't about Hicks. I mean, it does involve Hicks, but it goes beyond that."

"I'm not following....."

"From what we've gleaned, Hicks wasn't some lone-wolf killer targeting victims at random. It was actually some kind of complex game being played on the Dark Web. A morbid game, to be sure, but still a game. In fact, all references I could find referred to it as The Murder Game"

JJ plopped down in her chair, totally stunned. "A game? Murdering people was a game to him? And others? How many others, were you able to tell? And please tell me that you have the names of the others that were in this with Hicks."

"No names, and in fact, Hicks' name doesn't even appear in the details that we found. The players, if that's what you want to call them, are each associated with a color. Like, we believe that Hicks was Mr. Blue, and the others are Misters Red, Green, and Yellow. From what I've analyzed, I believe that all these guys – presumably male, but no guarantees there – killed their victims at the same time and using the same kind of weapon. I mean, the weapons varied with each cycle of the game, as did the locations and the victim personas, but it looks like the killings were synchronized."

Luckily she was seated, because her head started spinning and her stomach lurched upon hearing this new information. She was beyond shocked, beyond flabbergasted. She couldn't even begin to think of a word that captured what she was feeling. "So, you're telling me that these four people, including Hicks, killed these victims as part of a game? And if Hicks killed about 20 people, at least that we've identified so far, we're to assume that the other three killed just as many? We might possibly be looking at 80 homicides over the past few years?" The fact that there were three others besides Hicks, the same number of people that were in the photographs taken from his home, did not escape her. Certainly not definitive proof, but one more thread to pull.

"Yes, that's exactly what I think. Actually, a few others that have been working on the data all agree, as well. We found references to this group being referred to as The Slayers. Morbid, but seems accurate."

"And did you say that these killings used varying weapons and different victimology across the past few years? We noticed a similar pattern with Hicks, and we also determined that his murders seemed to follow a schedule of one killing about every other month. Sorry if I'm asking you questions that you've already answered, but my mind is going a million miles an hour in a million different directions,"

"The weapons definitely varied, as did the victims. If there was any pattern, we failed to see it. You'll want to verify the data, but what we've seen leads us to conclude that these so-called Slayers performed their killings every couple of months, and each time they killed roughly identical victims, using the same type of weapon, and synchronized almost to the minute. And get this: each time there were murders across all four time zones."

Bingo! "That's an important point. One thing that we noted while investigating Hicks' murders is that he did hits in three of the four different time zones, but never his own. He was from Austin, so Central Time. I'm guessing that these other three killers are spread out across the country and, like Hicks, always do victims outside of their respective time zones."

"I'm not sure why they would do that, but OK. I mean, I can understand maybe not doing a killing that's in their own backyard but worrying about time zones seems a bit extreme."

"I agree. Not sure that I see the logic. Maybe I'll figure that out as I dig deeper, especially if I can identify the other three members of this group." JJ was quiet for a minute, collecting her thoughts. "I wonder how they decide when and where and who and how they're going to do these targeted killings? Did you find anything that spoke to, like, a leader or president of the Slayers that made the assignments?"

"Well, no, but we did find something odd. There were references to someone or something called 'Oz', and it seemed that a lot of time and effort was being spent to provide data to him. Or it. To what end, we couldn't determine."

"Is there any indication that this Oz was providing information back out to members of the Slayers?" JJ knew that her question must have stumped Ruggiano because he didn't respond. "Let me throw out a crazy idea, just thinking out loud. But if you think there's some logic to it, maybe you and your team can dig a little deeper?"

"OK......" He sounded more than a little trepidatious.

"What if this Oz is actually some kind of randomizer program on steroids. You know, like those applications that you can put on your phone or PC to pick random numbers for raffles or contests. Maybe Oz has all the data and possible variations in its memory – presumably uploaded by Hicks and the members of the Slayers -- and then it generates the criteria for each cycle of the game? Is that plausible?"

"Actually, I think it is. Absolutely possible. We need to dig into it a little bit more to see if we can find a trail of this two-way communication, but I think you might be onto something. I'll talk with my team, and we'll dive into it."

"One more thing before you go. You referred to what these guys do as a 'game.' If it's a game, to what end? I mean, how is a winner determined? And what does the winner get? Here we have four guys flying all over the country, spending money on hotels, and eating out, and buying weapons, and for what? The thrill of a random killing?"

"So, you're thinking, what? That there is some way that the winner is getting some money out of this game? Like maybe they all put some money in the pot and it's winner take all?"

"I don't know. Again, I'm just thinking out loud. One thing I know for sure, though, is that when I'm investigating a crime, Step One is always 'follow the money'. Is there a chance that maybe you and your team haven't found everything there is to find on the PC and on the Dark Web sites they used? I mean, it's a deep, dark, scary place, and isn't it possible that these Slayers are sharing the game with a bunch of sickos? Maybe even letting them bet on the outcome? If it were me, that's what I'd do; it's an almost sure-fire way to drive huge sums of money."

"That's an interesting theory, and again, not outside of the realm of possibility from a technology perspective. Let us dive into that and see what we can find. It would be great to uncover a list of the people that, in simple terms, financed these murders. They may not have exactly contracted to get these people killed, but they certainly would have been a linchpin in financing it. I'll be back to you ASAP, hopefully by close of business tomorrow."

"Thanks, Ruggiano. I appreciate all your hard work on this. And for now, please keep this quiet until we're further along with the investigation. I can't afford any leaks."

After hanging up with Quantico, JJ's first call was to Kristyn. Once again, she didn't expect to reach her but was pleasantly surprised when she answered on the second ring.

"Wow, twice in one day. Aren't I the lucky one! How is it that the FBI's new super-sleuth serial-killer-catching diva has time for me?"

"Trust me: This is worth making time for. You may want to sit down for this, preferably somewhere private."

JJ told her the entire story, and just like she had been, Kristyn was absolutely stunned. Once she recovered enough her reporter instincts took over and she asked great questions, even came up with some new angles to explore. Her excitement, now that she was over her shock, was palpable. "Any thoughts about our next steps?"

"I think our next stop should be New York to check out Hicks' background at Columbia University. You able to fly up there on Wednesday for maybe one night, fly back on Thursday?"

"Definitely. If you can setup the meetings at Columbia, I'll make the travel arrangements and book a hotel. You ok if we share a room, just to make sure that neither of us catches a lot of flak about expenses?"

"Works for me." *If you insist. How can I say no to that offer?*

Chapter Twenty-Two

MONDAY, OCTOBER 31

T he three surviving members of the Slayers were on a video call much earlier than normal, but it couldn't be helped. They were in a time crunch; they'd been in a time crunch since deciding to tweak the rules of the game, create and launch a 'Top 10 Kills' contest, and move up the date of the next game. They'd all put in extremely long hours, more than they'd counted on when they'd aligned on this plan of action. They all agreed that they'd taken on too much, leaving them exhausted and their brains fried, but they got it done. Now all that was left was picking the winner of the Top 10 Kills contest and catching their flights to their respective hunting grounds for tomorrow night's executions.

It had been five days since the Slayers met to review the videos that Calvin had picked showing the best 15-20 kills from the last few years. It had been a tough assignment, and one that required a lot of discussion and give and take among them. After a few hours they'd narrowed it down to the Top 10, and Mark Saxe posted the videos on their secure site after adding some special touches that blocked them from being saved, forwarded, or recorded; they trusted their players, but they all believed in 'trust, but verify.' They had agreed ahead of time to make this a simple raffle contest, and once a player made the raffle 'ticket' purchase, they would be provided a unique, one-time key that would give them access to view the videos. Each raffle entry would cost $1,000 in cryptocurrency, and players could buy as many chances as they want. The Grand Prize winner would receive 25% of the wagered bets, while second place would get 15% and third place 10%. When the betting period ended at 6pm Eastern time on Sunday, more than 1300 unique bettors had wagered almost $1.5 million. They calculated that they would be paying out $750,000 and splitting the remaining $750,000 three ways. Calvin had definitely hit one out of the park with this idea.

Saxe drove the discussion in the interest of time. "All that's left to do is let Oz generate the winning 'ticket' numbers and then we can post the results before getting on the road. Agreed?" Calvin and Graham both nodded their agreement. "OK, consider it done. I'll post the winners and make the wire transfers to the top three finishers, as well as to each of us, then I need to head to the airport in about 30 minutes."

"Great work, Calvin. This was a fantastic idea, and I know that our bank accounts could all use the extra cash." Graham could hardly contain his smile and pocketing a cool quarter million.

"One last thing before we go, I just checked the site to see how much is wagered on tomorrow's game. The good news is that the rule changes that we put in place did not have any negative impact on the betting, thankfully. In fact, there's already more than $2 million in the pot, and we still have another 6 hours before the betting is closed. This is likely to be the largest pot ever." Mark double-checked one last thing on his PC and then continued. "I was concerned that the fact that we no longer had four of us participating in the executions might raise a lot of questions and maybe even drive the bets down. Turns out that's not the case."

"Have you noticed any online chatter about why there's now only three of us, or what happened to Mr. Blue?" Calvin had seen some questions on their site but, surprisingly, not a lot of speculation about why.

Mark spoke. "No, not a lot. I expected there to be a lot of conspiracy theories, like he'd been arrested, or he turned on us, or he got killed while doing a job. Surprisingly, I haven't seen many of those posts."

"I'm glad," added Graham. "We don't need our site turning into 'conspiracy theory central' like Twitter."

"I'm excited for tomorrow's game; I think Oz created a great challenge, though, admittedly, I'm thankful that a handgun is our chosen weapon," offered Mark. "With such a short window of time to find the target, the location, and the escape route, I appreciate not having to get super up-close and personal."

"Yeah, I agree. I just wish we had another week to catch our breath and plan these hits. I like to know a little bit more about where I'm going, get to know the police coverage and response time, and seemingly a million other variable." Graham was far from scared, but he had learned long ago that there was no substitution for good preparation.

Calvin concurred. "Don't disagree with you at all, my man. We just need to get there, get some rest, and then get a fresh start in the morning. Tomorrow we'll only have about eight hours to identify our target and reconnoiter the area, so make every minute count. And whatever you do, stay safe. The last thing we need is a repeat of the events from our last game." They both nodded in agreement.

"Before we go," added Mark. He lifted his coffee cup towards the screen in a virtual 'cheers' to his friends. "This one is for Jamarcus. Let's make this the best game, with the most creative and well-executed kills – no pun intended - that we've ever done."

Chapter Twenty-Three

O z had definitely lived up to 'his' reputation when selecting the variables for this game, especially since it was the first time that the game was being played with three players instead of four. Four was the perfect number of players for the way the game was conceived, that is, there was one player covering each of the four US time zones. In a nod to the changes wrought by the loss of Jamarcus, the remaining Slayers had agreed to set aside the rule that had been in place since the inception of the game, namely, that members never did a hit in the same time zone where they live. They instead programmed Oz to select only cities that were at least 250 miles from their respective homes.

The parameters for this game were simple and straightforward. Oz specified that the targets would be 42-year-old Caucasian females, the target cities would be Cleveland, Salt Lake City, and Richmond, VA, and the weapon of choice would be a Glock 9mm handgun. The last detail from Oz's output is one that *could* make the hits a little trickier: the killings were all planned for 5:35pm ET, which meant 4:35pm in Cleveland and 3:35pm in Salt Lake City. Broad daylight could be tricky, for obvious reasons. The planning around the location of the hit, as well as planning for a quick getaway in heavy afternoon traffic, could not be minimized.

***

Calvin flew into Cleveland on Monday afternoon, thankfully non-stop. That gave him a few hours that evening and at least a half-day on Tuesday for reconnaissance and planning. He recalled that a few decades ago the city was derided as the 'Mistake on the Lake', but more recently he'd heard about the great restaurants and bars, the fantastic night life, and even the resurgence of the local sports teams. Unfortunately, this visit wouldn't afford him time to play tourist. He needed to complete his mission and get out of town as quickly as possible. In fact, he'd even planned to drive the nearly 150 miles to Columbus as soon as he'd completed the job rather than wait around for several hours to get a flight. He always felt better putting some distance between himself and his kills, and it never hurt to spread the travel plans among different cities and airports. Following his usual practice, he booked his hotel for an extra night even though he planned to clear out by early Tuesday afternoon.

On Monday night he treated himself to a nice steak dinner at the Cleveland Chop House, and then spent some time walking around the area of the city known as The Flats. Even on a Monday night it was pretty crowded, and he considered it a viable target area. The only downside is that it would not be nearly as crowded in the late afternoon as at night, but Oz had set the rules and the time. It was between The Flats and the river front area; both had tons of restaurants and bars and lots of people to help in selecting a target. The cacophony of city sounds would mean that people would remain blissfully unaware that he had just fired his suppressor-equipped Glock.

By the end of the evening, Calvin had settled on The Flats as his hunting grounds and the Cuyahoga River as the dump site for his Glock. He'd taken note of the major roads that led to Interstate 90, and from there it was simple matter of jumping on Interstate 71 South all the way to Columbus. Satisfied that he'd done all that he could for the day, and totally satiated from the huge dinner and three glasses of Cabernet, he was happy to crawl into bed at the luxury Westin hotel that he'd booked using his ID and credit card under the name of Calvin Mattox.

Because he'd spent several hours planning for today's game when he'd arrived on Monday, he was able to spend a relaxing morning. Before he went downstairs for a late breakfast, he called the hotel spa and made an appointment for a massage at noon. Having almost 90 minutes before his massage, he performed one of his other rituals: cleaning his weapon. The gun was new and had only fired one box of ammo a week ago at the range, at which point it had been immediately stripped and cleaned. Still, despite that fact that it hadn't been fired since, he field-stripped the gun, lubed and cleaned it, and reassembled it. *Always prepared means no surprises.*

Around 2:30pm he left his room and placed the Do Not Disturb placard on the door. Pulling his rental car from the parking garage, he drove around The Flats until he found a parking spot on the block that he'd scoped-out the night before. Tucking the Glock into his coat pocket, with the suppressor in the other pocket, he exited the car and started strolling the area. His plan was to find a victim and make the hit no more than one block in any direction from where the car was parked. When it was about ten minutes before the appointed time, Calvin ducked into a McDonald's and headed straight to the restroom. Quickly reversing his coat, putting on a hat and glasses, as well as some black gloves, he headed back out to the kill zone. He felt certain that anyone viewing earlier camera footage from around the area would not easily recognize him as the same person.

Within minutes he spotted his target. Her name, not that he cared or even needed to know, was Jan Andrews. All that mattered was that she fit the target profile and was in the right place at the right time. Or the wrong place at the wrong time, depending on your perspective. As she climbed into her car, Calvin grabbed the door to stop her from closing it and then fired a single shot into her head. He closed the door and then walked away. It took him less than three minutes to reach his car, another two minutes to reach the dump site for the gun, and then he was on his way to Columbus. Another picture-perfect kill.

* * *

Mark went to Salt Lake City, arriving around 4pm on Monday, barely 23 hours before he had to make the kill. This was a city that he'd flown into twice over the years when he was visiting the picturesque National Parks that Utah is famous for, including Arches, Zion, Bryce, and Moab. All were stunningly beautiful and among his favorite destinations. This would be the first time, though, that he'd be spending any time in the state capitol. He wasn't expecting much; it wasn't known as a real party city, to put it mildly. Not that he planned to check out the party scene, but he was hoping that he wouldn't have to settle for bottom-of-the-heap chain hotels and restaurants. Luckily, he didn't have to, snagging a three-night reservation at the Grand America Hotel and having dinner at Santo Taco Taqueria. All things considered, a very pleasant evening. Part of him wished that he could take advantage of having the three-night hotel reservation so he could spend some time here, but there was no question that he'd be heading out of town immediately after completing the assignment.

As was his habit, he spent a couple of hours exploring and getting a feel for the city and possible target locations. He was considering Temple Square but found that the area was undergoing some renovation and construction, making movement through there much more challenging. The Mormon Temple was worth considering since there were always a lot of tourists around, but he was uncomfortable with the demographics as there were too many families. Hogle Zoo was quickly eliminated for the same reason. It took some time, but he finally narrowed it down to City Creek Center, the city's premier shopping mall. He could choose his victim in the massive parking lots surrounding the stores, or if that wasn't working, he could stake out the many high-end anchor stores. He assumed that Nordstrom, H&M, and other fashion stores would be target-rich environments for the 42-year-old female 'contestants' that he sought.

Mark slept-in on Tuesday morning and took his time getting ready. He followed much the same routine as Calvin and spent time cleaning his weapon and readying himself. For him it was almost a Zen experience, one of the most effective ways he'd ever found to attain the level of calm and focus that he relied on to be at his best. Shortly after 1:00 he headed out to grab lunch since he'd skipped breakfast and, likely, wouldn't be able to grab dinner before his flight this evening. He picked a casual BBQ place with good sightlines up and down the street. There was quite a bit of traffic at this time of day, especially in this area that was just a few blocks from I-15. *Too bad I can't do the job here and jump right on the interstate.* He was tempted to change his target area, but his training and discipline overrode that temptation. Better to stick with the planned location, the primary and alternate routes, and the dump site that he'd rehearsed in his head countless times.

City Creek Center was less than 15 minutes away, and he found the parking lot to be less crowded than last evening. Probably to be expected; mid-afternoon on a Tuesday is not exactly a popular time for retail therapy. If he'd been the one calling the shots for this game, rather than Oz, he would have scheduled this for a Saturday afternoon or early evening. But the rules are the rules. Since he had plenty of time, he circled the entire mall several times looking for the best spot based on the foot traffic, the number of cars, and proximity to the exits. He finally settled on the section near the Nordstrom's entrance and parked about 50 yards from the closest car.

As 3pm approached, Mark was growing concerned because he wasn't seeing many women that fit the target demographic, or if they did fit, they weren't alone. All members of the Slayers were emphatic, and had a perfect record, of having zero collateral kills. That meant that women walking in a group, especially with their kids, were off-limits. While his plan was to make the kill here in the parking lot, with the clock ticking down and no credible targets in sight, he called an audible. Grabbing his backpack from the backseat, he put on a blue hoodie and a pair of dark sunglasses and headed for the store entrance. Once inside, he switched from the hoodie to a ball cap and from the sunglasses to a pair of fake eyeglasses with black frames. Subtle, but reasonably effective for making himself hard to identify, especially if he kept his head down and never in full view of the security cameras.

As he walked through the main aisle near the makeup counter, the only suitable target was one of the employees in her white lab coat. *When did they start trying to make these women shilling makeup look like lab technicians? Who are they fooling?* She was lucky to be working, otherwise she may have been a target. Continuing into the women's clothing section, things started looking up. While certainly far from a target-rich environment, it was still an improvement versus what he'd seen so far. Finally, he spotted the perfect target, maybe even a choice of targets. Two women were at the register as one was paying for her purchases. As he got closer, he overheard a snippet of their conversation indicating that they were getting ready to go in different directions.

The lady that was paying said to her friend, "You should really try that black dress on, Alexa. It would look incredible on you. Why don't you do that, and I'll walk over to the shoe department and see if they have something strappy and sexy in your size to complete the outfit. God knows you deserve to treat yourself a little."

"I'll look around for a few more minutes to see if I find anything else, then I'll try the dress on *if* you promise me that it will be the last one, alright? You know that I don't feel right about spending this much money just to get back at my dead-beat husband," Alexa answered with a giggle. "I'll try it on, and I'll text you to come take a look."

"Deal. I'll see you back in a bit then. I might even have to try on one or two pairs of shoes for myself."

Mark was working hard to stay patient, but it was already twenty minutes past three. Any execution that was more than 10-15 minutes before or after the Oz-designated kill time had little chance of winning. Finally, Alexa headed to the dressing room, and for once the lack of crowds and the skeleton crew of store employees worked in his favor. After she entered the room, he slowly headed that way. Passing a couple of chairs positioned outside of the dressing room area, likely a spot for exhausted and impatient husbands to rest, he grabbed a small throw pillow from one and headed into the fitting area. He ducked into the empty fitting room next to hers and bided his time. Fortunately, it was just a couple of minutes before he heard her opening the door to her room, likely to check herself out in the 3 mirrors at the end of the short hallway. As she stepped out, he did the same, immediately grabbing her hair and pulling her violently back into her room. Before she could scream, he forcefully smashed the pillow down over her face and shot her twice with his silenced Glock. Between the suppressor and the pillow, the shots were virtually silent.

Mark stepped back quickly into the changing room he'd been using and pulled out a different hat, glasses, and jacket from his backpack. He was back in his car and heading away from the mall in less than three minutes. Not his easiest kill ever, but certainly not his hardest. Most importantly, it was another kill that would go unsolved. No witnesses. No prints or DNA. No bullets to be matched. Not even any useful security camera footage.

* * *

Graham traveled to Richmond, Virginia; he'd traveled through Richmond a few times on the way to the Outer Banks of North Carolina and to Busch Gardens in Williamsburg, VA, but he really knew little about the city. He did know enough, though, that he was not thrilled with Oz's choice for him. Not that there was anything wrong with Richmond, but he really preferred to fly in and out of places with direct flights, and that was a challenge for Richmond. He'd already made plans to drive from Richmond to the Westin hotel near Dulles airport, about two hours away. That would allow him to put some distance between him and the scene of the crime today and fly home non-stop on Wednesday.

Unlike Calvin and Mark, Graham knew who his target was going to be before he'd ever left home. Her name was Christy Payne, and while he didn't know her from Adam, he knew that she fit the demographic perfectly. He had seen a posting on LinkedIn mentioning that Christy, apparently one of the most respected women in the tech industry, was going to be a guest speaker at a 'Women in Technology' conference. At first, he'd had the idea – actually, more of a fantasy – of doing the hit while she was presenting in front of a couple thousand people in the hotel ballroom. The goal was always to minimize risk and collateral damage, and to get away with no witnesses or physical evidence left behind. Acting on his little fantasy would not be consistent with those goals. At least his job was made easier by knowing where she was staying and, at least to some degree, knowing her schedule.

While Christy was staying at the Jefferson Hotel, one of the finest hotels in the city, Graham chose to stay a couple of miles away at the Berkley. He reserved a room there for several nights but planned to be heading towards Dulles on Tuesday evening immediately after the kill, and fortunately Interstate 95 was within minutes of the Jefferson. Whereas the Slayers usually had to take time for reconnaissance of the area, checking police response times, and the other million-and-one details they need to know to be successful, Graham already knew that he'd be making the hit at her hotel. Still, he had some reconnaissance to do, but this time instead of driving around a city or walking around the area in the freezing cold, he'd have the luxury of sitting in their beautiful lobby and restaurants.

On Tuesday he had a plan in place, he just needed to sit and observe some of the details before he made his move. He walked around the Jefferson to observe their security procedures and coverage. He wanted to observe how their waiters, maintenance workers, and room service staff were dressed. How many security cameras did they have in the lobby, the hallways, and other common areas? All these details factored into his plan, but he had already settled on where he would do the deed: in Christy's room. Now it was just a matter of determining the best ruse for getting into her room and ensuring that she was alone. The last thing he wanted or needed was to create the perfect plan for getting her to open the door only to find out that she had others in there with her.

In the end, he went with a plan that was simplicity itself. No need to try to steal a maintenance worker's uniform or steal a pass key from a maid. At 4:50pm he called the front desk of the Jefferson and asked for Christy's room. When she answered, he engaged her in a short conversation, ostensibly as one of the people working on the conference room setup for her upcoming presentation. He heard nothing that indicated that she had others in the room with her. At 5:30pm, almost to the minute, he entered one of the side doors to the hotel wearing a sports jacket and tie and carrying a beautiful bouquet of flowers and a Jefferson Hotel bag from the gift shop. Being familiar with the location of all the lobby and hallway cameras, he made sure to hold the flowers to obscure his face. Taking the elevator to her suite on the top floor, he stayed vigilant as he made his way to her door.

Knocking on the door, he announced himself as one of the managers and said that he had a lovely gift for her that was sent by the conference sponsors. He made sure that she could see the flowers through the peephole, as well as his face. No matter, since she wouldn't live to remember it or describe him to anyone. She opened the door and graciously invited him in, and as she led him into the room, he noiselessly slid his pistol from his jacket. As soon as he heard the door close completely behind him, he shot her twice in the back of the head.

Graham took just a few minutes to ensure he'd covered all bases. He removed his pants, tie, and jacket and put on a pair of jeans, dress shirt, and sweater that he'd brought with him. He checked and re-checked the suite before leaving to make sure that there was no trace of him having been there. The clear latex gloves stayed on until he was out of her hotel room door and exiting the elevator on the lobby level. Minutes later he was in the car and heading for I-95 North, albeit at a virtual crawl since he was at the height of rush hour. Without question, traffic would probably suck the entire way to Northern VA, but at least he was moving away from the kill zone. Another successful hit, and, in his mind, a definite contender for the game winner.

Chapter Twenty-Four

T he 7am flight from DFW to New York LaGuardia came way too early for both JJ and Kristyn. They'd both been burning the midnight oil on this investigation, and the lack of rest was starting to catch up with them. JJ always required a little extra time going through Security because of her service weapon, but fortunately that didn't take too long this morning. They were on their way to their gate, or, more accurately, on their way to the Starbucks closest to their gate with time to spare.

They were scheduled to arrive in New York around 11:15am Eastern time, with their first meeting at Columbia scheduled for 3:30pm. Kristyn had booked them into the Empire Hotel, which was just a few miles from the University on the Upper West Side, so they planned to check-in early. This afternoon they were meeting with the Registrar to understand more about Hicks' life during his college years, including the classes he took, his academic record, membership in any campus groups, awards, and basically anything that would paint a picture of his college years. Tomorrow, they hoped to meet with as many of Hicks' professors and advisors as they could squeeze-in in one day. JJ had also reached out to the campus Public Safety team and secured a meeting with them to inquire about any unsolved crimes, particularly murders, that may have occurred during Hicks' tenure. They both had their fingers crossed that they'd get lucky and find some leads regarding the other men in the pictures that had been hanging in Hicks' house. It hadn't gone unnoticed that all the subjects appeared to be about the same age; could that mean that they'd spent time together at Columbia?

Just a few minutes after 3:30 they were shown into the office of the Registrar, a strikingly beautiful African American woman named Chanel Woods. She was tall, officious, and exuded competence and confidence. JJ and Kristyn immediately liked her.

As JJ shook her hand, she said, "Mrs. Woods, thanks for making time in your schedule to meet with us. This is Kristyn Reynolds from the Dallas Morning News; she and I are collaborating on the case I told you about, the case of Jamarcus Hicks and the murder of FBI Special Agent Mark Stevens at DFW airport a couple of weeks ago."

"Well, I have to say that this is the first time I've ever heard of law enforcement and the media working together on a case. I trust that you're making progress, since you've come all the way from Dallas to talk with me and others here at the University?"

"We are," replied Kristyn. "And we're hoping that you may be able to shed even more light on Hicks and help us determine if there are other crimes that he might be tied to."

As they sat down at the conference table in Woods' office, JJ jumped right into the conversation. "Mrs. Woods, all we really know about Hicks' college days is that he attended Columbia. We were hoping that you could fill-in some of the details, like the kinds of classes he took, the kinds of grades he got, if there were any academic awards or other special accomplishments."

Woods set a few file folders on her desk and pulled out a few pages. "Just to make it easier to share, I printed out some information from our systems. Here's a copy for each of you; you're free to take them with you." She handed them each a summary of the classes that Hicks had taken and the grade he'd gotten in each class. "As you can see, he majored in Computer Engineering and his GPA was exemplary. He made the Dean's List almost every semester. From all indications, he was a model student. I didn't find any disciplinary action, no complaints lodged against him by his instructors or other students, no issues brought to our attention from disgruntled roommates, nothing.

"Were you working here at the University while he was attending?" JJ was furiously taking notes and referring to the list of questions that she'd prepared in advance. Woods looked too young to have been in a senior position like Registrar that far back, but she could have been at the school in another capacity.

"I was here during his college years but in a different role. I've only been the Registrar for a little more than 4 years. I was working in this office in a more junior position during that time, but if you're asking if I knew Hicks or remember him, the answer is no. To be honest, I've met thousands of kids over the years, but there are only a very small handful that I remember. Usually, if I remember them, it's for all of the wrong reasons, as in, they've done something seriously wrong."

"That's understandable," said JJ. "Tens of thousands of kids passing through here every semester; you can't be expected to know them all. But let me ask you, would you mind looking at a few pictures that we have and let me know if you recognize any of the people in them?" She fished the photos out of her bag and laid them on the table for Woods to view.

"Hmmm, let me see. Well, I recognize this guy as Jamarcus Hicks, but only because I've seen his face a million times on the news over the past 10 days or so. These others," she said as she slowly scanned the faces intently, "no, I don't recognize any of them. May I ask who they are and what they have to do with this case? If I'm not overstepping."

Kristyn picked up the pictures and straightened them. "The honest answer is that we don't know, and they may or may not have anything at all to do with the case. We're hoping to identify them so we can determine if they're involved and, at the very least, learn more from them about Hicks and what drove him."

"Is there anything else interesting in the information that you were able to gather?" So far nothing that they had heard really provided JJ with anything useful.

Woods looked through the stacks of printed information and pulled out one item that she thought was noteworthy. "There is this, which is pretty unusual, but in a very good way. Apparently, Hicks helped create an online computer game that really took off and became very popular. Says here that it started with a class assignment but quickly grew into some sort of online viral sensation." She continued scanning. "Oh, my. Wow, this is impressive. It says that the game was eventually sold to a Silicon Valley-based gaming company for more than $50 million! And that it made him and his co-developers rich, as well as a few university professors and advisors that helped them get the deal. Pretty incredible for a bunch of underclassmen!"

JJ and Kristyn looked at each other, both with the growing feeling that they were onto something big. Kristyn asked, "Does it say anything about the game itself? I mean, does it describe the game and how it was played?"

"Yes, let me see. OK, the game was called Kill Starter – that's kind of a morbid name, if you ask me – and it was an online game where people would nominate the celebrity that they'd most like to see killed. Sounds sick, but from what I'm reading it was really just tongue-in-cheek and juvenile humor. Like people would send in their jokes and memes and reason for wanting to see a certain celebrity dead and then they would pick a winner. Looks like they did a new game every week."

JJ could barely sit still at this point. Kill Starter? It wasn't a stretch to make a connection between Kill Starter and The Murder Game. "We're going to want to talk to his professors and advisors, basically anyone that was involved with Kill Starter. Can you help setup meetings with them for tomorrow?" She tried to stay calm and under control, but it was proving difficult.

"Sure, I'll call them right now and ask them to make time for you. It seems that this might be an important lead for you, so I'll make sure that they all understand the urgency."

"Thank you, but please, don't share any of the details beyond the simple fact that we're looking for background on Hicks in relation to the events in Dallas. I'm sure you can understand." JJ didn't want her tipping their hand to the people they were going to interview; at this stage there's no way of knowing if they were merely teachers and advisors or, potentially, co-conspirators.

"One more quick thing before you make those calls," added Kristyn. "You said that the article reported that Hicks did this as part of a class assignment along with some co-developers. I'm assuming that those co-developers were other students. Does the article happen to list their names?"

Woods scanned the article again. "Yes, yes it does. In addition to Hicks there were three others. Mark Saxe, Calvin Mitchell, and Graham Robbins. It says that they were all computer engineering majors and all in the same year of study." She looked up and JJ and Kristyn. "And now apparently all freakin' rich, too."

Bingo! It was all that JJ and Kristyn could do not to jump up and high-five each other. They didn't have to say anything. They knew that this was huge and that digging up every last bit of information they could find on these three was their top priority. They knew, deep down, that they had just uncovered the surviving members of the Slayers. Now they just had to find the proof.

After Mrs. Woods setup some in-person meetings for them for Wednesday morning, they thanked her for her help and headed for the elevator. Barely a word was spoken until the elevator doors closed and then they barely suppressed squeals of delight and threw their arms around each other in a hug as they jumped up and down. They were beyond ecstatic.

"Oh my God! We got these bastards, Kristyn! Now that we've almost assuredly identified the elusive Misters Red, Green, and Yellow it's just a matter of time before we track them down. I don't think the world has ever seen anything like the Slayers! We're going to identify, arrest, and help prosecute people who murdered 80 innocent people."

Kristyn was just as excited as JJ. "My God, this is going to be huge, from a lead story perspective! I wouldn't be surprised if it didn't turn into a five-part series, maybe more. And that's before the trials. I can envision this being a story that plays out for a year, probably more. My bosses are going to be thrilled!"

"Wow, I don't know what to feel right now. I mean, I am super-excited, but I'm also feeling mentally drained, physically exhausted, and hungry as hell. Getting up so early and then going non-stop all day...

whew, it's almost like crashing after being on an adrenalin rush for hours."

"I know how you feel. But you need to rally." She smiled at JJ. "We need to celebrate this day, and I know exactly how we're going to do that. How does a fancy dinner and a beautiful bottle of wine sound? And it's all on my expense account – and pre-approved! Don't even think about saying no; I made the reservations before we even left Dallas, so there's no turning back now!"

"Tell me that we at least have time to go back to the hotel to freshen-up first. I feel gross from a day of travel. And how nice is this restaurant that we're going to? I packed for business, not a night on the town."

"You'll be fine, and while the restaurant is super nice, they're not too hung-up around dress codes. Business casual is what they show on their website. And we do have time to go back to the hotel. Our reservations are for 8pm."

"So don't keep me in suspense. It sounds like we're going a little fancier than Shake Shack. Although I could inhale one of their burgers right now......"

"We're definitely going a bit fancier than that. We're dining at Le Bernardin, a place that I've wanted to dine for years, so, admittedly, I kinda took advantage of the situation since we had to travel to New York. I'm sure you'll love it."

"I have no doubt! Le Bernardin is one of just a handful of Michelin 3-star restaurants in New York, and their chef, Eric Ripert, is a freakin' god. I can't believe you have us going there. I love it!

"I didn't know you were a foodie. Are you a killer cook, too?"

"Oh God no! I can't cook for shit, to be honest, but I watch tons of cooking shows and subscribe to several cooking magazines. There are so many restaurants on my bucket list you can't believe it, and the list keeps on growing. Le Bernardin has been on that list for years."

Once back at the hotel they took turns getting ready, and JJ was still swept-up in the excitement of the day. She kept pushing the exhaustion down, because she so much wanted to enjoy this once-in-a-lifetime meal and Kristyn's company. After such a great day, investigation-wise, and the promise of a world-class meal this evening, the only thing that made it less-than-perfect were the sleeping arrangements: their room had two queen beds instead of one king. Even if nothing happened, and if she were being honest, she was pretty certain that nothing would, just the thrill of being that close and feeling Kristyn next to her all night would be incredibly nice. And arousing. And distracting to the point of losing sleep. *Oh, well.*

Chapter Twenty-Five

K ristyn and JJ both slept like bears hibernating for the winter Tuesday night. After a stellar meal, accompanied by a beautiful bottle of wine, they finally crawled into bed about midnight. Even though they both said that they were still too excited to sleep, they were out in minutes. The alarm clock went off way too early for either of them, but they had several interviews to get through today and the first one was at 10am. As much as they both wanted to roll over and sleep for a few more hours – although JJ's thoughts veered slightly more towards the erotic – they coaxed each other to get up.

"Why don't you get in the shower first, and I'll order us some room service breakfast," offered JJ. "Not that I'm hungry after last night, but who knows what today is going to bring as far as finding time for lunch. Or dinner, for that matter."

"Good point. I'll jump in the shower, and just order me something basic, plus coffee and orange juice."

JJ was distracted as she looked through the room service menu, imagining what it would be like to be on the other side of that door and joining Kristyn in the shower, touching her, bathing her.... *Stop! You have to focus on the case!* Admittedly, she wasn't always the best at compartmentalizing, but she vowed to make the effort. Still, it wasn't easy. *Maybe she needs help scrubbing her back.... STOP!!*

They arrived at the Columbia office of Dr. Richard Miller at the scheduled time and the three of them squeezed into his tiny office, barely large enough to hold his desk and the guest chairs that he borrowed from a common area. As a professor of Computer Engineering, Mills had a deep expertise in all aspects of computer networks, computer coding, and the inner workings of cloud computing and security. He was also an avid gamer – not surprising since he was only in his early 40's – and had consulted on several multiplayer games and First-Person Shooter (FPS) games. Apparently, he was something of a rock-star in the gaming world. After just a few minutes of speaking with him, it was obvious that *he* thought of himself as a rockstar and a lady's man, too. They didn't share that opinion; they both considered him to be your basic, misogynistic douchebag.

"So, Dr. Miller......"

"Please, Agent Jansen, call me Richard."

I wonder if I can just call you douchebag? "Thank you, but for purposes of this interview, I need to keep this on a more formal basis. You understand, for the official notes and recordings." Not that she was making any recordings, but she wasn't going to let that fact get in the way. "So it's our understanding, after speaking with the Registrar, Mrs. Woods, that you were a teacher and advisor for Jamarcus Hicks for one or more of his classes, correct?"

"Yes, I was. He was a brilliant student, one of the best it's ever been my pleasure to teach. He not only understood computers and networking and coding, but he also truly understood business. That's rare for someone so young."

"Did you ever have any problems with him, or see him having problems working with others or getting along with others?"

"No, never, and that's one of the reasons why it came as such a shock when I saw the news about him being involved in the killing of that FBI agent in Dallas. Not in a million years would I have expected him to be involved in anything that was the least bit illegal or violent."

Kristyn jumped in. "It's our understanding from Mrs. Woods that there were three other students that worked with Hicks on his class project, this 'Kill Starter'. That would be Calvin Mitchell, Graham Robbins, and Mark Saxe. Do you remember them, as well?"

"Oh yes, absolutely. I spent many hours working with them. They were like the 'Four Musketeers', if you will. They were a 'one for all and all for one' group of guys. You rarely saw one of them without the others."

Pulling the photos from her purse, Kristyn laid them out in front of Mills. "Would this be them?"

"Yes, for sure. I knew that they continued to stay close after they graduated even though they lived all over the country. Lifelong friends, for sure." He then identified each one and Kristyn and JJ took notes while also labeling one of the pictures.

They spent another 90 minutes with Miller talking about the genesis of the Kill Starter game, how it worked, how it grew so quickly, and how they sold the company. According to Miller, he and another Columbia professor, Dr. Tim Bedford, were the ones who identified and solicited the Silicon Valley companies that made bids to buy Kill Starter. Dr. Bedford was a professor in the Columbia University Business School and a renowned business consultant and startup expert, so he took the lead in drafting purchase agreements. Miller made no secret of the fact that Hicks and the others had gifted him and Dr. Bedford a percentage of the sale price; while not required, or even expected, it was more than welcome. They each received $2 million, and since they both had their own respective LLC's for their outside consulting work, it was all legal and aboveboard.

Over the next few hours, they talked with two more of Hicks' professors and the campus police, but none had anything of value to add to what they'd already learned. They would have liked to talk to Dr. Bedford since he'd been directly involved with the sale of Kill Starter, but he was out on sabbatical and unreachable. By 3pm they'd finished their scheduled interviews and were just about to go online to get an Uber for the ride back to the hotel when JJ's phone rang.

"This is Special Agent Jansen."

"Hi Agent Jansen, this is Gerry Ruggiano from Quantico." He could barely contain the excitement in his voice, which was quite a departure from the last time they'd spoken. "Based on our last conversation, we've been doing some more digging into the Slayers and how they ran the game."

"Please tell me that you found something good!" JJ looked at Kristyn and gave her a thumbs-up, already anticipating good news. They sat down on a nearby bench, and she put the call on speaker so that Kristyn could hear both sides of the conversation.

"I'd say that it's way beyond good! First, we've confirmed the identities of the other three members of the Slayers, and I have their files ready to send to you with everything that we could dig up on them."

"Would their names happen to be Calvin Mitchell, Graham Robbins, and Mark Saxe?"

Ruggiano was caught off guard. "How in the world could you know that? But yes, those are the three surviving members that we've identified."

"Their names came up during the course of the investigation here in New York. Turns out that they were all friends in college and have worked together on other projects." JJ didn't want to take time to go through all of the details at this point. "I believe you have more?"

"Yes. Second point, what you suspected about the game was correct: there was online wagering, and the winners were paid *very* substantial amounts in prize money. And of course, the Slayers kept the lion's share of the revenues for themselves."

"Were you able to determine how much was wagered and paid-out since the game's inception?"

"We've determined that total revenues have been just shy of $12 million over the past four years, with revenues increasing every year since the game started. Of that, about 25% was paid out in prize money, so that tells my simple mind that the Slayers pocketed about $9 million. And who says crime doesn't pay?"

Kristyn jotted a note to JJ, which she quickly read and nodded her agreement. "Are you able to determine the last time that the Slayers played one of these games?"

"We did, and it's quite interesting. There are two recent games that were played, but one of them appears to have been more of a raffle. Apparently when the players bought a virtual 'ticket' they were granted access to view some videos from previous homicides committed by the Slayers. As I said the other day, morbid. And before you ask, the answer is 'no', we were not able to access those videos. Apparently, their system

SONNY HUDSON

had been programmed to be viewed just once per token, and then they were either erased or taken totally offline. Oh, and we found that more than $1.5 million was wagered on this raffle, and the Slayers paid out 50% of the total pot, but that still left them with $750,000 to split three ways."

JJ and Kristyn looked at each other, totally astonished. "Wow, they are definitely raking in serious money. Obviously, though, this money is all going unreported and untaxed, so that's one more nail in their coffin once we haul their asses into court". JJ thought for a second, then added, "You mentioned two recent games. What was the other one?"

"I thought you'd never ask! The last game was yesterday! The Slayers haven't picked a winner from the online bettors yet, but I can see that the three remaining members traveled to Salt Lake City, Richmond, VA, and Cleveland. I'm sure that if you do just the slightest bit of digging, you're going to find that a Caucasian female somewhere in the neighborhood of 42 years old was shot and killed yesterday afternoon in each of those cities; I can even tell you which of the Slayers was the killer in each case."

Once again it was all that JJ and Kristyn could do not to scream and jump up and down right there in the middle of the campus. "Gerry, this is incredible. Even more than I could have hoped for! I have one last question for you: in all that data that you were able to access, were you able to pull a list of all of their online players and those that received payouts from the games?"

His excitement was amped up to eleven by this point. "Yes! I've been able to identify nearly 1,500 different player logins and hundreds that have received payouts. It will take some continued effort to correlate all the player's email handles to their real identity, but we've already identified more than 500 of them. And we may not be able to track where the money went once the winners received it because they were paid in cryptocurrency, but from a legal perspective that's secondary. The most important thing is that we can identify them as players in a game that involved murder, we can identify which games they bet on and how much they bet, and we can identify who received payouts and the amounts. Fortunately for us the Slayers were excellent at keeping records of their financial transactions."

"I could just kiss you! You and your team are going to help bust this case wide open. How soon can you get me the information that you've pulled together? I'm still in New York but it would be great if I could work on this tonight and start things moving before I get back to Dallas tomorrow."

"Most of it is ready to go, so it should be on the server and accessible in probably 30 minutes. As I get more information and more of the players identified, I'll send it to you immediately."

She ended the call and turned to Kristyn. Before she could say a word Kristyn squealed and threw her arms around JJ's neck and they both started jumping up and down in delight again. At least this time they didn't have to worry about the elevator crashing down a few floors. The fact that people were looking at them like they were crazy didn't bother them in the least.

Back at the hotel, they decided to order dinner from room service and focus on the information that Quantico had sent. As before, there was a *lot* of data, but the good news is that it was already well organized. After a couple of hours of sorting through the information, Kristyn shared an idea. "We've got names and online handles and details about dates of the games, how much each player wagered, how much each won. What do you think about me putting together an article to run in tomorrow morning's paper that exposes the Slayers, the members, and even some of the online players and winners? I know that we've played this pretty close to the vest so far, but maybe it's time to shed a spotlight on the remaining Slayers, and maybe exposing their online players will put a damper on their ability to do any future games."

"Actually, that's not a bad idea. I'm sure Isaksen will shit a brick, but I'd rather beg forgiveness than ask permission at this stage. Maybe we don't speak to the scale of the Slayers' activities at this point or go into too much detail about the size of the wagers and payouts. We save that for later. But I like the idea of publicizing a few names of 'persons of interest' and having them picked up for questioning, including Mitchell, Saxe, and Robbins. I have to believe that at least some of the players will spill their guts about the Slayers with just a little push. For that matter, maybe one of the Slayers might flip on the others with the right motivation – like taking the death penalty off the table."

161

"Then it's agreed. I'll start on the article now, and I'm going to call my boss and give him a heads-up that this is coming and to save me front-page space for it. If I can get a draft there by midnight, we should be able to get this into tomorrow's edition as well as online."

"Great, and I'll keep digging into these names and dates and places. I'm trying to find someone that's maybe a household name, someone that will really catch the public's attention, as well as law enforcement's attention." Over the course of the next hour, she managed to find five names that she knew would spark huge interest. One was a Republican US Senator, another was a Federal Appeals Court judge, two were professional athletes, and one was a TV evangelist that was a millionaire many times over as he admonished his followers to believe in God and the 'prosperity gospel'. Almost at the point where she thought her eyes were going to cross from looking at so much data, she found something that shook her to her core. And then it made her smile.

"I think I have a great angle for your story. I think this player could use the exposure."

"I'll bite. What did you find?"

"A player that goes by *gamergod10inches*. Otherwise known as," she paused for dramatic effect, "Dr. Richard Miller."

"Holy shit!" and then neither of them could contain their laughter.

"That pompous, arrogant, prick! He gets paid by the Slayers when they sell Kill Starter – a couple of million bucks – and now takes an active part in this game." JJ thought for a second, and then added, "I'll keep pulling this thread, but not tonight. I'm willing to bet that Miller had more involvement here than just another online player. And I'd also be willing to bet that he's already reached out to the surviving Slayers to tell them about our visit today."

"True. Hopefully that won't be enough to make them flee the country. Personally, I think they're probably too cocky and self-assured for that, especially since we didn't know anything about their involvement with The Murder Game. But I'd love to be a fly on the wall when the police come to arrest him. I bet he cries like a little girl as soon as they put the cuffs on him."

"Yeah, and let's see how he handles jail. I'm sure he'll have lots of new 'friends' in there that would love to see him prove the accuracy of his online handle 'gamergod10INCHES'." They both cracked up at that.

Shortly after 11 they read through Kristyn's article together and did a few edits and tweaks, but both agreed that it hit the mark. She emailed it to her editor and crossed her fingers.

"You know that this is going to stir up a major shit storm tomorrow, right?" JJ looked at Kristyn to see if she looked worried. "We're about to expose three guys that are responsible for about 60 murders, maybe more. I wouldn't expect them to take this lying down."

"True, and for that matter, I wouldn't expect the online players that we're identifying to take this well, either. Hopefully the police and FBI can move on all of them quickly."

"I'll make sure that happens, especially with Saxe, Robbins, and Mitchell. The sooner that they're off the street, the better. In the meantime, watch your six. That goes for both of us."

"You're FBI. Do you think they'd have the balls to come for someone in your position?"

"They're going to be facing the death penalty times 60, so yeah, I don't think they'd have any hesitation to go after me, you, or the pope. Self-preservation is a powerful motivator."

Truer words were never spoken.

Chapter Twenty-Six

THURSDAY, NOVEMBER 3

Their return flight to Dallas wasn't until 10:05am, but Kristyn and JJ agreed that they should get to the airport early so they would have time to talk to their respective bosses without trying to do it from an Uber. Considering the sensitive subject matter, the strong personalities and emotions, and the tendency to let things devolve to the point of spewing four-letter words like lethal weapons, that was probably a wise move. They rolled up to the airport and made it through security by 7:30am.

"Damnit, Evan," Kristyn practically yelled at her editor. She was pissed, and it didn't help that she had to talk so loudly to be heard over the mind-numbing noise and constant overhead announcements throughout the airport. "I worked my ass off on that article to get it to you in time after checking and double-checking every single fact that I wrote, and then you take the chicken-shit way out and cave to Legal? Seriously, what the hell?"

Evan remained calm. He was used to having his reporters kick and scream about how their articles were edited, which page they appeared on, or any number of other perceived slights. He actually preferred the reporters that were passionate enough to fight for their articles, and on that point Kristyn never disappointed. "Look, I loved the article and I think it's going to be one of the biggest stories that we've done in years.

But I ran it by Legal last night, and trust me, they were none too thrilled to have me call them last night at 1am to have them review and bless it. They raised concerns about naming too many conspirators at this point and opening ourselves up to a ton of liability. Especially when the evidence that you cite has not even been vetted by Agent Jansen's superiors, much less the US Attorney. They said, in no uncertain terms, that we have to hold the article until early next week, at least."

"And since when does the media wait for the blessing of the Federal government before running an article, especially when it's uncovering a crime that has nothing at all to do with any Federal or State government? We're not uncovering any state secrets or outing any spies. This is about as far as you can get from the goddamn Pentagon Papers or WikiLeaks."

"No argument there. None. This is an incredibly important story, and what you have uncovered so far makes the Son of Sam or Unibomber stories look like a sorority pillow fight. We're going to make this a multi-part series, and you obviously have the lead. But we need to take a step at a time, and because of the seriousness of what you've uncovered, we don't want to be responsible for jeopardizing the ability to arrest and prosecute these people."

Kristyn looked over at JJ but looked less than thrilled with the conversation. Her goal was to get a commitment for a series on this case, which she got. But she was not happy for the delay in releasing the story, though she couldn't argue with the logic. She just hoped that JJ would see it the same way.

"You still there, Kristyn?"

"Yes, sorry, the cell signal cut out for a minute. So, just so I'm clear, the article will run with the names of the other three members of the Slayers? In addition, we're naming Dr. Richard Miller as one of the game players, correct, since we can tie him directly to all four members of the Slayers and to their earlier online game called Kill Starter?"

"That's correct, and......"

"And there is still mention of the fact that there are well over 1,000 game players still to be identified and their information shared with the police, FBI, and, very likely, Interpol?"

"Yes, that's correct, and....."

"And this will be front-page, above the fold, early next week? No chance that we can get into Sunday's paper since that is by far our biggest day for circulation?"

"Legal said early next week but they weren't more specific. No way would I plan on Sunday. But I promise: when it runs, it will be front-page, above the fold."

After hanging up with Evan, Kristyn sat back down with JJ. "Well, the good news is that they've committed to a multi-part series with me as the lead. The bad news is that they're not going to run the article until at early next week."

"I assume that they're like every other corporate legal team in America and scared of getting sued if they publish the names?"

"Definitely. The bar for successfully suing a newspaper is pretty high, but you know how these lawyers are: they look at how much it will cost to defend yourself even if you're successful."

"Maybe that's not a bad thing, as much as I was hoping for today. This will mean less chance for the Slayers and the online players to make a run for it before we can have arrest warrants in hand and round them up."

JJ read through the article for what felt like the hundredth time and decided that it was time to loop-in Isaksen to let him know what would be coming. "I guess it's time for me to bite the bullet and call Isaksen and take my forty lashes. I'm not sure that I even need to call him; if I stick my head out the window, I'll probably be able to hear him screaming at me all the way from Dallas."

"Nah, too much jet noise out there," Kristyn giggled. "Want me to come hang with you for moral support?"

"No, but thanks. Time to pull up my big girl panties and face the music. I'll be back in a few minutes, hopefully. Then maybe we can grab some coffee or breakfast before we have to board."

As she went in search of a quieter spot, JJ rehearsed the discussion in her mind. No beating around the bush. That wasn't her style, and Isaksen was generally a no bullshit kind of guy. She decided that the best tactic was to come right out with it, explain what was and what was not in the article, when it was likely to run, and the next steps that she had planned. She hoped that the fact that she was about to hand him three serial killers responsible for about 60 murders, all wrapped-up neatly in a bow – *well, almost* - would be enough for him to see the logic and righteousness of her actions. *Sure, when pigs fly.*

The conversation with Isaksen felt at times like a tennis match, with the volleys and returns flying back and forth, each player looking to smack a winner just out of their opponent's reach. At other times it felt more like the Nuremburg Trials, with JJ as the defendant – *probably already condemned* – and Isaksen as the prosecutor. Surprisingly, he never raised his voice. He was obviously angry, and he didn't mince any words, but he never yelled. She was shocked, but grateful. She was also grateful that he listened to her explanations and rationale; there were times that he didn't agree with her decisions, but he didn't berate her or question her common sense as he had in the past. The conversation was much more productive and professional than she had dared hope for, and though it lasted more than 30 minutes, she walked away with some level of validation.

"Agent Jansen, I'm setting aside time tomorrow for us to review this information in detail. Based on what you've said, I assume that there is far too much data for you to complete your analysis by tomorrow?"

"Correct, sir. I can get started and have some preliminary information for you tomorrow, but it will take me a couple of days to get through all 60 murders and correlate each to one of the Slayers. And as far as the online players that bet on these games and essentially financed the whole thing, there are literally more than 1,000 players. With your permission, perhaps we can have the Labs team in Quantico that uncovered the existence of online players take a shot at consolidating it for us?"

"That's not a bad idea. A bit outside of their charter, perhaps, but let me reach out to their Director to request their assistance. You said they've already uncovered quite a few players and been able to identify them, so hopefully they have that process perfected, and they can respond quickly."

"Right, and as I mentioned earlier, the Dallas Morning News' attorneys decided not to publish those names now, and that's probably a good thing. Arresting these people is going to be a US and international effort; we've found players in Europe, Asia, and Australia, so we'll want to involve Interpol, just as we've done in the past with international child pornography cases."

"Alright, then, I'll see you tomorrow morning. If you need any help from me, reach out immediately. Let's target Monday morning to have everything ready to brief the US Attorney and request arrest warrants for everyone involved."

"I'll get right on it, sir. And thank you for your understanding."

"Agent Jansen, one last thing. While I don't necessarily agree with your methods in pursuit of this case, I can't deny your results. But let me be clear: while I will do my best to have your back, when this is all over, I may not be able to protect you. You've gone way off the reservation here and ignored standard FBI practices and protocols, and to say that you've put your career, and possibly mine, in jeopardy with those actions, is an understatement. Bringing Ms. Reynolds into this and having her assume an active part of the investigation, that is beyond the pale. Frankly, it quite possibly put her life in danger, and that may well be the straw that breaks the camel's back. Again, I'm not challenging your results or even her contributions, but that may not be enough to save you from the oversight team."

"I understand, sir....."

"Then let's make damn certain that we have what we need to ensure convictions for these bastards, and try your best to keep a low profile from this point on. No matter how well this turns out, there are going to be people just waiting to tear you down. And it won't be personal; it will be because of your willingness to ignore FBI rules and regulations."

"You have my word, sir. I will make this whole case airtight; my goal is a 100% conviction rate. And I appreciate you having my back. I knew that what I was doing was coloring outside of the lines, and I'm willing to suffer the consequences. But I don't want anyone else punished for my actions."

"I appreciate that. Anything else before you catch your flight?"

"One thing, sir. When this article drops, the Slayers are going to realize that we're on to them and their game. For that matter, one of the people that we questioned, Dr. Miller, may have already told them that we're sniffing around; it turns out that he's actually one of their online players."

"So this Dr. Miller is actually a co-conspirator then. Maybe we should pick him up now and see if it's possible that he'll flip on the others. Thoughts? It would be nice to have one of their online bettors in custody, maybe sweat them a bit."

"I don't disagree, sir. How long do you think it would take for you to secure the warrant?"

"Hopefully not more than a few hours. I would want you to be there to help coordinate the arrest, but that would mean that you'd have to miss your flight today and travel home tomorrow instead. Would that be a problem?"

"No, sir, not at all. And I'd definitely want to be here to help with the arrest and questioning."

"Alright, then. Make the necessary arrangements to stay one more day and I'll let you know as soon as the warrant is in hand. And I'll coordinate with the New York office to help get this moving and ask them to reach out to you. Stay safe up there."

Chapter Twenty-Seven

THURSDAY, NOVEMBER 3

For the first time in their long and checkered history, the Slayers were panicked. They'd always been supremely confident, perhaps even cocky. That cockiness, that feeling of immortality, was history. The proverbial shit had hit the fan, and now they were all gripped by fear. They had always been so careful and so assured of their anonymity that they'd never even conceived of someone uncovering the game or their identities. Sure, they had their multiple aliases and ID's, multiple passports, stashes of cash and cryptocurrencies, and a packed bag always at the ready, but that was simply 'insurance'. The reality quickly sunk in that today was the day that their world would start crashing down. It was Mark Saxe who received the call from Dr. Richard Miller warning him about the FBI and a reporter snooping around and asking questions about Jamarcus and the rest of them, and Miller made no bones about the fact that he was getting out now while there was still time. Saxe wasted no time in reaching out to the others and kept it short and succinct: *911! We're burned! Move! Meet at noon ET.*

"I don't know how this happened. I never, ever expected anyone to discover our identities and the details of the game." Calvin said what all of them were thinking. "I thought our shit was totally safe and unbreakable."

"I did, too," added Mark. "No offense to Jamarcus, but this must have all been precipitated by the events in Dallas. They must have somehow tied the Georgetown murder to the alias he used for the airline and hotel, and then were able to drill down from there."

"I guess we underestimated the Feds," said Graham. "I guess we should have been more concerned when they recovered Jamarcus' cell phone and laptop and started making plans to leave the country then. Personally, I never gave it much thought."

"You're right. I guess hindsight really is 20/20. The question to you guys," said Mark, "is what are we going to do about it? And how quickly can we do it?"

Calvin spoke first. "Without question we need to get as far from here as possible. We have our aliases and passports, and virtually unlimited funds, so we can leave the country on a minute's notice. I know that it's always been part of our contingency planning, but we need to focus on countries with no extradition treaty with the US. Fortunately, there are dozens. The only downside is that there are only a handful that I'd consider as 'home'."

"I agree," said Graham. "I definitely want to be on a plane out of here ASAP, before they issue the arrest warrants and have our faces plastered across every transportation hub in the country. And as far as where to go, I've always had my heart set on the Solomon Islands. There's lots of worse places than the South Pacific."

"I'm thinking Indonesia," responded Calvin. "Literally thousands of islands to explore and escape to, and some absolutely killer surfing and fishing."

"Love those choices. I'm thinking the Maldives. About a million miles from everywhere, and one of the most beautiful places on earth. We can still get together once a year like we've been doing, we just need to make sure that we meet only in other non-extradition countries."

"And make sure that our travel itineraries only include stops or layovers in non-extradition countries, too. There have been instances where people got arrested because their flight connected through Australia or other countries with extradition." Calvin had obviously given this a lot of thought.

Mark had something else on his mind. "One other thing is bothering me. I'm not sure how you guys feel, but I don't think there's anything we can do for our online players, no way we can save them from the shit storm that's about to come crashing down. It's probably just a matter of hours, or at most a few days, before the FBI uncovers the identities of our online players, where they live, their bank account numbers, pretty much every bit of information we had on them."

"Not to be a dick about it, but at this point I think it's down to every man for himself. We could post a notice on our site warning them about the situation, but I think it goes without saying the FBI is, or very soon will be, monitoring our site and making plans to shut it down." Graham was not unsympathetic to the situation, just being realistic.

Mark and Graham looked at Calvin and stayed silent until he could respond. "I have to agree with Graham. Not much that we can do for them at this point. Arrest warrants will be issued within days, if not hours, both in the US and abroad."

"Yeah, but it really sucks that they stumbled onto Dr. Miller. They'll probably be coming for him really soon, and not a damn thing we can do about it. I just hope they don't come down too hard on him." Even after all these years, Mark still had a soft spot for Dr. Miller because of his guidance and support in creating, and selling, Kill Starter. "At least he has the money and resources to hire a great lawyer."

"That's true, and maybe he has his own escape plan in place. Like maybe popping across the border into Canada and then traveling from there under a different name. I certainly hope so; I hate to see him get burned." Calvin knew that it was out of their hands, but he had faith in Dr. Miller's resourcefulness.

"Let me throw out another idea for you guys: I know that we're all in agreement that we need to get the hell out of here sooner rather than later, right?" Graham asked. Seeing nods from the others, he continued. "OK, so before we disappear, I want to travel to Dallas to take out this FBI agent and reporter that are running this investigation before it's too late. If it's not already too late."

Calvin and Mark were shocked. Graham was usually the calm one, the voice of reason. Now here he was, advocating for the murder of the two people leading the investigation. But was the revenge worth the risk? Should they risk traveling to Dallas and delaying their escape, especially when one of the targets is an FBI agent? They'd end up with every local, state, and Federal cop in the US after them.

"You really think it's worth such a huge risk? Wouldn't the smart move be to cut our losses and get the fuck out of here ASAP?" Mark couldn't deny the rush that would come with killing the two people ruining their lives, but better to live as a free man – *better to live* – than to put it all at risk.

"I'm with Mark on this, Graham. I mean, I'd like to take them out as much as you, but I'd rather get out while the getting is good, if you know what I mean. We've got the money, our passports, and everything we need to start a new life. Staying here means we're likely to either end up in prison or dead. Actually, even if we end up in prison it will probably just be a short stop before we get the needle."

"Guys, we owe this to Jamarcus, and we owe it to every one of our players that are about to lose their fortunes and their freedom. Mostly though, I think we owe it to ourselves. This has been our work, our passion, our livelihood, for years. And now it's over, or soon will be. The writing is on the wall. I say it's worth the risk. I'd rather die fighting than run from this and let them shit all over the legacy that we built and the memory of our brother, Jamarcus. Fuck them. Let's make them remember us as the group that wouldn't back down, wouldn't run from a fight."

The three of them grew silent, deep in thought and weighing the risk versus reward. "If we're going to consider this, then I say we need to vote, and it has to be unanimous." Mark was not in favor, but he wouldn't let the others down if they voted for it. Calvin and Graham both nodded their agreement. They talked for a few more minutes, and then they took the vote.

"Alright, I guess we're doing this. Let's be extra careful when booking travel and use our 'last resort' ID's that we set aside for just such an occasion. We can't take any chances since our other aliases are likely compromised and flagged by the FBI." Mark was still not in favor, but he was going to do everything possible to ensure that they walked away from this alive. *Was there even the slightest chance of walking away alive when this is over?* That's probably not a bet that even Oz would approve of.

Chapter Twenty-Eight

FRIDAY, NOVEMBER 4

I n JJ's fantasy, she would watch as dozens, maybe even hundreds, of simultaneous arrests were made around the globe as the authorities closed-in on the online players and bettors from The Murder Game. Unfortunately, that fantasy would have to be on the back burner, because right now the only arrest warrant they had was for Dr. Richard Miller, and even that had taken much longer than she'd hoped or expected. Warrants for the Slayers and the other online bettors would hopefully come early next week when she was back in Dallas. In the meantime, they hoped to get Miller off the street and as incommunicado as possible, if it wasn't already too late.

JJ had gotten the green light from Isaksen to coordinate with the New York Field Office and NYPD on Miller's arrest. The calls had gone back and forth well into the night, but finally a plan had gelled and, most importantly, the arrest warrant was in the system. The plan was to have everyone meet at the NYPD's 28th Precinct building on Frederick Douglas Boulevard at 5am to review each agency's role in the arrest. Because the 28th Precinct was closest to both the Columbia University campus and Miller's home in Morningside Heights, it was chosen as the staging location.

The tactical plan called for hitting Miller's front door at precisely 6am. He wasn't considered likely to resist or get violent, but there was still considerable manpower and firepower assembled to bring him in. In addition to six FBI agents there were a half-dozen uniformed NYPD officers and an additional ten from the NYPD Apprehension Tactical Team, a.k.a, the A-Team. While some would consider it overkill, Miller was considered a high-value target since he was a co-conspirator and, potentially, the nail in the coffin for the Slayers.

By 5:50 they were in place covering both the front and back of his building. Kristyn stayed down on the street well out of the way – *thankfully* – while JJ went up with a half-dozen heavily armed men. They split up and two of them took the exit stairway to the East, two took the exit stairway to the West, and JJ and two others took the elevator. Miller's building, like so many in this neighborhood, was historic, extremely expensive, and highly sought-after. The fact that it was so close to Columbia University and barely a stone's throw from the Hudson River certainly didn't hurt its value, either.

They all arrived on the 10th floor and noiselessly approached Miller's door. JJ was wearing a tactical vest, but the A-Team members were in head-to-toe body armor and had the lead. Plus, serving warrants, especially for high-value targets, was one of their specialties. They spread out on either side of his door, and when they got the signal that everyone on the ground was in place and ready to go, Sergeant Gilberti, the leader of the A-Team, knocked on the door and announced himself.

"Dr. Richard Miller, this is Sergeant Gilberti of the NYPD. I have a warrant for your arrest and a search warrant for these premises. Please open the door immediately."

They waited, their pulses quickening. No matter how many times they'd done this, it still got their hearts racing and their adrenalin pumping. After about 20 seconds with no response, Gilberti knocked on the door again, this time more loudly, and made the same announcement virtually word for word. Still there was no response or any sounds coming from within.

"Dr. Miller, this is your last warning. If you don't open this door immediately, we will break it down and enter the premises. I need for you to answer me now or we will be coming in."

Gilberti was ready to move. "OK guys let's take it down. You know the drill. Let's watch each other's backs, and let's clear every room, every closet, and every possible hiding place. We want this guy alive if at all possible, but if he has a weapon and engages you, take him down. Any questions?" The Sergeant looked around. "Agent Jansen, please let my team take the lead and we'll signal you when it's safe to enter."

JJ nodded her agreement and took no offense to being the last one in. It was a tactical decision, and absolutely the right one.

Two members of the A-Team stepped up to the door with a heavy battering ram, and the others took a couple of steps back with their weapons at the ready. "On the count of three." As the ram hit the door there was a tremendous explosion that blew them both against the far side of the wall, killing them both instantly. Fortunately, the force of the blast was focused on the doorway so, other than the concussive force of the explosion and flying shards of wood and metal, the others were not seriously injured.

As the breach team staggered to their feet and rushed to check on their fellow team members, JJ made her way to the doorway – what was left of it – and tried to enter the apartment. There was still too much heat and smoke, so she was forced to back off. Her senses were reeling; she could barely hear for the ringing in her ears, her balance was off, and her head was already pounding. The noise from the building's fire alarm, the screaming of the residents rushing out of their apartments, and the cops screaming into their radios for EMT's and fire support only added to the hysteria.

Getting her legs back under her and regaining some of her equilib-rium, JJ made her way down the hall to one of the mounted fire extin-guishers and, tearing it from the wall, moved quickly to what was left of Miller's apartment. She wielded the extinguisher and was able to knock down the fire around the doorway, or what was left of it, and rushed in alone. She knew it was against the plan and against protocol, but she didn't care. She had to find out if Miller was in there.

Luckily, the damage to the inside of the apartment, which spanned more than 4,000 square feet, was not too extensive and there did not appear to be any structural damage. The force from the blast had been directed at the door, which meant that Miller fully intended to kill whoever came through it. JJ took only about five minutes to clear the apartment and assure herself that Miller was gone. It would be up to the

Crime Scene Unit and the Forensics teams to go over the place with a fine-toothed comb, but she was not at all confident they'd find anything useful. Still, in any investigation, you have to follow the process.

Her phone rang as she was heading back to the door, her throat and eyes burning like crazy from the smoke. She couldn't even see the display on her phone because her eyes were watering so badly.

"JJ, oh my God! Are you OK? We heard the explosion all the way down here. Are you OK!" Kristyn was crying and nearly hysterical.

"I'm OK. A few scratches, but otherwise OK. Unfortunately, a couple of others weren't so lucky."

"Oh, God, no. That's horrible." The crying turned into sobs. It took her a moment. "What happened up there?"

"The assault team knocked on the door, several times, but got no response, so they crashed the door with a battering ram. The door was rigged to blow when it was breached, and the two officers with the ram were killed. The force from the blast was directed at the doorway so there was minimal damage in the hallway where the rest of us were positioned. I just left the apartment and there's surprisingly little damage there."

"Did you find Miller?"

"No, he's not here. I'm sure he's been in the wind since we left the University on Wednesday, which is why I wanted to do this yesterday. If we could have hit him then instead of waiting on the US Attorneys to get off their asses and issue the warrants, we might not be in this mess. And two cops would still be alive." Her eyes were starting to water more, but it was no longer just from the smoke.

"When will you be down? Or do you need me up there to do anything?"

"I need to wait here for the EMT's and fire department, though luckily the fire is pretty much out. And I'll need to wait for the NYPD brass and the local FBI leaders to get here. I'll get away as soon as I can and meet you outside. Maybe we can wait in the lobby for the other police and FBI teams to get here." She was happy to try to get Kristyn access to the lobby, but she was glad that they wouldn't allow her up to Miller's apartment. No one should have to see the gruesome scene in that hallway. It was the kind of scene that could make even a seasoned Medical Examiner lose his lunch.

It was nearly a half hour before JJ made it outside. Kristyn spotted her immediately, her eyes having been glued to the entrance the whole time. She ran up to JJ and threw her arms around her and started crying again, this time so hard she almost couldn't breathe. "I heard that explosion and I was so scared that I'd lost you and everyone that went into that building! It felt like a lifetime before I could reach you." They held each other tightly for several more minutes, and finally Kristyn calmed down enough to be able to speak. "I'm so glad that you're OK. And I'm sorry that I'm such an emotional wreck."

"I'm fine, and there's nothing to apologize for. I'm just glad that you were down here where it was safe and not up there to witness that scene. It's the kind of thing that will stay with you for life. I know that I'll never forget it." JJ took her arm and started walking back towards the building. "Let's sit in the lobby while we wait for the other teams."

While waiting for the SAC from the New York City FBI office to arrive, JJ's mind was going a mile a minute. *It's not hard to understand why Miller fled at the first opportunity, but where would he go? Has anyone put out an APB yet? Should she reach out to the NYPD to ensure that they issue one? Would he try to travel out of the country? Does he have multiple ID's and passports like the Slayers? If he was trying to fly somewhere outside of the US – almost a certainty – he'd have to pick either JFK or Newark since LaGuardia doesn't handle international flights. On the other hand, Miller has the financial wherewithal to charter a flight, so we can't overlook the private airports. Teterboro was just across the bridge in New Jersey and actually closer than Newark or JFK.* The possibilities made her head spin.

"Do you think Miller will try to flee the country?" JJ asked Kristyn, pretty much just thinking out loud. "Or do you think he'll hideout somewhere waiting for things to blow over?"

Kristyn thought about it for a moment. "I don't know. I can see both sides. But my first instinct is probably to get out while the getting is good, before his name and face are all over every newscast and newspaper in the country."

"Yeah, I'm kind of leaning that way, too, but maybe he thinks his window of opportunity has already closed. He might be the paranoid type and already expecting every cop in the country to be looking for him and staking out every airport and train station on the off chance that he'll show up. I mean, he knew that we'd eventually show up at his home, so he fled from there after booby-trapping the place. Maybe he has somewhere else to lay low until the heat dies down? Just a theory...."

"Actually, that's a pretty good theory. When you consider that it's not always possible to fly out of the country on a moment's notice, especially to a non-extraditable country, he may be waiting for things to cool down."

"I've got an idea. I'll be back in a moment." JJ grabbed her cell phone and started pacing the lobby. She was having an animated conversation with someone, but after about 10 minutes it was evident that whoever she was talking to had caved to her argument, or maybe to her rank. She was all smiles as she walked back and sat back down with Kristyn.

"So did your idea pan out?"

"It did! I reached out to one of the forensic techs at the Quantico Labs that I've been working with and asked him to dig into Miller's financials, and he uncovered another home here in the city that was purchased using an alias. He's using the name Blake Ryznar, and he bought the place about two years ago. It's in a high-dollar condo building on Park Avenue that probably makes this place look like a hovel. Sounds like the perfect place to suffer through a few weeks of hiding out. I've got to notify everyone and get us there ASAP."

JJ knew that she'd need some extra 'juice' to get the NYPD and local FBI office moving on this, especially when it had been less than an hour since two members of the A-Team had been killed trying to arrest her suspect. Her first call went to Isaksen; she quickly explained the situation and he promised to get right on it. Several minutes later his counterpart, the SAC of the New York office, approached her in the lobby along with the Chief of Police for the NYPD. It didn't take long for JJ to make her case, and in minutes they had formulated a plan and started putting it in motion. While the entire New York contingent was distraught about what had happened to members of their team, they were hellbent on taking this guy down. Or taking him out.

JJ and Kristyn jumped into a black Suburban driven by the SAC's aide, along with the SAC and several other FBI agents. Members of the NYPD were in two armored vehicles and at least another dozen police cruisers. *So much for being subtle or having the element of surprise.* It seemed that every cop in New York was converging on Miller's building, The Palisades, on Park Avenue.

"Have you thought about how we're going to approach Miller's apartment, especially since it's on the 25th floor?" JJ was anxious to hear a plan. "We need to make sure that he hasn't rigged another bomb or barricaded himself inside with a cache of weapons."

Kristyn added, "Or possibly taken hostages."

"We could try to evacuate the building, but that could take hours. And who's to say that Miller wouldn't sneak out during the crush of people leaving?" The SAC was saying what everyone else was thinking.

As they turned the corner and pulled up to the main entrance it was almost impossible to park because of all the police and FBI vehicles pulling in. The Palisades took up an entire square block, so police units pulled up on all sides of the building. As they piled out of the car, JJ whispered to Kristyn, "I've got a bad feeling about this, and it doesn't help that we pulled up with half the NYPD. If Miller's in there, I'm sure he knows we're here and coming for him. That makes him even more dangerous. Promise me you'll stay here with the car. It's the safest place at this point."

* * *

Richard Miller, aka Blake Ryznar, had hardly slept the night before. He felt sure that he'd probably never have a good night's sleep again even if he was able to get out of this alive. He was growing concerned about all the sirens he was hearing, but this being New York City, sirens were a near-constant way of life. Even here on the 25th floor one could still hear their constant wail, and his paranoia was running rampant; he imagined that every siren was coming for him. And then his fears were confirmed. Dozens of police cars, black Suburbans and Escalades, and even several armored vehicles were pulling up to the building. It looked like they were planning to invade a small country or arrest half of ISIS.

Miller considered his options. His original plan had been to stay here for a week or two and then drive to Chicago, eventually catching an international flight from O'Hare. That plan had obviously gone to shit. He had a Glock semi-automatic and several hundred rounds of ammunition, but he had no illusions of being able to escape. He was nothing if not a realist; while shocked that they had tracked him down, especially this quickly, he knew that it was game over. Taking hostages was not in his nature; he had no problem killing cops or anyone trying to take him down, but he considered himself above such low-class thug tactics like hurting innocent victims.

He decided that he was going to set the terms, not the police or FBI. He dug in his wallet for the business card that Special Agent Jessica Jansen had given him. This whole clusterfuck started with her, and he intended to make this a day she'd never forget. He grabbed his cellphone and dialed her number.

JJ was still outside of the building with the others as they planned their strategy. She answered her phone on the first ring. She didn't recognize the number but took the call anyway. "This is FBI Special Agent Jessica Jansen."

"Special Agent Jansen, how good to speak with you again. This is Dr. Richard Miller. I see you've stopped by to see me, along with what appears to be hundreds of your closest friends."

JJ was shocked, to say the least. She quickly muted her phone and then yelled for everyone to be quiet before informing the SAC that Miller was on the phone. He gave her a quizzical look, to which she responded by saying, "I'm as shocked as you are, sir."

Returning her attention to Miller, she said, "I'm surprised to hear from you, Dr. Miller. Should I take this as an indication that you're going to surrender peacefully when we come upstairs for you? We have a warrant for your arrest, so it's all nice and official."

"In due time, Agent Jansen. In due time."

What kind of game is he playing? Why is he stalling? "Time is something that we don't have a lot of Dr. Miller. And, in case you're not aware, your bomb killed two NYPD officers a little while ago when we went to your apartment, so now you've put yourself in a much worse position. Originally, we were coming to arrest you just for your participation in The Murder Game. We were even going to offer you the chance to be a material witness against the Slayers in exchange for reduced charges. But now you've totally screwed yourself. I'm just hoping that you'll give yourself up and not give these pissed-off cops a reason to shoot you."

"Well, I could say that I'm sorry about those dead officers, but that would be disingenuous of me." The smirk and sarcasm in his voice was palpable. "But rest assured that I have absolutely no plans to put any of the residents of this building in harm's way. There will be no hostage taking, no 'shootout at the OK Corral' kind of ending."

"Well, I'm glad to hear that. We don't need anyone else to die here today. And believe it or not, Dr. Miller, that goes for you, too."

"That's very kind of you, Agent Jansen. So, I've decided, in order to make this easy for you as well as the people living in this building, I'll come down to you."

"No, absolutely not. You wait right there, and we will have officers come up to your apartment. Do not, I repeat, do not try to leave your apartment under any circumstances."

"Oh, Agent Jansen. Just when I thought you had at least some semblance of a brain you prove to be just another feckless civil servant. I said: I'm. Coming. Down. To. You. And here I come!"

JJ heard screams from people on the street and looked towards the building. "No!!"

Chapter Twenty-Nine

B y late Friday afternoon, all three members of the Slayers had arrived in Dallas. They flew on different airlines and intentionally planned their arrivals to be staggered across several hours. They were taking no chances on being seen or caught on camera together. They stayed at different hotels in the downtown area and avoided any contact until their video call at 9pm.

"I'm guessing that you guys have seen the news out of New York about Dr. Miller by now, right?" Mark was still a bit shaken.

"I saw it while I was sitting in the airport but couldn't hear the TV, so I pulled it up on my phone. I can't believe that he'd kill himself like that. Especially not by jumping from 25 floors up." Graham shook his head, still partly in disbelief. "I know that he owned a gun, probably had it with him. If he wanted to off himself why not use it? That's a lot less terrifying than throwing yourself off a building."

"Did you guys see the part where the cops tried to arrest him at his apartment near the University? He rigged a bomb to go off when they tried to break down his door and it killed two cops. I guess the bomb-making skills that we taught him were finally put to good use. To be honest, I never thought he'd have the balls to do it." Calvin loved the guy, but never expected him to have the backbone for something like that.

"How the fuck did they track him down that quickly? Obviously, they'd know about the place in Morningside Heights, but the condo at the Palisades? It wasn't even in his name, or even an alias that he'd used previously." Mark had to grudgingly admire the FBI's computer forensics team for their capabilities. He wished they were a lot less capable.

They commiserated about Miller for a while longer, reminiscing about the good times in college, including their first foray into the gaming world, 'Kill Starter'. Finally, Calvin dragged them back to the matter at hand. "Let's talk through the logistics for targeting Agent Jansen and this reporter, Kristyn Reynolds. I don't know about you, but I have zero interest in treating this like one of our games. I vote for making it fast, simple, and effective."

Graham nodded his head. "I totally agree. We should purchase our usual Glock semi-automatics and decent sniper rifles, then it's just a matter of determining the time and place. You guys want to hit them one at a time or together?"

"I say we plan for one at a time," replied Mark, "but if the opportunity presents itself where we can do them both, we take it. And then we get the hell out of here."

The Slayers spent another hour planning the timing and logistics for the hits. While Graham advocated for moving quickly, Calvin and Mark were on the side of careful planning and reconnaissance. Their argument was persuasive; after all, it was their discipline and preparedness that had allowed them to stay off the radar for all these years. They wanted to scope-out their homes and workplaces, the routes they take to and from work, and a million other details. Plus, they needed to book their flights out of the country and prepare themselves for a life on the run and forever looking over their shoulder.

Finally, they came to agreement: Monday would be D-Day. Kristyn would be the first to die, for no other reason than that they thought she'd be easier to take out versus an FBI agent. They imagined that Agent Jansen would be racked with guilt and blame herself for Kristyn's death. At the same time, she'd be overwhelmed by her own terror, knowing that she was now in their crosshairs. Where once she likely felt safe and secure in the fact that she was FBI and thought of herself as untouchable, she would now see the absurdity in that thinking.

The Slayers couldn't wait to get their revenge. Revenge for Jamarcus. Revenge for Richard Miller. Revenge for their online players that were about to have their lives ruined. And revenge for the impending loss of the game that they loved.

* * *

JJ and Kristyn caught the last flight to Dallas, and they were beyond exhausted. When they had first discussed traveling to NYC on Tuesday to meet with Columbia University, they had planned for just one night. As the case evolved, one night quickly evolved into three. The time they'd spent there had certainly been productive; they'd confirmed the identities of the three surviving Slayers, as well Miller's involvement as one of The Murder Game's most prolific online gamblers. The downside, of course, was that Miller had killed himself rather than surrender and turn state's evidence, plus they'd lost two members of the NYPD A-Team that led the raid on his primary residence.

"I'm so glad that I took an Uber to the airport. I'm so tired I don't think there's any way I could drive home. I'd probably rather sleep in the airport than get behind the wheel." Kristyn was talking but her eyes were completely shut.

"If I had to drive tonight, I'd just grab a room at the DFW Hyatt and head home in the morning. Want to share an Uber tonight?"

"Sounds like a great idea." Shifting the subject, Kristyn asked, "So what's the plan from here? I'm ready to take these guys down and pray that they never see the light of day again."

"My vote is that we get some rest tonight – what's left of it – and get together tomorrow afternoon and all-day Sunday if you can. We need to compile the evidence detailing the murders committed by the Slayers so that I can present it to Isaksen on Monday and, hopefully, get in front of the US Attorney to secure the arrest warrants."

"I like it. Why don't you come over to my place tomorrow and just plan to stay the night? That way we can spend more time working and less time driving back and forth."

JJ blushed. *I'd like to spend more time ravishing you......Stop!* "That sounds like a great idea. I think that between the two of us we can get through all of the information by Sunday evening." *If I can keep my hands and my mouth off of you....STOP!*

Chapter Thirty
SATURDAY, NOVEMBER 5

W hen the alarm went off at 10:30am on Saturday morning JJ was barely able to function. It had been after 3am before she finally got home and into bed, and even though she was exhausted, she didn't sleep as well as she'd hoped; it was one disturbing dream after another. She relived the explosion and the carnage multiple times, as well as the horrific sight of Richard Miller jumping to his death. Her mind roiled with all that she had seen and heard and learned, and then it roiled some more with the seemingly endless work still to be done. After a few cups of coffee and a long, hot shower, she was starting to feel almost human again. Unfortunately, though, that did little to quiet her mind and shake the gruesome images and memories that had tormented her all night.

JJ got to Kristyn's house shortly before 3pm, and when the door opened, she was taken aback. It was the first time that she'd seen Kristyn looking less than perfect. She looked tired and pale, with visible bags under her gorgeous eyes. It actually made JJ fall for her even more, made her long to hold Kristyn and keep her safe and free from all this craziness. "Are you ok? You look like maybe you didn't get a lot of rest. Though I guess I shouldn't talk."

Kristyn tried to smile at JJ's little attempt at humor. "I didn't. I don't think I slept more than a couple of hours all night. The stress and anxiety are beyond anything I've ever had to deal with, and God knows I've dealt with a lot in my job. I always considered myself to be pretty strong, but maybe I was just kidding myself. Maybe I'm only strong when I can hide behind my keyboard."

"You're strong, and you're smart, and you're tenacious. You're as capable as any investigator I've ever worked with, and you have great instincts. Don't sell yourself short; you would've made a helluva cop or FBI agent."

Kristyn let out a light giggle, even as her eyes started to water. "I appreciate that, but I think I'm much too chickenshit to ever do what you do. But I do love working with you; this case has really energized me in ways that I haven't felt in years, maybe ever. Of course, it's also scared the shit out of me at times." She smiled again. Slowly she was lightening the mood.

"Why don't we order a pizza before we get down to the drudgery? I think we could both use some time to turn our brains off. I only had coffee and a piece of toast this morning, so I could definitely eat."

It was nearly 6pm before they got down to the real work at hand. They'd managed to eat the entire large pizza and a bottle of Cabernet, but it was just the medicine they needed. While they both would have loved to just kick back on the couch, stream some movies and drink more wine, there was work that had to get done or this case would continue to drag on forever. Or at least until the Slayers added them to their list of victims.

They started by calculating how many victims they had to track. Before Jamarcus Hicks had been killed, there had been a total of 20 games, meaning there were 80 victims. Earlier this week the surviving members of the Slayers had done another game, meaning three new victims for a total of 83. Since they'd already accounted for Hicks' 20 kills last weekend, that left 63 homicides to track. At this point they had the process and routine perfected and were able to move quickly. By 11pm they had cleared almost 40 of the 63 murders and added them to the master spreadsheet.

"I don't think I can look at any more names and dates and places and other data tonight. Feels like my eyes are crossing. Ready to call it a night?" JJ felt like she was fading fast; last night's not-so-restful sleep was catching up to her. Several glasses of wine probably wasn't helping, either.

"Yeah, I think we've done enough for one night, and we don't want to make any mistakes because we're too tired to focus. That could come back to bite us if this becomes part of the court case."

Even tired her mind is like a steel trap. "Maybe we just move over to the couch for a while and relax? Maybe one last glass of wine?"

"That sounds good to me. I'm tired, but I think my mind is still running a hundred miles an hour, so no way I could go to sleep right now. I'll grab the wine."

They sat on the couch, closer than before. JJ was feeling so many things: physically and mentally exhausted, aroused to the point of distraction, and scared to death of saying or doing the wrong thing and scaring Kristyn off. Not to mention ruining any chance of having their friendship evolve into a relationship, if a chance even existed. They talked for well over an hour and the conversation flowed easily; any talk about the case was assiduously avoided. It was time for more pleasant thoughts. And JJ was having the most pleasant thoughts....*Push them down!*

It was well after midnight and Kristyn had grown quiet. JJ gave her a quizzical look, and finally Kristyn spoke. "I want to ask you something, and you have to promise to be honest." She looked at JJ and saw an affirming nod. "Last night I had the worst sleep I've had in years; I tossed and turned all night, and when I did nod off for a few minutes here and there, I had awful nightmares. I didn't even see the terrible things that you did in New York, so I can only imagine how rough your night was."

"That's true. All night it was one terrible, terrifying dream after another."

"I couldn't stop myself from crying as I thought about you and what you must be going through." She hesitated for a moment. "I'm not scared, in the normal sense of the word, to sleep alone tonight, but I am scared of having another night of anxiety and restlessness. Would you be comfortable sleeping in my room tonight, with me? Please say 'no' if it makes you uncomfortable, but I think I would feel better just knowing that I had someone there with me. I guess I sound pathetic...."

"No, you don't sound pathetic at all. You just sound human." There were a million thoughts running through JJ's mind, most of them erotic, but she realized that now was not the time to press the matter. Kristyn was hurting and scared and exhausted; what she needed was a friend and a human touch, not someone trying to pressure her to take things to the next level. "To be honest, I think I'd rest better knowing that you were there, too."

And she was right: JJ had the most peaceful sleep she'd experienced in months. Maybe years.

* * *

There were no awkward looks or awkward words when they woke up Sunday morning, no embarrassment. There had been nothing sexual about the night, but for JJ it was one of the most sensuous experiences of her life. "Morning, sunshine. How'd you sleep?"

Kristyn stretched and yawned. "Oh my God, so much better than the night before. Thank you so much for staying here with me; having you here made me feel safe and warm and connected. I hope you slept well, too."

"Oh, definitely. Between the exhaustion, the food, the wine, and snuggling in a warm bed next to you, I had a great night's sleep. Being with you is better than any sleeping pill."

They dressed and headed out for brunch, agreeing that they had earned a reward after all the progress they'd made last night. Neither were in the mood for a light little breakfast of fruit and stale pastry; they wanted real food, and lots of it. They chose a restaurant famous for its huge Sunday brunch buffet, and they both got more than their money's worth. Kristyn had a huge Bloody Mary with enough garnishes on it to qualify as another entrée. JJ stuck with iced tea, figuring that the lighter drink left more room for her to hit the dessert table.

"Oh, God, I ate way too much. Someone is going to have to roll me out of here." JJ knew that she'd eaten far too much, and a moment later a small belch escaped her. "Woah! I'm sorry! That was embarrassing."

Kristyn couldn't help but laugh. "Well, that was certainly lady-like."

She giggled some more. "Although I feel like I could match you burp for burp right about now." That made them both laugh.

They were back at Kristyn's by 2pm and dove back into the data. The spreadsheet had grown into an anal-retentive, Type-A person's dream come true: color-coded, well organized, and thorough. But it would all be for nothing if it didn't convince the US Attorney to arrest the Slayers and prosecute them to the fullest extent of the law, but they were confident. If ever there was a case that screamed for the death penalty, this was it. They had correlated 83 murders to each of the 21 games and the four Slayers. In every case they could tie the victim, the city, the date and time of death, and every other detail of the killing to the Slayer that committed the murder, including the alias they were using at the time. Kristyn even had the foresight to note which Slayer 'won' each game as well as a corresponding list of the top winners among their online players. When they were done, they had essentially boiled down hundreds of pages of documents and terabytes of data into one glorious spreadsheet.

They sat back and admired their work. "You know," said JJ, "I know that this a massive spreadsheet, but I think even Isaksen will be able to understand it."

"I'm sure he will, at least since you'll be there to walk him through it. It seems to me that the evidence we've compiled is irrefutable."

"Let's just hope that the US Attorney sees it that way. Sometimes they are totally chickenshit, not willing to take any chances if it puts their batting average at risk. They'll either refuse to prosecute or, maybe if they're feeling a little bit ballsy, go for a plea deal. It pisses me off to see all of the FBI's hard work be for nothing because the lawyers don't have the stones to step up to the plate."

"Yeah, that would suck." Kristyn realized that it was already after 7pm. "Hey, what do you think about ordering some Chinese, or maybe some Indian food, and relaxing for while? I'm hungry, which is pretty shocking considering the massive brunch I ate! And maybe we can stream a movie?"

"You sure you want me invading your space for a few more hours after you've already had to play host to me last night and all day today? I don't want to wear out my welcome," JJ added with a smile.

"Oh, you don't have to worry about that, I promise. In fact, since it will be getting late by the time we eat and watch the movie, why don't you just stay the night again? And you know we'll have to drink a couple of beers or glasses of wine with dinner, so by that point you probably shouldn't drive anyway."

"You do realize that I have to work for a living tomorrow, right?" JJ smiled.

"Not a problem. We'll just set an alarm, and I'll make us a quick breakfast before you head home. I do need to go to the office tomorrow, but I'm not on any set schedule. I mainly want to spend some time compiling my notes from the past week and start the draft of my article."

"If you're sure it's OK, and I'm not cramping your style, I'll stay. But I probably need to get up around 6am so I can get to the office by 8:30."

"No problem. Are you OK if we do another one of our special slumber parties again like we did last night? You know, you stay in my room instead of the guest room?"

Oh, lord, keep me from temptation! "That's fine, but only if you're sure you're comfortable with it. Are you feeling the same anxiety as last night? Is that why you want me there with you?"

"No, I'm much better today. It's just that it's nice knowing that someone else is close in case the nightmares come back. I can't really explain it, but....it was really nice having you there."

JJ blushed. "Yeah, I thought it was really nice, too. OK, you got me for one more night. While you order dinner, I'm going to make sure our work is backed up to the cloud and FBI servers. I don't want to take any chances."

"Good idea. I'd die if we lost all of our work after the hours we've put into it."

JJ agreed with Kristyn. There had been a lot of tough, stressful days, and there will probably be more before it's over. But there had also been a lot of great days, and nights, and tonight was shaping up to be another one. *If the sexual tension and arousal don't kill me first.*

Chapter Thirty-One

At 8am sharp JJ reached out to Isaksen's administrative assistant, Angie. She hoped that her improved relationship with the SAC would make Angie a bit more civil. No way that she expected her to be friendly, but civil was at least a start, especially on a Monday morning that followed an intense week and weekend of work.

JJ could tell, just from the tone of Angie's voice, that even 'civil' was out of the question. And that was before JJ had even identified herself. *Why do some people wake up in the morning mad at the world and intent on making everyone around them miserable?* "Good morning, Angie. I hope you had a nice weekend. I need to see SAC Isaksen this morning, as early as possible. This is in relation to the serial murder case that I've been working."

"It seems that you and everyone else wants a piece of him today, and everyone seems to think that they have the only important case in the entire Bureau. I will tell you like I've told the others, some going all the way back to last Thursday: his calendar is booked solid with staff meetings and calls with his superiors in DC. He has no available time on his calendar today, period. His earliest availability is not until late afternoon tomorrow."

It was all that JJ could do to remain outwardly calm. "I understand that he's busy, but this can't wait. This case has grown from one suspect and 20 murders to four suspects and 83 murders. I have the entire case laid-out for him and, hopefully, the US Attorney. It's imperative that we get those arrest warrants moving before the suspects flee the country, if we're not already too late."

"Did you say 83 murders?!? And you have the investigation documented and ready for the US Attorney?"

"Yes, that's exactly what I'm saying."

"Admittedly, that is unusual, to say the least. I can push out his 9:30am call and slot you in there, but the best I can do is 30 minutes."

A thousand things flew through JJ's mind, but she decided to keep it professional. "Thank you very much, Angie. I'll be there at 9:30. I appreciate your help." She had little doubt that, once seated with Isaksen and reviewing the case, he would cancel pretty much everything on his schedule for the rest of the day. This is the biggest case of his career. For that matter, it's the biggest case for the Dallas office since the JFK assassination nearly 60 years ago.

For the next 90 minutes JJ reviewed every detail of the case for the umpteenth time, determined to present the case accurately, succinctly, and confidently. She anticipated every possible question and told herself to resist the urge to embellish the facts or conflate opinions with facts. This was, without question, the most important presentation about the most important case of her life. Only with her attention to detail and ability to 'sell' the facts could they hope to secure arrest warrants and a successful prosecution. Whereas in the past she lacked confidence and self-assurance due to the way she'd been treated by Isaksen and her fellow Agents, today she was supremely confident in her case and her preparations. She'd put in the hours, and she'd put in the miles to delve into every aspect of the Slayers, their game, and the players that supported them.

As promised, at 9:30am sharp JJ presented herself at Angie's desk and was immediately led into Isaksen's office. He motioned her towards the conference table and they each took a seat. "Agent Jansen, I hope you're doing OK after what you went through last week in New York. I know that the things that you witnessed are terribly unsettling, so I hope you've had some time to decompress and relax a bit."

"Honestly, sir, I haven't. There was just too much that had to be completed by this morning, which is what I'm here to show you."

"I'm very serious here, Agent Jansen. As soon as practical, I want you to take a few days off. Maybe a whole week. You've been under a lot of pressure and a lot of stress, and the events of last week only exacerbated that. We can't afford to lose you; to say that you're key to this investigation is an understatement."

"Thank you, sir. I promise as soon as we have these guys behind bars I'll head to the beach and sleep for a week. That's a promise."

"OK, let's see what you've got. And don't worry about rushing through it; I've had Angie clear my calendar for the rest of the day."

Yes! "Perfect. Let me walk you through the case and the evidence, and then if you agree that we have enough to take to the US Attorney I'd like to meet with her to secure arrest warrants ASAP. With the resources that these guys have, they could go anywhere in the world and live quite comfortably. I'm just praying that they haven't already fled."

"I assume that you've had all of their aliases and passports flagged in case they try to travel anywhere?" Seeing JJ nod in the affirmative, he continued. "Just so you know, I've already reached out to the US Attorney and set up an appointment for us today at 3pm. I feel certain, based on the work you put together for Jamarcus Hicks, that you will have built a case that will stand up to whatever questions or concerns the US Attorney and her team might raise."

In all her years at the FBI, she'd never had a superior express that kind of admiration or confidence in her. She could feel herself blushing at the praise. "Thank you, sir. That means a lot." She shared her spreadsheet on the large wall monitor for easier viewing. "I know that this is a bit of an eyechart, so I'll try to step through this slowly and highlight the particular cells that I'm speaking to."

She opened the worksheet labeled "Mark Saxe' and started to explain. "What we have here, sir, is separate worksheets for each of the original four members of the Slayers: Jamarcus Hicks, Graham Robbins, Calvin Mitchell, and Mark Saxe. These individual worksheets detail the murders that each member is responsible for, including date, location, method of execution, and more. Then, when we move to the worksheet labeled 'Master', that gives us an all-in-one view of all 83 murders. In other words, all of the data that we saw on the individual worksheets is also included in the Master. It really puts into perspective how this group committed murders at the same time, using the same kind of weapons, but in different cities across the US, when you view it all at once like this."

"And what am I to make of the different colors that you've used on this Master sheet?"

"The colors that I used correlate to the code names that they used on their game site. That is, they didn't use one of their aliases, they were simply referred to as Mr. Blue, Yellow, Green, and Red. That's how the online players referred to them and placed their bets."

"In some cases, I see that you've added a cell with a hyperlink to associate it with the murder. What is that link for?"

"In simple terms, sir, we got really lucky. Our Lab guys were able to recover some videos that the Slayers took of the executions. Apparently, they used these video clips to document the exact time and location of the hit and then uploaded it to one of their secure servers. From the best that I can tell, these videos played a part in helping determine the winner of each game. The videos were supposed to be deleted after each game, for security purposes, but it seems that someone, maybe all of them, wanted to keep these videos as some sort of morbid souvenir."

"As if we needed more evidence that these are some sick, twisted individuals." Isaksen shook his head in disbelief. "I see another work-sheet at the bottom that says, 'Online Players'. Tell me about that."

"Yes, sir. For each of the 20 games I have listed all of the people that placed bets as well as the game winners and the amounts that they won. I think it's safe to assume that none of these winnings were ever declared on their income taxes, so if we should need it, the IRS may give us another lever to pull with these players. As you can see, there are hundreds of players that place one or more bets on every game. Thanks to the incredible work of the team in Quantico, we've been able to iden-tify more than a thousand individuals that have played the game at least once. Even though they used aliases and were playing a game on the Dark Web, our guys were able to track them all down. On the last work-sheet, which is labeled "Online Players ID" you'll find all of them listed by their screen name, their real names, and their contact information.

I'm sure that the US Attorney would love to have this information, too."

"I agree. And I'm sure they'd love to put the full-court press on some of these online players and persuade them to become witnesses for the prosecution. Your observation about the IRS being another possible lever is spot-on."

"Without a doubt, sir. That's why we went the extra mile to identify all of them and include them here with the other evidence."

They spent another two hours reviewing the details that JJ and Kristyn had compiled. Isaksen asked good probing questions, both for his own learning and in anticipation of similar questions or concerns from the US Attorney. For every question or concern JJ was able to answer with conviction; her knowledge of the case and the hours of preparation were apparent. He even asked some questions specifically to elicit her opinion, and for each question she provided thoughtful and well-reasoned answers.

Isaksen stood up and paced the room, collecting his thoughts. He circled back up to the big screen monitor and admired the detail and organization. "So let me summarize this vast treasure trove of evidence that we've reviewed, and don't hesitate to let me know if I miss anything or misinterpret any of the facts as you presented them." He hesitated a moment while gathering his thoughts. "The evidence shows the details for 83 murders, including the name of the victim, the city where they were killed, the date and time at that location, the weapon used, the name of the Slayer that did the killing, and the alias they used on that job. In addition, we have the identity of the winning online bettor for each game, how much they won, and the names and identities of every online player that has ever bet on even a single game. And finally, for at least some of the murders, you have added a link that takes us to a video clip showing the actual murders from a body camera worn by the responsible Slayer. Does that about capture it?"

"I'd say that you're right on the money, sir. No pun intended."

"You know that this is going to be the single most important piece of evidence when this goes to trial, right? You will be the government's most important witness. Expect countless hours of prep and countless days on the stand."

"Not something that I love, admittedly, but it's something that I have to do. I have to see this through to the end, and I want to see these guys fry for what they've done. Not trying to get ahead of myself, sir, but I can't imagine the US Attorney *not* wanting to pursue the death penalty for this case. If ever a case screamed out for the death penalty, this is it."

"I totally agree, Agent Jansen. And we are in Texas, so you know how our courts love to hand out death sentences," he said with a grin. "Why don't you grab some lunch and relax a bit before we meet with the US Attorney. You've earned it. I know that this morning has been intense and draining. Before you go, let me just say that this is as fine an example of police work as I've ever seen. The thoroughness and attention to detail is beyond reproach, and your interpretation of the data and the way that you pulled it all together into an unimpeachable narrative...." he trailed off. "Let's just say that I wouldn't be surprised to see this become a case study taught at Quantico for all new agents."

"Thank you, sir. I appreciate the support. Let's hope the US Attorney is as enthusiastic."

"In my experience with her, she is extremely smart and shrewd but a little too political for my taste. She tends to only get personally involved with prosecutions that she feels certain she can win. If it's a case that her office has to take but she thinks there's a chance of losing, or even just a chance of bad optics, she'll pawn it off on one of her underlings."

"I would think this case, one of the biggest serial killer cases ever, would be the kind that she'd want her name and her face attached to. Especially if she's got political ambitions. And show me a DA or US Attorney that doesn't."

"Very true, Agent Jansen. But I feel confident that once she sees the evidence that you've put together, she'd have to be a fool to turn this one down. And she's a lot of things, but a fool isn't one of them.

Chapter Thirty-Two

MONDAY, NOVEMBER 7

The office of the US Attorney, located in the Earle Cabell Federal Building on Commerce Street, is about 10 miles from the FBI Field Office, and JJ and Isaksen drove separately. JJ didn't want to press her luck; Isaksen had been thoughtful and supportive today, but she wasn't sure how they would 'gel' alone outside of the office. She had rarely seen him engage in small talk, and certainly never with her. She was envisioning a long, uncomfortable silence if they rode together, and that was not something that she wanted to subject herself to.

As the US Attorney for the Northern District of Texas, Maria Dasher was the chief federal criminal prosecutor covering 100 counties and nearly 100,000 square miles. With approximately 250 attorneys on her staff across five different divisions, she had the reputation of being very smart, very ambitious, and a total ball-buster. She relished that reputation and worked hard to ensure that people feared and respected her. Despite the fact that she was feared and handled with kid gloves, there was near universal agreement that she was a top-notch legal mind and skilled litigator.

When JJ and Isaksen were ushered into her office, they were momentarily taken aback by the sheer scale and sumptuousness of it. It was filled with stylish, high-end furnishings and decorative touches that looked like they sprung from the pages of Architectural Digest. Her only nod to tradition was obvious on one of the walls: dozens of 'vanity pictures' showing her next to countless government officials, celebrities, and even a few Dallas Cowboys. JJ was surprised that there wasn't a campaign poster for her rumored future run for the Texas State Senate.

Seated around the large steel and glass conference table, they got introductions out of the way quickly. Surprisingly, the US Attorney had insisted on being called Maria rather than by her last name or some honorific. JJ was somewhat surprised by that, expecting her to be more formal and demanding of deference.

Isaksen kicked things off. "So, Maria, as I explained earlier when we spoke, Agent Jansen has uncovered what is, unquestionably, the most prolific groups of killers we've seen in decades, maybe ever. It all started when she was assigned to the killings at DFW a few weeks ago."

"I remember that well," interjected Maria. "Special Agent Stevens from the DC office, as I recall. And the person that killed Stevens was then shot and killed by two officers from the DFW force, correct?"

"Yes, that's correct. We assumed that this was just a case of festering air rage or two guys that crossed paths and exchanged some words, but we quickly found out that that wasn't the case. Agent Jansen worked with the DFW police and quickly learned details about the suspect, the late Jamarcus Hicks, and his multiple ID's and passports. The case probably would have been closed at that point, but fortunately for us, Agent Jansen insisted that she be allowed to continue digging to find out the 'why' behind this incident. It took her a while to convince me, but thankfully I gave into her request."

"I applaud your instincts and initiative, Agent Jansen."

"Thank you, ma'am." Two people complimenting her in one day on how she performed her job? JJ assumed that she was either dreaming or having some kind of out-of-body experience.

"Why don't you run me through the evidence that you've uncovered, and we'll see about issuing those warrants. That, of course, is only step one. I'm certain that you and I will be talking a great deal as this case progresses; I'll need to be as expert as you on every aspect of the investigation and evidence. I can only imagine how much evidence there is if, as you say, it covers 83 different murders."

JJ was impressed by Dasher's steel-trap mind and quick grasp of the facts. There was not a word of criticism about the methods used – even when JJ mentioned some aspects of Kristyn's involvement – or her interpretation of the evidence. In fact, Dasher was effusive in her praise of the detail and organization of the spreadsheet and how it laid out all of the relevant details. It took less than an hour to cover the entire case and have the official blessing of the arrest warrants for Saxe, Mitchell, and Robbins.

"Agent Jansen, I must compliment you on the exemplary work that you've done, especially the way in which you've compiled the vast amounts of data into a relatively simple and straightforward exhibit. I can't tell you how much easier you've made future trial preparation; usually I have to put this kind of exhibit together to walk a judge or jury through the millions of moving pieces typical in these large Federal cases. And it's obvious that you have a mastery of this information, so I have no doubt that you'll be an excellent witness when I get you on the stand." She saw JJ squirm a bit. "Do you have a lot of trial experience, Agent Jansen?"

"No, ma'am, I don't. I mean, I certainly have some experience, but it's not in my comfort zone. But as I told SAC Isaksen, it's part of the job and something that I'm 100% committed to. I may need a bit more practice and coaching than some of the other Agents you've worked with in the past, but I will work hard to make sure that I'm as prepared as I can be."

"I will work with you, as will my team. I have every confidence that you'll do fine. She stood up, her not-so-subtle way to indicate that the meeting was over. "My office will send you the requested arrest warrants within the hour, and I hope you're able to locate these monsters and have them off the streets asap. And Agent Jansen, I'm going to have my assistant reach out to you to set another meeting for us to dig a little bit deeper into this huge list of online players and gamblers. I noticed that they were from all over the globe, so we'll want to work with Interpol and other international authorities. It would be nice to have some of these players as witnesses for the prosecution, which I assume is one of the reasons that you worked so hard to compile their names and contact information. Again, very well done."

"Thank you, ma'am. And yes, I definitely agree that some of these players, especially the ones from within the US that have large winnings and probably eager to avoid jail for tax evasion, are likely ripe for flipping to our side."

JJ and Isaksen took their leave, and both were more than satisfied with the outcome of the meeting. It's what they'd expected and hoped for, but still, they were experienced enough to never take anything for granted.

"Great job in there, Agent Jansen. You two had a good rapport, which is more than I can say for most people that have met her," Isaksen with a smile. "I trust that as soon as those warrants are in hand you will coordinate with the locals for each of the suspects?"

"Yes, sir, though I don't expect them to still be there. I feel pretty certain they're already in the wind, but I'll raise all of the alarms and alerts to get every cop in America looking for them."

"At least if they're on the run they're not focused on another game and killing even more people. That's one small blessing."

* * *

The Slayers were anything but on the run. They were on the hunt, and it was Kristyn Reynolds they were hunting. When planning a hit as part of The Murder Game, they followed Oz's requirements for the type of weapon. But this was no game, this was vengeance. For the attacks on Kristyn and JJ they planned to keep it simple by purchasing easily obtained Glock semi-automatic handguns. And, just in case a situation should arise where they need longer-range capabilities, they also purchased Remington M24's. *Plan for the worst and hope for the best.*

It was nearing 5pm and all three were in the large Escalade SUV that Calvin had rented. They had been staking out Kristyn's office all afternoon, the plan being to attack her as she pulled out of the Da;;as Morning News parking lot as she left for the day. They'd done a thorough job of reconnaissance and knew the kind of car she was driving and where she was parked. They also planned multiple exit routes for making a quick getaway regardless of traffic conditions.

The plan was simple and straightforward: Graham would stakeout the parking garage and watch for Kristyn to exit the elevator and head towards her car, then notify Calvin and Mark via the two-way radios they each carried. If the opportunity arose that Kristyn exited the elevator alone and no one else was around, Graham had the greenlight to take her out. They considered that unlikely, especially at the end of the workday, so the plan was to take the shot after she exited the garage but before she turned onto Harwood Street. They would then head straight to an old industrial area a few miles away where they'd torch the Escalade and exit the area in another rental car they had parked nearby.

"I wish we could have targeted them both at the same time. I'm worried that the FBI bitch will run for cover as soon as she hears about Reynolds, and we'll miss our opportunity." Graham was in the garage with a direct line of sight to the elevators and to Kristyn's car, but he was growing impatient and agitated.

"Yeah, that would have been ideal," agreed Mark, "but right now we don't know how long it will be before they're together at a time and place that we can do them at the same time. Unfortunately, it's going to have to be one at a time."

"Yeah, you're right, but let's make sure that we're hitting Agent Jansen tonight or tomorrow at the latest. We need to finish this and get the hell out of here. When we kill these two it's going to bring a lot of heat, for certain." Calvin said what should be obvious, even if they hadn't acknowledged it.

"Graham, is the garage crowded? It looks like a lot of people are starting to head out." Mark had noted a steady stream of cars exiting over the past 10 minutes.

"Yeah, definitely. Looks like a fucking convention down here. Probably no chance in hell that I'll catch her alone, but at least I'll see her as she heads to her car."

Graham didn't have to wait much longer. As Kristyn emerged from the crowded elevator, he heard a phone ringing and observed her reaching into her purse to answer it. He wasn't close enough to hear the conversation, especially with the noise of car engines and screeching tires throughout the garage, but it didn't matter. He just wanted to get back in position for when she exited the garage.

"Guys, the target is heading to her car now. I'm heading back your

way. I don't have a clear shot, so we stick with the original plan."
Graham was back in the SUV in less than a minute.

As Kristyn climbed into her car, she continued the conversation.
"I'm so happy for you! That's incredible news that Isaksen supported
you and the US Attorney is moving forward with the warrants. From
what I've always heard, she's not the nicest person or the easiest to get
along with."

"That's what I've heard, too, including from Isaksen. But as it turns
out, she was pretty decent, not to mention whip smart. I like her, so far,
which is a good thing since I'll be spending a lot of time with her if and
when this goes to trial."

"I'm so proud of you! I had no doubt that you'd blow them all away
with the work you've done and all of the detailed analysis."

"You mean all the work that *we've* done. Don't forget how instru-
mental you were in this whole thing. For obvious reasons I couldn't say
too much about your involvement, but I felt bad that I couldn't play
your role up more. I know that someday that will still come back to bite
me, but, oh well. That's the price we pay, right?"

"Absolutely, but if we get these guys off the street, it will be totally
worth it." Kristyn put the car in reverse and started backing out of her
space. She set the phone on the console. "I'm just leaving work, so bear
with me one second while I get my badge out for the security gate."

"No problem. I'm ready to head home, too, although I think rush
hour traffic is going to be terrible from here."

Kristyn exited the garage and turned right, and as she did, the
Escalade pulled out from the curb and into the left lane. They knew
that she would go two blocks before turning right to head towards the
highway, so that gave them a window of about 30-45 seconds to take the
shot and head for their exit route.

"So JJ, maybe tomorrow night we can meet for dinner to celebrate
this great step forward in the investigation. It definitely seems like something worth celebrating!

"That sounds like fun! God knows I could use it. I'll make the reservations and then text you the details. Would 6:30 work for you?"

"Sounds perfect." Kristyn noticed a large SUV moving quickly in
the left lane, now almost parallel to her. She thought it might be some

kind of official vehicle since black Escalades are almost ubiquitous. Watching the SUV while still trying to keep one eye on the road in front of her, she saw the passenger side windows both lower. "JJ, I think something weird is going on here...."

At that moment Graham and Mark opened fire from the front and back windows, unloading more than a dozen shots into the driver's side doors and windows of Kristyn's car.

JJ knew immediately what she was hearing, and instinctually knew who was doing it. "Kristyn," she cried. "Kristyn, oh my God, talk to me! Kristyn!"

Chapter Thirty-Three

It was hard to see through the tears as she drove as fast as she could from the Courthouse building to the office of the Dallas Morning News. It was all that she could do to hold it together and not plow right over other cars and pedestrians that got in her way. Luckily it was less than a mile from the Courthouse, so she was there within minutes. The first ambulances and police cars were already pulling up to the scene. The sound of multiple sirens promised that even more were on the way. JJ got as close to the scene as she could with the gridlock, slammed her car in Park and leapt from the car. She ran flat-out the length of the block, her feet and legs screaming in protest, but she didn't care. She would not stop, would not slow down, until she reached Kristyn. *God, please let her be alive!*

As she got closer, she could see that Kristyn's car had hit two parked cars and come to a stop just behind a third, the right front wheel up on the curve. Bullet holes were visible along both the driver's door and the one behind it, and the windows of both were completely blown out. *Not good*, she knew, and she could feel the tears turning into sobs and her fears turning into panic. She held her FBI badge above her head and yelled, "FBI, Special Agent Jansen. Let me through!"

The two Dallas officers who were first on the scene waved her forward and before they could say a word, or before the EMT's were even aware that she was approaching the car, she yelled, "Is she alive? Please tell me she's alive!"

The EMT that appeared to be in charge said, "She's alive, Agent Jansen, but we need to get her to the hospital, stat. She's got two gunshot wounds, hopefully not life-threatening. We're going to take her to Baylor Medical Center as soon as we're sure that she's stable and OK to transport."

Without waiting for permission, JJ moved right into the middle of the fray and reached into the car to touch Kristyn. She got no objections from the EMT's or cops. "Kristyn! Can you hear me?"

"JJ?" Kristyn answered weakly. "You're here? How?" She talked slowly, painfully, with her eyes still tightly clenched in pain.

"I heard the gunshots when we were on the phone, and then when our connection dropped, I knew that something bad had happened." She started crying harder. "I was so afraid that I'd get here and find that they'd killed you. I could never live with that, never live without you in my life. Hang on, we're going to get you to the hospital and make sure that you're taken care of."

"It was them, JJ. I couldn't see their faces, but I know it was them." The pain was evident in her voice. "I saw the two passenger side windows lowering and then I saw their guns. I hit the brakes and ducked down as low as I could hoping that they'd miss me. But they shot so many times. So many times." Kristyn fell silent, mercifully losing consciousness and escaping the pain, at least for the time being.

"Agent Jansen, can you step back please so we can get her ready for transport. We want to make sure that there are no injuries from the crash itself in addition to the gunshot wounds. Do you want to ride with us in the ambulance or just meet us there?"

"I'll follow you. You guys probably have your hands full without having another passenger in the back with you. Please keep her alive, no matter what it takes."

As often happens, the driver's door and the passenger door were completely jammed, so they had to use a hydraulic tool to pry one open before they could begin to extract Kristyn from the car. Once inside, it took the better part of 10 minutes for the EMT's to staunch the bleeding from the two bullet wounds and stabilize Kristyn's head. Being extra cautious, they placed her on a backboard as they extracted her from the car and then carefully placed her in the back of the emergency vehicle. As the ambulance began to pull away, the driver yelled to JJ, "Agent Jansen, we'll see you at Baylor Medical, and we've already communicated all of her information and vitals to the ER doctors there. She'll be in great hands."

JJ waved and said a silent *thank you* to them, her voice once again failing her as she fought back the tears. Turning to the two first responding officers, she asked, "Have you spoken to anyone who witnessed the shooting and able to share any useful information?"

"Let me reach out to the other officers on scene, Agent Jansen. Most of them arrived after us and we've been here with the victim the whole time. Give me just a moment." He reached for his mobile radio. "This is Officer Kyle Daugherty, Central Division. Anybody on the scene of the shooting on Commerce spoken to any witnesses?"

"Daugherty, this is Sergeant Ward. I've got two witnesses here who stated that they saw the whole thing and are willing to share what they know. One of them claims to have video of part of the attack, though it might not be very high quality. I'll walk the witnesses over to you."

"Thanks, Sergeant Ward. I'm here with FBI Special Agent Jansen, and I know that she would love to hear what the witnesses have to say before she heads to the hospital to be with the victim."

Minutes later JJ was interviewing the two witnesses and reviewing the video clip that one of them had recorded on her iPhone. Their stories were consistent, which is surprisingly rare, even in broad daylight. Both agreed that the shooters were in a black Escalade and that they pulled beside Kristyn and fired at least a dozen shots. Neither of them saw the shooters from their angle but they did see the big SUV turn the corner a block up and head towards the Interstate. *No surprise there.* The cops would follow-up and try to track it down, but in all likelihood, they'd ditch the car and either burn or bleach-bomb it. Still, JJ thanked the witnesses profusely for their help; many people refuse to get involved for any number of reasons.

As the two witnesses stepped away, JJ approached Sergeant Ward. "Sergeant, I'm not sure who you need to talk to, but it's imperative that we assign protection for the victim, Kristyn Reynolds, 24/7 while she's in the hospital. I can't go into all the details but suffice it to say that these guys will try again. She's a reporter that has been covering a large serial murder ring, and in addition to helping uncover the story, she's also going to be a key witness for the prosecution."

"You really think she's still in danger? This was a pretty brazen attack, broad daylight with dozens of witnesses. Maybe they high tailed it out of here?"

"Normally you'd be right, but not these guys. They traveled to Dallas specifically to kill her, and once they find out that she survived, they're not going to stop." She didn't bother to mention that the Slayers had traveled to Dallas to kill her, too. No need to muddy the waters with that detail.

"I'll reach out to my Lieutenant and Captain now, Agent Jansen, and then get back to you ASAP. Based on what you're telling me, I don't think it will be a problem."

JJ thanked him and then made one last but very important call. "This is Jansen, sir. I'm not sure if you heard about the shooting that happened about an hour ago near the Dallas Morning News building?"

"I just heard about it a few moments ago, but none of the details."

"Sir, the victim was Kristyn Reynolds...."

"The reporter that you've been working with on this case, the one that traveled to New York with you?" He didn't have to add, *you mean the reporter that has put both of our careers in jeopardy by participating in an official FBI investigation?* But it was implied.

"Yessir. I'm on my way to Baylor Medical Center now, she's already been transported."

"So, she is still alive then?"

"Yes, but suffering from at least two gunshot wounds. I won't know the extent of her injuries until I get down there, but the EMT's believed that both were survivable. As far as how long she'll be hospitalized, whether or not she'll suffer any long-term or permanent effects, etc., it's too soon to know. I hope to know more soon."

"Have we been able to positively identify the Slayers as the shooters?"

"There is no doubt, sir, but to answer your question, no, we don't have that proof in hand yet. We don't have any witnesses that can identify them, but we know for certain that there were three of them, so that aligns. It's still early in the investigation and the Dallas PD is canvasing witnesses and every business on the block to see if any security cameras recorded the attack. But like I said, there is zero doubt. It's them."

"And once they find out that she survived, they're going to try again. And let's not forget one other minor detail: they're going to be looking for you, too."

"No doubt, sir. But right now, my concern is ensuring that Kristyn is safe. I've asked a Sergeant with Dallas PD to work with his leadership to put a 24/7 guard on Kristyn's hospital room. I think he'll get it done, but a call from you to their Chief might help grease the skids."

"I'll take care of that immediately. And Agent Jansen, be sure to keep your head on a swivel. I'm going to have a couple of our Agents shadowing you; not so close as to get in your way, but close enough to provide backup if and when needed." Before JJ could object, he added, "And no argument on this point. It's non-negotiable. I am not going to lose an agent, especially one that is so important to this case."

JJ knew there was no use in arguing, especially since any argument would be half-assed at best. Having someone watching her back was actually a welcome 'intrusion'. "Thank you, sir. No argument here."

It took JJ almost 20 minutes to get out of the gridlocked area and travel the mile to the hospital. After presenting her FBI credentials she was immediately escorted to the room where Kristyn was being treated. JJ was surprised to see that she was awake and somewhat alert, and at the sight of seeing her friend alive, the tears once again started flowing despite her best effort at remaining professional and stoic.

"Hey, you," said Kristyn groggily. Obviously, they'd administered something for the pain, but not so much as to make her incoherent.

"Hi," sniffed JJ through the tears. "How do you feel?"

"Probably not up to dinner and dancing tonight, if that's what you're asking. But these doctors seem to think that I'll live. I'm not sure that I'll want to when these narcotics start wearing off, though." She tried to smile, but even that caused more pain.

"Maybe we'll put it off until tomorrow night, unless you're still milking your injuries for sympathy at that point," JJ replied with a grin.

JJ signaled the doctor to step outside of the room, and when they were alone, she introduced herself and showed her FBI credentials. "Dr. Evangeline, what can you tell me about her injuries?"

"She was shot twice, once in the left shoulder and one other shot that grazed the left side of her head. She's very lucky, to say the least. The scalp wound is essentially superficial; because it's a head wound it bleeds a lot, so that made it look a lot worse than it was. We were able to close that wound with just a few stitches. You probably wouldn't even notice except that we had to shave her head around the area, but in the scheme of things, hair is just an inconvenience. It grows back."

"That's great news. But I'm guessing that the shoulder wound is a bit more concerning?"

"It is, though again, I'd say that she was extremely lucky. The bullet was a through and through and doesn't appear to have done too much damage. We're going to take her down for some scans to be certain, but my preliminary guess is no permanent damage. She will need physical therapy, for sure, but it could have been much, much worse. Shoulder wounds can be pretty devastating because of all the bones and muscles and nerves in that area. I'd say that she's one very lucky lady, all things considered."

"Thank you, Doctor. I also want to make you aware that she's going to have around the clock protection while she's here." She saw the concerned look on his face. "It's just a precaution, but we can't be certain that the people that tried to kill her won't try again. We want to have a strong show of force to deter them from trying. I'm sure you can understand that."

"Yes, very understandable. I'll inform the hospital administration and our security staff right away. This won't be the first time that we've dealt with this kind of thing, and in this crazy world I'm sure it won't be the last."

"Thanks, Doctor. One last question: any idea how long she'll need to remain here in the hospital? Or let me put it another way: How soon do you think we can safely take her out of here and care for her at home? I'm talking about professional care, not just a friend watching over her. We'd make sure that she had around the clock care, so think of it as FBI protection with a staff of doctors and nurses thrown in, too."

Dr. Evangeline thought about it for a moment. "I can't say with any certainty until we've completed all of the scans, including an MRI, as well as blood work. We'll also be keeping an eye out for infection. But if I had to guess, I'd say that if everything looks as good and stable as we hope, she might be able to be discharged in 36-48 hours provided that you've arranged for the professional care that you mentioned. Normally we'd be looking at one week, at least, and even then, we'd be releasing her directly into the care of the physical therapy team."

"Fair enough. The sooner we're out of here, the better for everyone, including the hospital staff and patients. I'll start working on the home health care arrangements and keep you and her attending physician in the loop. Do you expect she'll be here in the ER much longer or moved up to a room?"

"We're going to take her for a preliminary CT scan now, but the MRI will have to wait until tomorrow. I expect that she'll be in her room in about an hour."

"OK, I'm going to run home to grab a few things and then I'll be back. The police protection details are already onsite, so I'll brief them before I go. One request, though, Dr. Evangeline. For everyone's protection, we need your administration to ensure that her real name is not used on any records, especially her room number. As far as this hospital is concerned, 'Kristyn Reynolds' doesn't exist. The only person that needs to know the alias you create is me. The people who are after her have world class computer skills, so they are going to dig into every possible system and record to find her. We can't let that happen."

Dr. Evangeline's head was spinning. Crazed killers coming for his patient? Police all over the hospital property, including outside of her room? FBI demanding that the patient be registered under an alias and then discharged into protective custody, *supposedly* with qualified medical staff to oversee her care? He couldn't even begin to fathom the administrative nightmare and hospital liability that this would cause. Maybe his mom was right when she said that he should have become a lawyer instead of an ER specialist; better hours, more money, and in most cases, less chance of being caught in the crossfire.

Chapter Thirty-Four

"With all due respect, sir, not just 'no', but hell no! I will not run and hide, especially not while Kristyn is lying in the hospital. I didn't object, hell, I even welcomed, your idea about having some agents shadow me and watch my back, but I'll be damned if I'm going to be sidelined and relegated to protective custody." JJ was practically breathing fire at the very idea of being forced into hiding.

"It would only be for a short time, until we bring these three men into custody....." Isaksen couldn't even get his complete thought out before JJ jumped in again.

"You don't know when we'll apprehend these guys, or even if we'll ever catch them! I won't be pushed aside, and I'm not trusting anyone to protect Kristyn and oversee her recovery from the attack."

"Agent Jansen, we all want nothing more than to ensure Ms. Reynold's safety and recovery. And contrary to what you may believe, we do have other competent Agents in the Bureau."

"I'm not arguing that point, sir. I know that we have a lot of great Agents, and any one of them would go to the ends of the earth to protect a witness. But one thing I can do that no other Agent can is get inside their heads, predict how and where and when they might strike next."

"Like you predicted the attempted hit on Ms. Reynolds yesterday?"

Ouch. That was cold and cruel, intentionally hurtful. Worst of all, it was also true, and she knew it. "Yes, I was wrong, and it almost cost Kristyn her life. I thought that they'd be heading out of the country after the debacle with Dr. Miller. They certainly have the means and the tools to travel anywhere in the world, so I expected them to head to their non-extraditable country of choice."

"My point exactly...."

"But it's a mistake that won't happen again!" She tried to keep her voice under control, but it was a losing battle. "The word is already out there that Kristyn survived the attack, so they're either going to attack her while she's in the hospital or when she's discharged and back home, regardless of the protective ring we put around her."

"And what does your gut tell you about the most likely scenario?"

"I think they'll attack while she's in the hospital, and for one simple reason: they don't know how long it'll be before she's released, and they can't afford to delay their escape forever. The longer they stay here targeting Kristyn, and me, for that matter, the more they risk being caught. They're already pushing their luck, and they know it."

"In this instance, I believe that your gut instinct is correct." He grew silent for a moment. "OK, for the moment, we will refrain from ordering you into protective custody. I assume that you wish to continue staying with Ms. Reynolds while she's in the hospital as the last line of defense?" He said that as a weak attempt at humor, but that didn't make his point any less valid.

"Yessir. I have a rollaway bed setup in her room, and I'm heavily armed. Plus, there are two Dallas PD officers stationed outside the door at all times, and roaming patrols around the grounds."

"And I still have your 'shadows' there in the hospital, too, and trying to remain unobtrusive. I trust that you know Special Agents McAuslin and Narcum on sight, correct? They're scheduled to be onsite today until 6pm, at which time they'll be replaced by McNine and Sisneros."

"I know all four of them, sir. And I won't hesitate to contact them if I see anything of concern."

"While you're watching over Ms. Reynold's, give some thought to how they're going to attack. As you said, you know these guys and their methods and their proclivities better than anyone. How will they attempt to get past the police that are spread all over the premises? How about the two officers stationed at the door to her room?"

"I'll get right on that, sir. I asked the hospital to take precautions, like erasing all references to her in the hospital systems, but to be honest, I don't think that will slow these guys down for long. Based on what I've learned about them, I think it's a virtual certainty that they've seen through that ruse and accessed all the information they need to plan their attack."

"Along with your thoughts about what they'll do and how they'll do it, consider our tactical options. How do we turn the tables on them while keeping Ms. Reynolds, as well as the hundreds of other patients and staff, safe and out of harm's way?"

After hanging up with Isaksen, she replayed his last points over and over in her head. She closed her eyes and concentrated on the seemingly infinite possibilities, playing a mental chess game of move/counter move. She tried to think strategically: how would she plan the attack if she were in their shoes? Which variables could she control, and which ones not? Which behaviors from their past killings might serve them well in this instance? She grabbed a yellow legal pad from her bag and started jotting notes and random thoughts.

1. *Trying to hide Kristyn's name wouldn't stop them. Any female admitted yesterday with gunshot wounds, regardless of the name on the records, they would assume to be Kristyn.*
2. *They know the extent of Kristyn's injuries and whether or not she's ambulatory*
3. *They know her room number, and they know the layout of the hospital*
4. *They may not know exactly how many police are onsite, but they've identified most of them and noted their movements and shift changes*
5. *They would split-up and enter the hospital through multiple entrances, raising the odds of at least one of them making it to Kristyn's room.*

6. *Pretending to be visitors would not work to get them close to Kristyn's room. They would disguise themselves as doctors, orderlies, or other members of the hospital staff. They might assault or kill staff for their uniforms and their ID's, or they might arrive at the hospital in scrubs or similar medical garb.*
7. *They will use semi-automatic pistols, their weapon of choice whenever possible. Rifles are too hard to conceal, and using a knife is too risky with such a large police presence*
8. *They probably don't know that I'm here with Kristyn*
9. *In past games there has never been collateral damage. Will they be reluctant to open fire in crowded areas?*
10. *They will have multiple getaway vehicles parked near multiple exits*
11. *They will be in constant communication via some type of two-way wireless*

JJ grabbed her phone and called Isaksen. "Sir, I think I know how they're going to attack, and I have a plan for how to stop them."

* * *

"Alright, it's time to go. They should be starting the shift changes now for most of the nursing staff, so let's take advantage of the situation. Remember to keep your head down and no looking up towards the security cameras. And it's critical that we not be recognized, so check one last time that your disguises totally mask your identity. It may not be good enough to beat facial recognition software, but that's not a concern here. We just need to change our appearance enough to go unnoticed by the cops that are crawling all over the place." Mark was not in favor of a second attempt on Kristyn's life, at least not now and not here in the hospital. Too many people, too large of a building, too many cops, and too many things beyond their control. It went against the disciplined process and standard operating procedures that had served them so well and kept them totally off the radar since the inception of The Murder Game.

"And don't forget that we're wearing medical technician scrubs, not doctor or nurse scrubs, so don't get sucked into a medical conversation with anyone. If a hospital visitor asks you something about patient care or any other medical topic, shut it down right away and keep moving." Calvin had been adamant about avoiding scrubs that were color-coded to identify them as doctors, nurses, or surgeons.

"I'm in place," announced Graham. "I'm parked on the street about 100 yards from the west entrance. I just dropped a 'pin' in the app so you guys can see where I parked, and you guys should do the same. And remember the rally points that we designated in case we get separated. No man left behind, right?"

"Right. And I've just re-confirmed that the target is in room 624 in the North wing. Let's rally on Six North near the public restrooms in T-10 minutes. Let's go!" Mark exited his car and started towards the main entrance. He was wound as tight as a banjo string, and while he usually loved every minute of their games, this was different. This was madness.

It actually took closer to 15 minutes for all three of them to reach the 6th floor. Part of their cover required them having a piece of medical equipment, like a Portable X-Ray machine, that they were transporting to a patient's room. That proved to be only a slight delay since they had acquired detailed blueprints of the hospital during their online searches, and disabling the RFID trackers on each machine was child's play.

"I'm going to move down the hall closer to her room to get a better view. I expect that there will be at least one cop guarding her room, plus there are bound to be any number of hospital staff and visitors around. I'll radio you with a status update and then we can finalize our plans." Calvin was running on nervous energy and was anxious to get this done.

As he got close to room 624, Calvin noted that there were two cops guarding the door, so that made things a bit more difficult. Luckily there were not a lot of other people in the hallways since it was between traditional visiting hours, so just the occasional nurse moving between rooms. He keyed his microphone and spoke to Mark and Graham. "We have two cops on her door, one on each side of the doorway. Not a lot of other people around. I think it's definitely a 'go'."

"How do you want to handle the two cops standing guard?" asked Mark.

"I'm going to walk down the hall past her room, and Graham, you start walking this direction. When I see you approaching, I'll slowly start heading back towards you, and when we're in range we'll hit them with the Tasers and cuff them. Mark, we just need you to watch our six and make sure no one sneaks up on us."

"Roger, I'm moving now," said Graham. Turning to Mark, he added, "This is it. Let's make it count!"

The two officers took notice of the men approaching from opposite directions, but they didn't look anything like the pictures they'd seen of the suspects. These guys had different hair styles and color, different facial hair, and even different facial features. Cops may be trained to be observant and naturally suspicious, especially in a stressful situation like this where there was an eminent threat, but the two officers took no extra notice. As Graham and Calvin closed to within about 10 feet, they raised the Tasers that they had concealed and fired, delivering 50,000 volts that immediately incapacitated them. It took only seconds to put the flex-cuffs on them and race into the room. They were ready to fire multiple shots into Kristyn's prone body when the realization hit them: the 'person' in the bed wasn't a person at all, just a CPR dummy. They'd been duped!

"Fuck! Let's get out, now!" shouted Calvin.

As they rushed to the door, they heard several shouts of, "Drop your weapons and get down on the floor! Do it now!"

JJ was two doors down and across the hall, and her FBI 'shadow' team were directly across from her and barely 20 feet from Calvin and Graham. Other police and FBI were closing in from other ends of the hall, weapons out and at the ready.

Calvin and Graham had no intention of giving themselves up and spending the rest of their lives in prison sitting on Death Row. They came out firing, sending JJ and the others diving for cover. Despite their own firepower and experience, Calvin and Graham stood no chance. JJ had planned the tactical response to perfection, and they were caught in a pincer with shooters in front of them, behind them, and cutting off the intersecting hallways.

The gunfire was intense, but blessedly short-lived and tightly focused. It was over in less than 10 seconds. Several police officers were down, but fortunately none with life-threatening injuries. The assassins' bodies were riddled with bullet holes, each suffering at least 8 wounds, any number of which could have been fatal. Blood covered the floor and was splattered on the walls, and those walls and doorways were littered with bullet holes. Blessedly, no patients were injured for one very simple reason: there were no patients in the rooms on this wing of the sixth floor. JJ had worked with a very reluctant and frightened hospital administration to ensure that all patients were secretly moved as far away as possible just in case the worst happened. And it had. Even Kristyn, the target of the assassination attempt, was in a totally different part of the hospital, surrounded by a half-dozen officers.

When the shooting stopped, JJ ran quickly to verify that Calvin and Graham were dead, and then she quickly directed others to aid the two officers that had been Tasered as well as those that had been injured in the gunfight. "Listen-up everybody! We've got two of the killers down and accounted for, but we need to find the third one. He's here some-where and we cannot allow him to escape. Get on your radios and secure this building ASAP. Nobody in, nobody out. And it goes without saying, consider this man armed and dangerous. Take no chances: if he engages you, in any way, do not hesitate to take him down!"

By the time the calls went out to secure the building Mark Saxe was almost to the lobby. When he had seen the heavily armed and armored teams closing in on Calvin and Graham, he knew that there was no saving them, no hope for their escape. He could have taken out some of them from his position, but they had an overwhelming advantage in sheer numbers and firepower. It wouldn't have changed the outcome; he just would have been one more body added to the heap. Dying along-side his friends, his brothers, is how he'd always expected, even romanti-cized, about going out. But if there was any chance of getting the vengeance that they'd sought, he'd have to stay alive.

He walked as calmly as the high-stakes situation allowed, always keeping one hand on his gun in case he was recognized and forced to fight his way out of here. His car was parked clear across the other side of the hospital, too long of a walk under the circumstances. The place was already crawling with cops, and more were on the way, evidenced by the many sirens he heard. He needed to get out of here before they put

219

up a blockade of the hospital parking lots and the surrounding streets. If that happened, then all bets were off.

Mark was brilliant and capable of making quick decisions, though his usual practice involved more observation, analysis, and strategic planning. *Plan the work and work the plan* were words he lived by, but this time his back was up against the wall. If he was going to get out of this alive, he had to improvise. He moved quickly through the parking lot, hoping against hope to find a car with the doors unlocked and the keys in the ignition. *Like that ever happens.* Just a couple of rows away he spotted a 20-something girl alone and heading towards a car. She appeared to be a nurse, based on the color of her scrubs, and she was crying and nearly hysterical. Surely that was from the chaos going on inside, and while he had no desire to make her bad day even worse, this was do-or-die time. *It's her or me.* Coming up behind her, he put a hand over her mouth and the gun to her head. She got the message. And because she got the message, she was allowed to live. Unconscious, but alive.

Seconds later he was exiting the parking lot and heading away from town. Despite his penchant for killing and his tough exterior, he's the kind of guy that feels things deeply. And he was really feeling the pain of losing his two best friends, especially so soon after losing Jamarcus. He couldn't stop himself from crying, practically blubbering. It was all he could do to continue driving, but he knew that his life depended on it. As did his shot at avenging his three friends.

Chapter Thirty-Five

TUESDAY, NOVEMBER 8

W ithin minutes the police were swarming all over the hospital and the surrounding areas, and the onsite commander immediately issued an All-Points Bulletin (APB) for Mark Saxe. He ordered that a perimeter be established five blocks in all directions in the hopes of trapping him, but it was too late. Saxe was already more than a half mile away.

Police searching the parking lot found the injured nurse and she was able to provide details about her car and how Saxe had surprised her and stolen it at gunpoint. She was assisted into the ER where it took several stitches to close the head wound from where he'd struck her with the gun. Doctors told her to consider herself lucky and insisted that she be admitted for at least one night for observation. The police standing outside of the room heard that comment from the doctors and gave each other a knowing look: *she's lucky that he chose to let her live.*

Every news channel in the Dallas area, and pretty much around the state, ran 'Breaking News' alerts about the shooting at Baylor University Medical Center, and within the hour they were able to show the pictures and share the names of all three of the Slayers. The pictures came from the investigative work done by JJ and Kristyn, including their college pictures and those taken from Jamarcus Hicks' home. It would still take hours, at least, for law enforcement to find any record of their movements via security cameras in the area. Not knowing the aliases that they'd been using, where they were staying, the cars they were driving, and myriad other details made things frustratingly slow. The media's insatiable appetite for information and sound bites to fill the maw of the 24-hour news cycle only exacerbated the frustration.

After coordinating with other law enforcement personnel for the better part of an hour, JJ excused herself to take care of something that she considered just as important: checking-in on Kristyn and filling her in on all that had happened. She knew that Kristyn would already be aware that something major had transpired since alarms went off throughout the hospital, and it was all over TV and social media. Surely the police guarding her room provided her at least some information, as well. Knowing that Kristyn was such a news junky, JJ had no doubt that she was likely glued to the story and already working on a first-person account for the paper, albeit with just one good arm.

Walking into Kristyn's room, which was down two floors and in a totally different wing from her 'official' room that had been in the hospital's systems, she showed her badge and credentials to the two Dallas PD officers. "You're looking much better today," she said upon seeing Kristyn sitting up in the bed and looking more alert and in less pain. "How are you feeling?"

"Not bad, considering, though I'd kill for a shower right about now. The pain has been manageable with the wonderful drugs they're giving me. I think I'd be hurting, though, without them."

"Oh, you would, without a doubt. But the pain will lessen over the coming days, but until then we'll make sure that you have what you need to stay ahead of the pain."

"So enough of my little problems. Tell me what happened."

JJ gave her the details on what had transpired upstairs, including the fact that Calvin Mitchell and Graham Robbins had both been killed. When asked, she didn't sugarcoat the fact that Mark Saxe had gotten away and was still at large. "He must have gotten out just ahead of us locking the place down, and he assaulted a nurse in the parking lot and stole her car. Thankfully, he didn't kill her, just left her unconscious. It could have been a lot worse, especially if he'd chosen to take her hostage."

"Yeah, I'd say that she was very lucky. And you said that the police and FBI that were part of the assault team upstairs are all OK? Even the ones who were guarding my decoy room?"

"Yes, those guys will recover. They were Tasered and had flex-cuffs on their wrists, but they'll be OK. A couple of our men were hit by gunfire but none of the injuries are too serious. Except for Saxe getting away, it was almost a perfect operation."

"Thanks to you! It's like you're not an FBI agent, you're some kind of brilliant military strategist," she giggled. "The female General Patton."

They both laughed at that. "Hardly," said JJ. "But at this point we'll take whatever win we can get. Now it's just all-hands-on-deck to track down and apprehend Saxe."

"What are you thinking?"

"First thing I want to do is get you the hell out of here. I'm going to talk to Isaksen in a bit and arrange for you to be transferred to an FBI safe house. We've got a full medical staff that will be onsite 24/7, so you should get the same level of care that you get here. He and I have already set this up and gotten all of the approvals, so now we just need to get moving."

"Are you worried that Saxe would make a third attempt? Gee, does he hate me that much?"

"Yes, and yes," JJ said with a smile. "But that's only because he doesn't know how wonderful you are." They both laughed at that. "Seriously, I don't think he'll try anything here in the hospital again, but you can never be 100% certain. I think the smart move for us is to transfer you to the safe house – and it's a *nice* house, too, so you'll be more than comfortable – until this is over. When the doctors think that you're ready, we can even have you start PT."

"Will you be there, too?"

JJ felt her heart flutter and her face blush. "Absolutely. You don't think I'd dump you off on a bunch of strangers, do you?" JJ couldn't think of anyplace she'd rather be.

* * *

"Agent Jansen, that is totally out of the question. I cannot have you dangling yourself out there as bait and putting your life at risk, not to mention everyone else that might happen to be in your proximity if Saxe targets you."

"But sir...."

"I admire your willingness to do whatever it takes to finish this, but I do not want to lose you in the process."

"I appreciate that sir, but let's be realistic. The only thing keeping Saxe from leaving the country is his need for revenge; truthfully, I'm not even certain that's enough to keep him around. The smart move would be for him to be on the first flight out of here. As we discussed before, he's got the money and the means to do it."

"And you think that he's so hellbent on revenge that he'd risk his freedom, maybe even his life, to come after you and Ms. Reynolds again?"

"I do. Luckily, Kristyn should be out of harm's way at the safe house. If time were no issue, Saxe would hang around until he eventually tracked her down, but time is not on his side. Every cop in America is looking for him, and his name and face are on every newscast and in every newspaper. He knows that time is running out. If he's going to get any revenge, he's going to have to target me."

"Is that supposed to make me feel better?"

"No, sir, but at least we know where to focus our efforts. If I'm out on the street he's going to come for me. I just think we need to help him out a little."

"What do you mean?"

"I think we tell him where I'm going to be. Or, more accurately, we place a story in the media that gives a time and location where I'll be tomorrow that he won't be able to resist. He knows that it's probably his last shot. No pun intended."

"So, you're basically inviting him to try to kill you. That's insane! You know there's no way we can protect you from every eventuality. It's damn near impossible to stop a determined assassin, especially ones with his skills."

"I don't disagree, sir, but if we don't do something to flush him out then he's gone forever. I'll take every possible precaution, but as you said, it's not without risk. But it's a risk that I'm willing to take if it will end this and keep anyone else from getting killed."

"Have you already given thought to the location of this crazy plan? Hopefully somewhere with minimal risk to the general public."

"I have. And it's a location that shouldn't raise any suspicions: the Cabell Federal Building. As part of our story to the media I'll be going there to meet with the US Attorney regarding this case. If I don't miss my guess, he'll see that as an excellent location for taking me out with a long-range shot from one of the surrounding buildings."

"You're certifiable! A hidden sniper perched *somewhere*, and God only knows *where*, with you in the crosshairs? He could easily kill you and dozens of others, including the other Agents there to protect you."

"I don't think that will happen, sir. I've studied these guys backwards and forwards, and the one thing that stands out, the one thing that actually surprised the hell out of me, is that Saxe and the others *never* killed anyone that wasn't a target in their game. Zero collateral damage. Even today, when he stole that car from the hospital parking lot, he could have easily killed that nurse but chose not to. The Slayers considered themselves above that whole shoot-em-up, gangbanger shit, like they had some kind of moral compass that kept them from killing anyone other than the intended target. I think he'll take a shot at me but not at anyone else, at least not until we corner him. We can make sure to leave my protection detail spread out enough that a skilled sniper can easily avoid hitting anyone else."

"To your point, they could have easily killed those two officers stationed outside of Ms. Reynold's decoy room, but instead they just put them out of commission while they executed their plans."

"Exactly, sir, and it wasn't until Mitchell and Robbins were trapped, when it became about their survival, that they started shooting up the place. But before today? Never a shot fired at anyone other than the target."

Isaksen thought this through for a moment. "I don't like this, not one bit, but I have to concur with your assessment of the situation. If Saxe is smart, and we know he is, he's going to flee sooner than later. And if we don't catch him now, who's to say that he won't start this dreaded game up again, recruit some new assassins to replace his friends?

We know that he's going to flee the country, but with his fake ID's and passports and huge cash reserves, he might easily make his way back here someday. We need to end this. Now."

"Let's get on a call with the HRT commander and Dallas PD to create a plan, and then let's loop-in your Communications Director to get my trip to the Courthouse placed with the press ASAP. We need to make the evening news for the local stations, and we need to make sure it gets out to the national news and cable networks, as well. And make sure she gets it splashed across whatever social media outlets we use, too. We have to cover all bases to maximize our chances of Saxe seeing it."

Am I crazy? Obsessing over the details of a message that might get me killed? And why now, when for the first time in years I feel like I have something in my life worth living for?

Chapter Thirty-Six
WEDNESDAY, NOVEMBER 9

Why did the scenes from *'Dead Man Walking'* keep running through her mind when she needed to be focused? As the convoy of vehicles got closer to the Court-house, the scenes with Susan Sarandon in her nun's habit and Sean Penn slowly entering the death chamber to receive his lethal injection were on a continuous loop in JJ's head. She kept trying to go to her 'happy place' mentally, but it was no use. As soon as she'd focus on a beautiful beach in the Caribbean the visage of Sean Penn grimacing as the needle plunged into his arm would come screaming back.

More than one person had told her that she was crazy, maybe even suicidal. She couldn't fault anyone for thinking that; she was putting herself out there as a target, a sacrifice, to catch a deranged killer. The fact that most of the people questioning her sanity didn't give two shits about her and had, for years, heaped abuse and ridicule on her, didn't bother her at all. She'd kept the details of her plan hidden from Kristyn so as not to worry her, but just the fact that she was still working the case had Kristyn pleading with her to let others handle it. *Don't be a hero. Don't be a martyr. Don't sacrifice yourself for these people that won't remember your name a week later. Fuck Saxe. Let him go, let him be some-body else's problem. You've done enough by shutting them down and ridding the world of three of these monsters.* She didn't blame Kristyn, though. What she said had the ring of truth to it: *You could be signing your own death warrant.* The hardest part for JJ was knowing the pain that she was causing Kristyn, and her fear that she'd never live long enough to see her again.

Isaksen and the HRT commander had tried to insist on a real show of strength by rolling up with a convoy of SUV's and all manner of police cruisers, motorcycles, and even an armored personnel carrier. JJ pushed back, hard, telling them that the last thing they needed was to look like a Presidential motorcade.

"If we show up with that many vehicles and people, we'll look like we're invading a small country! That might scare him off, and that's the last thing we want. We need him to show his hand, and for that we need him to think that the risk is worth the reward. If there's one thing I've learned about Saxe, it's that he's *willing* to die but has no death wish."

"So how many vehicles do you want for your escort?" asked the HRT commander.

"Two, at the most. The others should stay hidden, and keep in mind that he's going to be perched somewhere up high, either on top of a building or an upper floor of a nearby building, so he'll have a view covering several blocks in all directions. If he sees all those cars and SUV's he's liable to call the whole thing off and flee."

"Anything else?" asked Isaksen.

"Just one more thing. We made it a point to put the word out there about where I'd be going and the time I'd be going there. Obviously, he'll have to be in place before we arrive, so we need to be there and setup even earlier. Probably 2-3 hours earlier, just to be safe. Maybe we'll get lucky and see him moving into place and we can arrest him then without incident, but I doubt it. He's too skilled. But at least we don't want him seeing us moving our teams into place. If he sees that, we'll probably lose him forever."

She turned to Isaksen, who was riding beside her in the backseat of the Suburban. "Sir, I really wish that you'd reconsider and stay in the car instead of being part of the escort team. You really don't need to put yourself out on the front line like that; you have plenty of Agents and Dallas PD here to do that. You have a family to consider, not to mention an entire Field Office that counts on your leadership."

"Nonsense. I would never ask my Agents to take a risk that I'm not willing to take myself, and this has to be the riskiest thing that I've ever seen an Agent do. At least willingly." Then he added with a smile, "And I've had agents go deep undercover for a year or more with narco-terrorists."

"You do have your vest on, though, correct? There's crazy, and then there's stupid-crazy. Being out there without a vest definitely crosses the line to stupid-crazy."

"Yes, I have my vest on, and like the rest of your detail, I'll put on the rest of the body armor as we approach. I just wish that you were wearing full body armor, too."

"No, I can't do that. I'll just have to have faith in my vest and the fact that he's an excellent shot. He'll go for a shot center mass, especially with the breeze we have today. A head shot would be too risky, too much chance of missing me altogether and giving my protection detail time to get me clear. At least I opted for the Level IV vest that has more stopping power. It's so big I had to borrow a shirt to fit over it. Better safe than sorry, though, because this won't be a little cap pistol. This will be a hunting or sniper rifle with a helluva lot of stopping power."

The two Suburbans pulled up to the curb near the Federal building. The protective detail followed their standard protocol, stepping from the vehicle in a show of force and being highly observant. Several members of the detail took a quick sweep of the perimeter, ensuring that everything was clear. They looked for anyone trying to conceal themselves, any potential explosive devices, and any obvious signs of someone watching them from adjacent buildings. They fully expected that Saxe was nearby and watching them, so going through the motions was mostly theater. Once they were sure that the immediate area was clear, several of them went back to the second Suburban and opened the rear door for JJ to step out.

The procession started walking towards the Courthouse steps. As JJ had instructed, the protection detail was close but not too close to her. She wanted Saxe to have a clear shot and, even more importantly, she didn't want any of the others to be hit. Her eyes continued to scan the surrounding area. After conferring with the FBI's HRT and, especially, their long-range snipers, they had identified the most likely locations where Saxe might setup to ensure that the sun was at his back, he'd have the best angles, and have the best chance of making a quick and clean getaway. To make sure that they had the best chance of determining where shots came from, HRT had even deployed their ShotSpotter gunshot detection technology to zero-in on the exact location in seconds rather than the minutes, or even hours, it used to take with the traditional methods of measurements and triangulation. To say that the FBI and Dallas PD were using every trick and tool at their disposal was an understatement.

They were still about 100 yards from the building, but as JJ and the HRT team had calculated, Saxe couldn't wait much longer or else the angle would be too steep from the surrounding buildings. JJ fought the urge to slow down or in any way change her pattern. The primal part of her brain was telling her to turn and run and find cover, but she fought against it. The rational side of her brain told her it would not matter anyway. Saxe could and would shoot her if she tried to run away, and he might unload on the others just because she pissed him off.

Through her earwig she heard, "I think I saw movement, to your left, next building over. On the roof. Perimeter teams start moving that direction but keep out of sight."

Now she couldn't help but tense up. She tried to continue scanning the area in a natural motion, but she did not detect any movement on the indicated roof. As she focused back to see how much further to the Courthouse steps, she felt a crushing blow to her chest before she heard the crack of the rifle. Before she even started falling she felt a second crushing blow that hit just inches away from the first shot. The last thing she heard was the sound of the second shot as she hit the ground.

"Shooter! Shooter. On the roof, left of the Courthouse! All teams, converge!"

There were no more shots, indicating that Saxe was focused on escaping the area. Isaksen and two other agents bent down and scooped-up JJ and rushed her to cover behind the lead Suburban. Even before Isaksen set her down he was screaming into his radio for an ambulance, and fortunately several of them were staged less than a minute away.

The EMT's arrived as Isaksen and the others were working to remove her vest. They had felt for, and thankfully found, a pulse, but she remained unconscious. The EMT's took over and gently removed the vest, pleased to see that there was no blood from a bullet penetrating the vest. The vest had done its job, and both bullets were still wedged there.

JJ slowly came to, and she groaned loudly. This was as bad as any pain she'd experienced since her car accident, the kind of pain that she'd hoped to never feel again. Despite her high pain threshold and stoic nature, the intensity had her fighting back tears.

"Stay down and still, Agent Jansen," the paramedic instructed her. "I need to check you out before we move you. Once we load you in the wagon for the trip to the ER, I'll see about giving you a little something for the pain and discomfort if you still need it."

JJ groaned. "If I still need it? You think the pain is going to stop in the next few minutes? Ow! Ow." She groaned again as she moved ever so slightly trying to get comfortable.

"We'll move you as soon as the Commander gives us the all-clear. I'll have our guys move the ambulance up as close as possible so we can be ready to go."

Luckily it was a short wait. The radio chatter was constant as law enforcement was swarming over the area and the adjacent buildings, but no more shots were heard.

"Let's get her loaded up and go while it's clear. Anyone need to accompany Agent Jansen in the ambulance?"

"I'll go. She's my Agent." Isaksen was stepping up.

Chapter Thirty-Seven

The area around the Cabell Federal Building looked like a war zone. Police and FBI vehicles ringed the blocks surrounding the building, and several helicopters flew overhead. Inside the Federal building and other office buildings in the area, people were sheltered in place behind locked doors, cowering like frightened school children during an active shooter incident. Even the prisoners that had been brought from the jail for court hearings were taken to secure locations to shelter in place.

No one had yet sighted Mark Saxe, and their frustration was mounting. They knew which building that he'd fired from and had already secured the site, but they still didn't know if he'd made it out of the building before they'd stormed it or if he was still hiding somewhere within. The laborious and dangerous task of clearing the building floor by floor and room by room had already begun, with dozens of police working in teams to check each room and each person's ID. The bigger question was what to do with the people once they'd cleared the offices where they were sheltering: should they keep them there, move them to some other space inside the building, or try to escort them out of the building to safety?

On the streets around the Federal Building, local TV news vans screeched to the curb and the camera operators and on-air reporters scrambled for the best spot to record and report on the chaos. To add to the chaos, TV news helicopters started flying into the same area where the police helicopters were searching for Saxe. Finally, they were warned off in the strongest possible terms by the Dallas PD, with one police chopper pilot threatening to 'shoot them out of the sky' if they didn't leave the area immediately. While it may have been an idle threat made in the heat of the moment, it got the point across.

The Dallas PD SWAT commander had assumed control of the situation, along with the FBI HRT commander. They worked well together, no egos getting in the way of doing what needed to be done. They were in constant communication with their teams, and both were growing increasingly frustrated with the lack of progress. Their biggest worry was that he had somehow managed to escape the building before the police had entered, but they didn't understand how that could be possible. He had been on the roof, they had shutoff the elevators within 60 seconds, and they'd had teams flooding every stairwell and fire escape. The teams were down to the last few offices, and the large team that was covering the sub-basement and boiler room areas had also come up empty.

"Who is this guy, Harry Fucking Houdini?" groused Captain Dylan Hughes, the leader of the Dallas SWAT team. "We've checked almost every person in the building at this point, from top to bottom, even including the building's leasing agent and security guards, and we got squat."

A call came over the radio. "This is Lieutenant Sanders, DPD. I'm on the roof of the building where the shooter was staged, and I may have found something. You might want to check this out, and I think you should send up the forensic team, as well."

"We're on our way, Lieutenant. Be there in less than five."

Everyone assembled on the roof, and Lieutenant Sanders gave the commanders an update. "We didn't find any brass, not that we expected to, but we identified the exact spot where he took the shot from. He shot from this wall over here that's looking down on the target's approach, and we found a few scratches that probably came from his rifle; forensics can confirm that. Normally I'd expect to see more scratches, but he must have put a towel or something under the stock to minimize the scratching."

"But what can you tell us about where he's gone?" Hughes didn't want to be a hard-ass, but he was out of patience. "That's our main concern at this point."

"Yessir, let's all step over here," as he pointed to a wall that was on the opposite side of the roof from the Federal Building. "Look here. See these scratches? Three of them in kind of a triangle? I think it's possible that he used some sort of high-tech, lightweight grappling hook and a long-ass rope to rappel down the side of this building. See how it's well blocked from the street, and the building next door? No windows on this side. He could have gotten out of here without being seen during all of the commotion."

"He would have had to make his exit immediately after firing the two shots, probably before we'd even zeroed in on him." Hughes thought this through. "It's about 60 feet to the ground, give or take, so if he rappelled using military issue or professional mountain climbing gear, he could have dropped that distance in a couple of seconds. Damn."

"But where's the hook? And the rope? How could he have recovered those?" One of the dozen or more officers asked the question that was surely on everyone's mind.

"I don't have a clue. It might be something custom that we've never seen before." The HRT commander was baffled as well, but it didn't really matter *how* he escaped at this point, the only thing that mattered was finding him.

"OK, Forensics team, go over this entire roof with a fine-tooth comb, paying particular attention to the areas where we think he rested his rifle and where this grappling hook, or whatever the hell it was, was attached." Hughes turned to the others. "Let's get back downstairs and see if the other teams have finished clearing the building. We need to pray that Saxe is still somewhere within the area that we've cordoned off and we can keep him hemmed in."

* * *

While the assembled law enforcement teams continued their search and finished clearing the building where he'd taken the shot, Saxe was slowly making his way towards the outer reaches of the police perimeter. So far, he'd had no problems even after being stopped two different times and asked to produce his ID. With each step his confidence grew, but he knew that he wasn't out of the woods yet. There were still cops everywhere, and they were literally collapsing the perimeter one step at a time. He had no doubt that he'd be stopped again, maybe multiple times, and he wasn't certain that they'd let anyone move beyond the established perimeter.

Saxe kept putting distance between himself and the small army of law enforcement people still blanketing the Federal building and the other buildings in the vicinity. He tried to walk quickly, as most of the crowd was doing, but not so fast as to call attention to himself or have anyone give him a second glance. For the hundredth time he reached into his jacket pocket to check that his Glock was still there, and it gave him comfort, much like an old friend, to know that it was there and ready to go. A part of him wished that he could hide the sniper rifle underneath his jacket, but he knew that wasn't practical. He'd already disassembled it and concealed it in the backpack slung over his right shoulder. The backpack was heavy, but he couldn't even consider leaving it behind: it would be a treasure-trove of evidence for the police if they found it.

Head down. Just a few more blocks to go and you'll be home free!

* * *

"Captain Hughes, come in. This is CSI Fredericks."

"This is Hughes. What have you got, Fredericks?"

"It may be nothing, sir, but I thought you'd want to know about anything we find, any possibilities that we come up with. Would you have time to come up here and we can show you?"

"Yes, I'll be right up there."

Captain Hughes didn't waste any time. If the Forensics team had uncovered any kind of lead, he needed to know about it and act on it immediately. Every minute that passed put Saxe that much closer to freedom. When he got to the roof an officer pointed him to CSI Fredericks. "Let's see what you have."

"It's actually three things, sir. Any one of them may not be that conclusive, but the three of them together makes me think that it's more than a coincidence." Fredericks led Hughes over to the wall where Saxe had setup his shot. "We found this just a couple of feet away, and it may have no relation or bearing on our case, but we bagged it anyway." She held the bag up for Hughes to see.

"Is that what I think it is? A fake fingernail?"

"Yessir, it's one of those cheap, drugstore press-on types. Available pretty much anywhere."

"OK, what else do you have?"

"We recovered one hair fiber, or should I say one artificial human hair. It's from a synthetic wig, a pretty cheap one if I had to guess. The color appears to be auburn, as best I can tell. No way to know if this is the entire piece of hair until we look at it under the microscope, but if we assume it is, I'd say that we're looking at a wig that's shaped into a short bob. Although there's no way of telling if the wig was styled differently by the person wearing it, but I'm pretty sure that it at least started as an auburn bob cut."

Hughes was confused at first, but now he was feeling more and more confident that what Forensics had uncovered were important leads. "You said that you had a third thing. Can you show me, please."

"Walk this way sir." Fredericks guided him towards the other side of the roof in the direction of where they expected Saxe had rappelled down. "Look here, sir. I know it's not easy to see with this type of roof material, but I've identified a few footprints that could belong to our shooter. They certainly appear to have been moving in the direction of the assumed exit point. What I noticed was that the shoe that made those prints was approximately a size 11 or 12. What's unusual, though, is the contour of the shoe, the shape of the print itself."

"What do you mean?"

"I can't be 100% certain, sir, but my best guess is that these prints were made by a women's shoe rather than a men's shoe. It would have to be a size 13 or 14, maybe bigger, which is highly unusual. There's a very small percentage of women that wear shoes that large. It probably wouldn't be hard to track down recent sales in the area."

Hughes had heard enough. He quickly pulled up information on his tablet to confirm his suspicions, and it took only a moment to find what he was searching for. Immediately grabbing his radio, he announced loudly, "All units! All units! This is Captain Hughes. I have new information related to the suspect, Mark Saxe. We are not, I repeat, *not*, looking for someone that looks like the man in the pictures that you've been provided. We believe that Saxe is disguised as a female, approximately 6' tall, with reddish or auburn hair, possibly styled into a short bob-type cut. No report on what he may be wearing. We need to focus on the women inside our perimeter, ASAP."

"Are we cleared to approach if we spot him, sir?" asked a Dallas PD officer who was working a couple of blocks away.

"I want everyone out there to pair-up. No lone rangers, and don't even think about approaching Saxe alone. No exceptions. You spot him, you call it in. Consider this man armed and extremely dangerous. He's got nothing to lose, so that makes him especially dangerous. And remember that there are hundreds of civilians around right now, so we need to do everything possible to end this peacefully."

* * *

Saxe didn't know what had changed, but he noticed a change in the movements of the cops still swarming the streets. Their heads were in constant motion scanning the crowds, looking like a bunch of meerkats checking out the surroundings before emerging from their dens. They were now moving in groups of two or three, and they had drastically picked up the pace. He continued to do everything he could to blend-in with the crowd, but slowly took the Glock from his pocket and concealed it under his jacket. Then he heard something that made him freeze in his tracks.

"Mark Saxe! Stop and put your hands up, now! This is the Dallas Police Department, and we will not tell you again. Hands up and turn around slowly and face me."

Saxe did not move a muscle. He looked around slowly and saw what appeared to be half of the Dallas PD and FBI closing in on him.

"I said, put your hands up, now. If you move, we will shoot you. That's a promise."

More and more cops closed in, each one of them poised to shoot. In addition to dozens of officers with Glock semi-automatics, there were some with shotguns, others with MP-5's. *I wonder if they had this much firepower when they were taking down Osama bin Laden?*

He continued to stall, continued to consider his options. It didn't take long to recognize that he was out of options. *Not the way I hoped to go out, but if this is it, then let's make it epic!. I am not going to go to prison, and I am not going to let them kill me on their schedule with a goddamn lethal injection.* "Sorry, officer, but I don't like the idea of going to jail, sitting for years on death row. That's not how I choose to live what's left of my life."

"It's either give yourself up and be placed under arrest, or we'll drop you where you stand. The decision is yours."

"I think there's a third option, which I much prefer." He quickly lifted his Glock and, before the police could react, stuck the barrel in his mouth and pulled the trigger. The cops were stunned at how quickly he had moved and how he had not hesitated for a single instant. The result was grotesque, even for the hardened law enforcement personnel that were on the scene.

"This is Captain Hughes. Report!"

"Captain Hughes, this is Corporal Pennington. We spotted Saxe just moments after your report about his disguise. Several of us confronted him, and we called for backup. We tried to get him to give himself up, but he pulled a gun from his jacket and shot himself. He stuck the gun in his mouth, sir. Not a pretty scene."

"Did he make any move to fire at you or the other officers, Corporal?"

"No, sir. We were all expecting him to try that, a 'suicide by cop' kind of play. He saw the number of cops and guns surrounding him. He was looking for a way out, plain and simple."

Hughes breathed a sigh of relief. *Good riddance, motherfucker.*

Chapter Thirty-Eight

S he wasn't sure what the doctors had given her for the pain, but it was definitely working. That is, until she moved ever so slightly and then she was reminded that she'd just taken too large bullets to the body. JJ was beyond grateful for the stopping power of the Level IV vest that she'd been wearing. If she'd been wearing her usual 'day-to-day' Kevlar vest, she might not be here to complain about the discomfort. She was also more than a little bit thankful for Mark Saxe's skill as a shooter, as morbid as that sounded; if he'd been off by a bit and shot her anywhere except in the vest, she might be dead. Even a shot to the shoulder or the leg could prove fatal with the weapon he'd used. She'd heard stories before of people being shot in the leg with such weapons, usually in a war setting, and dying from shock and blood loss.

The doctors in the ER had taken numerous X-rays and determined that she had two broken ribs but no internal organ damage, which was fortunate. When they helped her remove her clothes and put on one of those atrocious hospital gowns, it was immediately evident where the bullets had struck. There were large bruises, each bigger than her fist, where each had hit. The doctors told her that they'd like to keep her overnight for observation, but she declined.

Isaksen stayed with her, as promised, and at one point his tough façade cracked enough to show some compassion. He was very solicitous and helped her move about the area, making sure that he carried her belongings, giving her a proverbial shoulder to lean on. "I'll give you a ride home, and I'll make arrangements to have your car transported back to your house."

JJ thanked him and he stepped out of her room so that the nurse could help her finish getting dressed. She heard his phone ring as he moved out into the hall.

Isaksen came back about five minutes later and sat down in the exam room. He looked at JJ and the sense of relief on his face was evident. "It's over, Agent Jansen. Saxe is dead."

JJ knew that the politically correct response was to mourn, or at least pretend to mourn, the death of any suspect. In the case of Saxe, or any of the Slayers, for that matter, she couldn't muster the strength to fake that emotion. "May he rot in hell. What about our guys, sir, and the others there tracking him? Was anyone else hurt?"

"No, great news on that front. They confronted him out on the street, and rather than trying to shoot his way out and escape, he took his own life. Stuck a gun in his mouth and pulled the trigger."

"I'd much rather have him kill himself than risk him killing our people or innocent bystanders. I'm just glad that it's over, either way."

"I can't argue with that."

JJ pondered things for a moment. "There are a couple of things still bugging me, though. Like how the hell did he get down off that roof? And how did he get away from the immediate area when there were literally dozens of police and FBI looking for him? It's not like we didn't have relatively recent pictures of him that we'd shared with the teams."

"I asked the same questions. Everybody was still shaking their heads about his exit from the roof. The investigators and forensic teams found evidence that he'd used some sort of grappling hook as an anchor to rappel to down the back of the building, but they had no idea how he recovered the grappling and the rope until about 15 minutes ago. They found it all stashed in a dumpster not far from the building, and when they checked it out, they realized it was like nothing they'd ever seen."

"How so?"

"Apparently this must be something that he made himself. Too bad he didn't patent it and launch this as a business because every police department, army, and mountaineering team would love to have it. From what I've been told, the grappling is controlled by a computer or app that sends an instruction to collapse its arms and fold in on itself, that way it can be pulled loose from where it was set. Plus, instead of the usual heavy rope that we see, which is bulky and takes up space, Saxe actually used parachute cord that is a fraction of the diameter of conventional rope but just as strong."

"Wow. Ingenious. Too bad that killing people was his hobby instead of mechanical engineering."

"As far as how he managed to walk away, the forensics team uncovered the clues, and in record time. Bottom line, Saxe did a masterful job of disguising himself, well beyond the usual fake beard and glasses. He was dressed as a woman: wig, full makeup, women's clothes and shoes, the whole nine yards. Fooled everyone."

"The pictures that I've seen of Saxe, and the information that I have on him, makes me think that he'd be a.....*how should I say this?*....less than attractive female and one who would stand out due to his height and build."

"I get your point. Especially since early reports are indicating that he'd been stopped by at least two different officers for ID checks in that area and no suspicions were raised. If the forensics team hadn't uncovered a couple of key pieces of evidence so quickly, namely, a fake fingernail and a strand of synthetic hair, he probably would have waltzed right out of the cordoned area and out of the country."

"I say it all the time because we'd be lost without them: God bless our Forensics and Labs teams."

"Let's get out of here, Agent Jansen. The doctors say you're cleared to go, so let me give you a ride home."

"Thanks, sir, but if you don't mind, I'd rather head over to the safe house where we took Kristyn yesterday so I can check on her, help take care of her."

"That's not a problem. And I hope this goes without saying: I expect you to take the next few days off, take time to heal and recover. There is nothing we need that can't wait until Monday, and that includes the US Attorney. She'll probably be trying to figure out what to do with this case and how she can use it to advance her career, but I'll handle anything that comes up until you're back."

* * *

JJ could barely contain her excitement at seeing Kristyn when she arrived at the safe house. Only the stiffness and shooting pain that came with every breath and every movement kept that excitement in check. Still, entering the house and seeing Kristyn up and moving about, albeit slowly, made her heart leap. "Hey you! Looking like you're ready to roll out of here and run a marathon! How are you feeling?"

"Oh my God, I am so glad to see you! The guards told me what happened, especially the part about Saxe killing himself and putting this nightmare behind us."

Kristyn moved as fast as she could to greet JJ and embrace her, though they quickly realized how that wasn't going to work too well. There was a symphony of 'ouch' and 'easy' and general groans from both. Kristyn couldn't lift her injured arm to hug JJ nearly as tight as she wanted, and even the half-hugs that Kristyn was giving her send jolts of pain through JJ. The pain brought them both to the verge of tears, but at the same time they broke down in laughter at the absurdity.

"I don't know if we're more '*Golden Girls*' or '*Three Stooges*'," laughed JJ. "But we definitely sound old with all these grunts and groans."

"I cannot believe what happened to you. Thank God that no one here told me what you were planning until it was all over and they knew that you were OK. If I'd have known what you were scheming, I would have been down there trying to drag you away. That was the most insane thing I've ever heard of. But once again you pull this great 'General Patton' strategic move, and it all works out. You're like a cat with nine lives."

"It was no big deal, really. Just putting myself out there and counting on this psycho killer to be an excellent shot and taking two large caliber slugs to the vest. Just another day in the life of your average FBI agent." She smiled, hoping to lighten the mood.

"Well, then thank goodness for Saxe's excellent marksmanship!

We'll have to drink to that. Maybe not tonight – we probably have enough narcotics in our system to knock down a wildebeest – but soon."

"Since the threat is over, we can get you out of here in the morning and back home to your place. We can still have the medical staff there to take care of you and oversee your recovery."

Kristyn looked a little shy, a little sheepish. "Would you be able to stay there while we both recover? I'd really love to have you there."

JJ's pulse raced and her heart fluttered, and it wasn't from the pain or the narcotics. "I'd like that a lot."

They sat beside each other on the couch, a bit of an awkward silence. Finally, Kristyn reached over and lightly touched JJ's hand, then slowly intertwined their fingers. "I don't want to be forward, or make this awkward or uncomfortable, but I feel like there's been kinda this vibe between us for a while. Is it something that I'm imagining, or do you feel it, too?"

JJ was never shy, but she was a bit caught off-guard and tongue tied. "Honestly, yes, I have felt this attraction, but I never wanted to push it on you. The feelings caught me by surprise, because other than one sorta bi-curious relationship in college, I've never been attracted to another woman. I was trying to sort out my feelings but didn't want to make you uncomfortable or have you run for the hills. I really love and value our friendship as well as our working relationship. I didn't want to mess that up by clumsily hitting on you."

Kristyn smiled. "Why would you assume that you'd scare me off or send me running for the hills?"

"Because you were married and obviously into men, not women. Plus, you said that you'd been hurt when your ex-husband came out as gay and ended your marriage. I didn't want to put you through a similar situation."

Now Kristyn smiled even more broadly. "My poor, clueless FBI agent. It's easy to see why you're an Agent and not a profiler," she said with a giggle. "The truth is, I've dated at least as many women in my life as I have men, including a few long-term relationships. And while I married a man, my preference has always been women. And now that I've finally met a woman that is beautiful and fierce and independent and brilliant, I know that I want her to be a part of my life. So, in simple terms, I'm feeling the same vibe."

JJ was practically a puddle. "Oh, I wish we weren't in so much pain right now, for both of us, because I'd throw my arms around you and never let you go."

"Well, then at least there's one good bit of news: my lips aren't hurting, so you can start there."

JJ leaned in and tenderly, tentatively kissed Kristyn. She sat back and looked at Kristyn with half-glazed eyes. Seeing nothing but a smile and not even a hint of resistance, she kissed her again, this time more passionately.

"Ow, ow, ow," moaned JJ. "Sorry, it just hurts as I lean over."

"Want to stop?" Kristyn added seductively.

"Oh, God no! Not ever. But I think we better find a better place, and a better position, if we're going to continue down this road. I want to make you scream," giggled JJ, "but I don't want it to be because of the pain in your shoulder."

"And I don't want your screams to be from those bruised ribs, either" responded Kristyn as she leaned in for another kiss.

For the first time in what felt like forever, JJ was in bliss. *Oh, this is the start of something great!*

Epilogue

L ife was a whirlwind. Even though they were both recovering from their injuries, JJ and Kristyn made virtual appearances on morning news shows, the 24-hour news networks, and every local TV news channel. There were interview requests from the New York Times, the Washington Post, and dozens of other top papers around the country, plus top magazines like Time, Vanity Fair, and more. Luckily Kristyn was experienced in this world, so she knew how to handle the requests and prioritize them. JJ would have been lost and overwhelmed without her.

Even as she was recovering, Kristyn continued writing her first-hand account of what many had dubbed, 'The Crime of the Century'. She believed that the moniker was a bit premature, being barely 22 years into the century, but the media's penchant for hyperbole was in high gear. There was talk about her series being a shoo-in for a Pulitzer Prize, and a lot of that talk, and the less-than subtle promotion, was from her own paper.

It wasn't long before Hollywood came calling. And calling. Kristyn and JJ had received offers of representation from at least 30 talent agents, and after conducting interviews with their top picks, they settled on a high-powered, well-connected agent from the famed Creative Artists Agency (CAA). The agent, Diana Glassman, was soon negotiating with a number of production companies that were practically begging to bring the story to the big screen. They offered money – *lots of it* – and producer credits, screenplay credits, basically anything that would put their offer over the top, to get Kristyn and JJ to sign with them.

They finally struck a deal, the kind of deal that guarantees a large amount of money upfront and a backend percentage based on the movie's revenues and profits. Their agent oversaw every aspect of the negotiations and contract language to ensure that they wouldn't get the usual Hollywood treatment, aka 'Hollywood creative accounting'. Once the deal was inked, Kristyn submitted her resignation to the Dallas Morning News so that she could dedicate herself to working on the screenplay. The paper reluctantly accepted her resignation, but they admitted that they were going to continue to lobby, however quietly, for her to win the Pulitzer. They wanted it badly for their own bragging rights and, more importantly, to help drive increased advertising revenue.

* * *

For the first few weeks after the case ended, JJ was the toast of the FBI. She was celebrated and feted by the Dallas Field Office and HQ in Washington, DC, including a ceremony in DC where she and SAC Isaksen were presented with multiple awards. Isaksen was awarded the FBI Medal for Meritorious Achievement. JJ was recognized with more awards than any Agent had ever received, including the same Meritorious Achievement Award and the FBI Star, the Bureau's equivalent of the military's Purple Heart. She also received the FBI Shield of Bravery and the FBI Medal of Valor in recognition of the personal danger and risks she had faced bringing the case to closure.

JJ appreciated the awards and recognition, but she was waiting for the other shoe to drop. Experience had taught her that at the FBI, as in life, it always does. Heroes are built-up only to be torn down again. She'd seen it countless times in politics, in Hollywood, and even in the FBI's own little world. She expected her 'honeymoon', her new popularity, to come crashing down at some point. And that point came even sooner than expected.

The official notification of the investigation by the Office of Professional Responsibility (OPR) arrived just a week after the Hollywood deal was signed. Coincidence? She wasn't sure. Regardless, the official reason stated for the inquiry was not a surprise: involving a civilian in an official FBI investigation without authorization. It also specified Kristyn's unauthorized access to FBI files and information, endangering her life and increasing the government's liability, and allowing a civilian to be seriously injured during an unauthorized operation.

When the day came for her to appear at the OPR hearing, she surprised the panel by showing up alone. She'd been offered representation and could have even brought in her own lawyers, but she didn't bother. She already knew that the case was just a formality and that their decision was a foregone conclusion.

JJ answered each question posed to her, and when asked to provide her version of various events during the investigation, she was honest and direct. At no time did she apologize for her actions, and she had no plans to. Every step in the investigation and the results of every action were part of the official record, a record that she had created and knew inside out. But this wasn't about results, this was about finding justification for putting her out to pasture. By the time the session had ended the first day, it was clear to her that they were hoping to pressure her into resigning.

The second day of the inquiry things took an unexpected turn, catching JJ completely off-guard. Soon after the questioning started, the focus seemed to change from JJ's handling of the case to Isaksen's supervision of her investigation. *They're trying to force him out, too.* Isaksen was sitting in the room, as he had been during every minute of the inquiry, and he tried to remain impassive. The shocked look on his face betrayed him.

"So, Special Agent Jansen, at what point did you notify SAC Isaksen about your involvement of Kristyn Reynolds in your investigation," asked the OPR investigator.

"At no point did I inform SAC Isaksen of Ms. Reynold's involvement."

The panel looked surprised, as did Isaksen. That was not the answer that they were expecting, and like all good lawyers, they only asked questions for which they already knew the answer. "Let me rephrase my question, Special Agent Jansen: during the long course of your investigation, what did SAC Isaksen know about Ms. Reynolds' involvement and when did he learn of it?"

"As I stated, at no time did I inform SAC Isaksen of Ms. Reynolds' involvement in the investigation. He only learned of her direct involvement after the fact."

"If we are to believe what you stated, how did you explain the fact that Ms. Reynolds was targeted by this group and almost killed?"

"It was a very simple explanation. She's an award-winning investigative journalist who'd been digging into this case as part of her job, including accompanying me to New York, without SAC Isaksen's knowledge, to investigate Jamarcus Hicks' past. The late Dr. Richard Miller, a co-conspirator in the case, notified the Slayers of our interests and questions, which ultimately lead to her becoming a target."

"Let me shift the inquiry a bit. Isn't it true that you have been treated harshly by SAC Isaksen over the years? When I say harsh, I am referring to things like excessive ridicule, being passed over for assignments and promotions, and basically being ignored by him and other Agents in the Dallas Field Office?"

"I would not say that, no. I admit that we didn't have a warm and friendly relationship, but I believe that my past challenges, most notably my two stints in rehab and my own reluctance to establish relationships within the office, was the primary reason that I didn't live up to my potential. I had a lot of self-doubts and ongoing mental and behavioral challenges. I consider myself very fortunate that SAC Isaksen continued to have me as a member of his team rather than forcing me out."

The members of the OPR panel were looking for a reason to sacrifice Isaksen, but JJ was having no parts of it. She could have easily thrown him under the bus, but she wasn't about to do that. She was out, of that she had no doubt. But she wasn't taking anyone else down with her. Not her style.

They took a break for lunch, and once they were clear of the panel's prying ears, Isaksen stopped JJ in the hall. "Agent Jansen, you really don't need to fall on your sword for me. They've made it clear that they want to force me out, too. Bring in a new SAC and start fresh."

"You don't deserve that, sir. You lead one of the highest rated Field Offices in the entire Bureau, and now that this case is closed, your profile is higher than ever."

"High profiles can be a double-edged sword. Some people naively thought that I'd end up with a promotion out of all this, maybe end up in DC, but I didn't share their opinion. Still, it was inevitable that some of my decisions would come back to bite me; I was aware of Ms. Reynolds' involvement, but I chose to turn a blind eye because of the results that you were delivering. I knew better, I just chose to let you continue with what was obviously working."

After the lunch break the meeting – which felt more like the Nuremberg Trials – was about to resume when JJ stood up and asked to address the panel in private. The members of the panel looked at each other, unsure what to make of this unusual request. Finally, the Chairman of the panel spoke. "Special Agent Jansen, that is highly unusual, to say the least, as the work of this panel becomes part of the official record, both for your protection and ours. Are you certain about this?"

"Yessir, I'm certain. And it will only take a few short minutes, and then we can have everyone rejoin us and go back on the record."

"OK, I'll allow it. Can we please have everyone leave the room please, other than Special Agent Jansen and the members of the panel." Seeing a questioning look from the assistant that had been diligently taking the transcripts, he nodded her way and said, "That includes you as well, Cathy. We'll call you back in when we're ready to go back on the record."

JJ nodded at SAC Isaksen as he headed towards the door and gave him a reassuring smile. "Thank you for indulging me, Mr. Chairman. This should only take a few moments."

"Of course, Special Agent Jansen. Please proceed."

"Let me start by saying that I respect the work that this panel is doing and believe that you are approaching it fairly and without malice. I take no issue with the questions that you've asked me or my treatment by anyone associated with this inquiry. I have admitted, several times and on the record, that I went outside the bounds of our rules and practices. Fortunately, everything turned out OK and the case was successfully closed, but the ends do not justify the means. For that reason, I am submitting my resignation, effectively immediately, to help put these events behind us and not cause harm or embarrassment to the Bureau or any of its people."

"But Special Agent Jansen...."

"Allow me to finish, if I may. You have my word that there will be no legal challenges or ramifications from my resignation. I am leaving voluntarily rather than being forced out, so I think we can agree that the Bureau is in the clear on that point."

"OK, but..."

"But let me add one caveat: my offer is contingent on SAC Isaksen being absolved of all responsibility in this matter and any disciplinary action that this panel may be planning or leaning towards must be dropped in its entirety." JJ looked at each member of the panel and saw their shocked expressions. "As I have stated during this hearing, I alone am responsible for the events and the bending of the rules during this investigation, *not* SAC Isaksen. He has been nothing but supportive of the work I've done on this case, but I repaid that trust and support by keeping him in the dark."

"Is that all?"

"No, just one more point. And on this point, I want to be clear. *Crystal clear.* I don't want there to be any misunderstanding or misinterpretation on anybody's part." She looked around the room to make sure that she had everyone's full attention. "If members of this panel, or anyone else in the Bureau, for that matter, decides to drag SAC Isaksen into this and discipline him in any way, then I will bring a lawsuit against the Bureau for the years of abuse, ridicule, and gender bias that I have suffered. I can promise you that I have everything well documented, as does my therapist, and you can be assured that I'll release her from confidentiality to testify on my behalf. If I'm forced to bring such a lawsuit, my attorneys will make certain that it's for tens of millions of dollars and my publicist and agent will ensure that it's front-page news. I don't think this is the kind of publicity the Bureaus wants or deserves. I love the FBI, and the last thing I want is to do it harm. But I mean what I say: this witch hunt that you seem to have for SAC Isaksen ends today."

JJ took her seat. "Unless you think that we need to discuss this further, or unless you want to reject my offer outright, I think we can let the others back in the room now and make our announcements. Do you agree?" She was almost daring them to argue or try to push back on the plan, but no one did.

Everyone filed back into the room, most looking confused and apprehensive about what was happening. Isaksen looked at JJ as he walked past, and she once again gave him just a small, self-satisfied smile.

The panel announced that they were concluding their business and that JJ had voluntarily tendered her resignation, effective immediately. They made a point of stating that she was not being dismissed and that they were not recommending any disciplinary or punitive actions against her. They further commended her on successfully closing this very complex case in such a short time frame. "Usually, cases of this complexity and breadth take months, if not years to solve," said the Chairman. "The fact that Special Agent Jansen closed this case within weeks is highly commendable, as evidenced by the many awards that the Bureau has bestowed upon her."

"We further find that there is no probable cause to believe that SAC Isaksen has any culpability regarding the issues raised during our inquiry. Special Agent Jansen has stated, repeatedly, that she knowingly kept Kristyn Reynold's involvement a secret from SAC Isaksen, her immediate supervisor, because she knew that he would not approve. It is the decision of this panel, and our recommendation to the Director of the FBI, that this matter be closed concurrent with Special Agent Jansen's resignation. Further, neither SAC Isaksen nor any other member of the Dallas Field Office will face disciplinary action in this matter. We consider this matter closed."

It was done. She was done. After all the years she'd invested in her education and training, and all the years invested in being an Agent, she thought she'd feel more of a loss. She thought she'd be devastated, an emotional wreck. Being an FBI agent was her life, her identity. Or at least it was. Now she was ready to move on. She was ready to start a new life, and she was excited about the prospect of doing it with Kristyn by her side. They would work on the screenplay together, and with their agent's help, create their own production company to help bring the movie to the screen and, not coincidentally, get a bigger piece of the pie. Maybe she'd even find a way to keep one toe in the water, so to speak, and work on some interesting criminal cases. Maybe some cold cases. And always with Kristyn by her side.

As JJ made her way out of the building, for perhaps the last time, SAC Isaksen called her name and moved quickly to talk to her before she could leave. "Agent Jansen, I'm not sure exactly what you told the panel, but you did not have to take a bullet for me in there. I don't want you to sacrifice your career to protect me."

"Look, they needed a sacrificial lamb, and I was happy to offer myself up. I've got other irons in the fire and I'm ready to start a new chapter in my life. This gave me the push I needed to do that. I just didn't see any reason why they should drag you down with me."

He looked on the verge of tears. "I can't thank you enough for protecting me. After my behavior over the years, it's more than I deserve. I can't begin to tell you how much I regret how I've acted and mistreated you, and how I've turned a blind eye to other's mistreatment of you. I'm ashamed."

"Water under the bridge, sir. Don't give it another thought. I'm just glad you're going to remain in charge of the Field Office and able to finish out your career with the Bureau in Dallas. Besides, depending on my next adventures, it may be good for me to have friends in high places at the FBI." She smiled widely. "Investigating crimes is part of my DNA."

"Well, I would consider it a privilege to be considered your friend. A friend for life. And I'll try to be a better friend than I was a boss, and that's a promise."

"Deal. But one thing needs to change: if we're going to be friends, I'm not 'Special Agent Jansen'. Call me JJ."

Acknowledgments

To Fred Zalupski, who always goes above and beyond when reading my early drafts and provides constructive, accurate, and extremely valuable feedback. In this case, 4 ½ pages of handwritten notes! *The Murder Game* is a better book thanks to his contributions.

To Jeff Dirgo, my old friend and coworker, who helped me tremendously by reading and providing feedback from very early in this project. His suggestions and passion for *The Murder Game* helped to keep me motivated and moving forward. Hopefully you'll be seeing a book from Jeff in the future; he's a talented writer with lots of great and creative ideas.

To Barbara Burgess for her great insights and suggestions regarding the characters and their actions and motivations. She picked up on things that got past me, and most importantly, she raised great questions regarding why I'd taken the story and characters down the path that I'd chosen. In many cases, those paths were changed, and made considerably better, from Barbara's input.

To Jessica Ollinger, for taking time out of her incredibly busy schedule to read the draft manuscript and provide valuable feedback and insights. She also helped to get me back on track when I was considering a different title and basically second-guessing myself. I value her opinion highly and always hope to have her in my life and part of my early reader team.

To my good friend, Robert Saxe, for once again volunteering to read my draft manuscript and provide feedback. I can always count on him to support my writing and provide open and honest feedback. Also to Sherry Deskins, a friend from all the way back to the elementary school days, for volunteering to be an early reader and being a fan of my first book, *Let the Truth Be Told*.

To Ward Cherry, for all practical purposes my 'nephew' and now a proud member of the Virginia Beach, VA police force, for his guidance and expertise on many of the details I used for police gear and methods.

To Paige Comrie (winewithpaige.com) for creating my new website (sonnyhudsonauthor.com) and providing her expertise on the social media and marketing side. I am SO lucky to have met Paige! What an incredible talent: great writer, incredible photographer, creative content creator, and more. She's WAY more than just another 'influencer'; I like to think of her as a 'DMG' (Digital Media Goddess). It was so incredible of her to agree to work with me on this book project, especially since her business is focused squarely on wine. I hope to continue working with her on future book projects. Do yourself a favor: if you're into wine, even just a little bit, you should definitely follow Paige on Instagram and sign up for her newsletter on her website.

To my good friends Patrice and Samantha Breton for opening their beautiful guest house in Calistoga CA (Napa Valley) to me — during the pandemic, no less — where I felt relaxed and inspired and so productive. I wrote four chapters during my stay there, and it really helped me kick-start The Murder Game and build momentum. Patrice and Samantha are the proprietors of my favorite winery, Vice Versa (https://www.viceversawine.com/), and have been friends for many years. When people use the phrase 'salt of the earth' to describe someone, they could easily be talking about this couple. And I also need to thank them for introducing me to their good friends John and Stacey Reinert while I was there earlier this year. John and Stacey are the proprietors of another one of my favorite wineries, Brilliant Mistake (https://www.brilliantmistakewines.com/). If you've ever met someone and realized, almost immediately, that they are people that you will love and want in your life forever, that's John and Stacey. (And yes, the fact that we met over an incredible lunch at Bottega (Yountville, CA) and enjoyed 5+ bottles of wine over the course of the afternoon and evening didn't hurt!). More importantly, they've given me support and encouragement on this journey to bring The Murder Game to completion.

Last, but certainly not least, I have to thank the wonderful members and staff of James River Writers (JRW), based in Richmond, VA. I've learned so much from the other writers and subject matter experts over the past year or so, especially about the 'business' side of being a writer. Special thanks to the staff at JRW: Katharine Herndon (Executive Director), Brynn Markham (Program Director), and Catie-Reagan Palmore (Membership Director).

About the Author

Sonny Hudson is an author of crime/murder mysteries and political action thrillers. Readers compared his first book, '*Let the Truth Be Told*', to novels by such masters as Robert Ludlum, Tom Clancy, and Vince Flynn. '*The Murder Game*', with its tight, fast moving story and strong characters, will appeal to fans of crime and murder mysteries from top authors like David Baldacci, James Patterson, Stuart Woods, and J.D. Robb.

Sonny is a resident of his native Virginia and has spent a long career in the technology sector. His writing weaves technology into the action driven stories, but never lets technology become all-powerful and omnipotent; the same goes for his characters. He lives by the words, "Perfection is boring; it's our weaknesses and flaws and capacity to fail and fall short that makes life, and characters, interesting."

To stay up to date on Sonny's work, follow him on www.sonnyhud sonauthor.com. You can sign up on his website to receive his monthly newsletter and be the first to know when new books are coming down the pike. (Hint: think mid-2023 for the next book in the Jessica Jansen series, '*Glitz. Glamour. Murder.*'!)

facebook.com/sonnyhudsonauthor

twitter.com/sonnyhudsonauthor

instagram.com/sonnyhudsonauthor

Coming Soon

Hollywood Has It All…

GLITZ. GLAMOUR. MURDER.

Book #2 in the Jessica Jansen series

Coming Summer 2023